THE DOG WHO BIT A POLICEMAN

By Stuart M. Kaminsky

The Toby Peters Mysteries

BULLET FOR A STAR
MURDER ON THE YELLOW BRICK ROAD
YOU BET YOUR LIFE
THE HOWARD HUGHES AFFAIR
NEVER CROSS A VAMPIRE
HIGH MIDNIGHT
CATCH A FALLING CLOWN
HE DONE HER WRONG
THE FALA FACTOR
DOWN FOR THE COUNT
THE MAN WHO SHOT LEWIS VANCE
SMART MOVES
THINK FAST, MR. PETERS
BURIED CAESARS
POOR BUTTERFLY
THE MELTING CLOCK
THE DEVIL MET A LADY
TOMORROW IS ANOTHER DAY
DANCING IN THE DARK
A FATAL GLASS OF BEER

The Abe Lieberman Mysteries

LIEBERMAN'S FOLLY
LIEBERMAN'S CHOICE
LIEBERMAN'S DAY
LIEBERMAN'S THIEF
LIEBERMAN'S LAW

The Inspector Rostnikov Novels

DEATH OF A DISSIDENT
BLACK KNIGHT IN RED SQUARE
RED CHAMELEON
A COLD, RED SUNRISE
A FINE RED RAIN
ROSTNIKOV'S VACATION
THE MAN WHO WALKED LIKE A BEAR
DEATH OF A RUSSIAN PRIEST
HARD CURRENCY
BLOOD AND RUBLES
TARNISHED ICONS
THE DOG WHO BIT A POLICEMAN

Nonseries Novels

WHEN THE DARK MAN CALLS
EXERCISE IN TERROR

Nonfiction

DON SIEGEL, DIRECTOR
CLINT EASTWOOD
JOHN HUSTON, MAKER OF MAGIC
COOP, THE LIFE AND LEGEND OF GARY COOPER

THE DOG WHO BIT A POLICEMAN

STUART M. KAMINSKY

THE MYSTERIOUS PRESS

Published by Warner Books

A Time Warner Company

Mysterious Press books are published by Warner Books, Inc.,
1271 Avenue of the Americas, New York, NY 10020.

Visit our Web site at http://warnerbooks.com

 A Time Warner Company

The Mysterious Press name and logo are registered trademarks of Warner Books, Inc.

Printed in the United States of America

First printing: July 1998

10 9 8 7 6 5 4 3 2 1

Library of Congress Cataloging-in-Publication Data

Kaminsky, Stuart M.
    The dog who bit a policeman / Stuart M. Kaminsky.
        p.   cm.
    ISBN 0-89296-667-X
    I. Title.
    PS3561.A43D55   1998
    813'.54—dc21   98-13385
                                                                        CIP

If any one of us knew of a proposed political murder, would he, in view of all the consequences, give the information, or would he stay at home and await events? Opinions may differ on this point. The answer to the question will tell us clearly whether we are to separate, or to remain together . . .

—Fyodor Dostoevsky, *The Possessed*

My continued thanks to Jeff Rice for his enthusiastic and excellent research on Russia and its people.

THE DOG WHO BIT A POLICEMAN

Prologue—
Marseilles, France

"*Les chiens*, dogs," said the oldest man sitting at the booth in the corner of the restaurant. He shook his head.

The three men had the rugged, weatherworn faces of fishermen, mountain climbers, or laborers. They were none of these and had never been. In spite of the fact that one of the men was half black, it was clear that the three were related.

One man, the youngest, who was at least forty-five years old, wore a blue turtleneck shirt under an unbuttoned black sport jacket. The other men were old. The half-black man was about seventy. The third man, who had said "dogs" in a voice of uncertainty, was close to eighty. The two old men wore white polo shirts under sport jackets. All three men were lean. All three were armed, making no effort to hide the holsters and weapons under their jackets.

Noise filled the room. Smoke filled the room. The people who filled the room laughed, talked, drank. Everyone—fishermen, shopkeepers, petty criminals, drug dealers, pimps and prostitutes—was careful not to look at the three men who sat talking, eating shrimp, and drinking wine.

These were special men, dangerous and dour men known to the underbelly of Marseilles. The waiter, who had known and served them for more than two decades, approached them cautiously, said nothing, and brought them whatever they ordered. The oldest man always ordered and said, "Bring whatever is fresh." He didn't bother to order wine or after-the-main-course shrimp or squid.

And the waiter had done as he had been told, and as he had not needed to be told. He filled the wine glasses when they were empty and retreated quickly after he had done so.

"You are certain about the money?" asked the half-black man.

"If we can take over independent operations in Moscow, Bombay, Osaka, New Orleans, Hamburg, Buenos Aires, and Cairo," the youngest man said, "we will be insured of an initial income of thirty million a year."

"Francs?" asked the oldest man.

"American dollars," said the youngest man. "And we can expand. Take over or start operations in Taiwan, Sydney, Singapore. It is almost limitless. This could mean more than the drug income, the protection business, the . . . almost limitless."

The oldest man drank his wine and shook his head, still not convinced.

"And we must go to Moscow?" asked the half-black man.

"We must start there," said the youngest man. "It is well organized, and the young lunatic who has taken over has ambitions much like ours. We absorb him or eliminate him. We meet with him, see his operation, judge him. If we don't like him or what we see, we deal with it."

Silence at the table while the three men ate and thought. A man across the room laughed loudly. It was too hearty a laugh to be natural.

"He's crazy, this Russian?" asked the half-black man.

"*Mon oncle,* you will judge for yourself."

"When?" asked the oldest man.

"Immediately," said the youngest man. "Tomorrow or the next day. The sooner we act, the less trouble we are likely to have."

"We take our own men?" asked the half-black man.

"Yes," said the youngest man.

The oldest man finished his glass of wine and the waiter appeared instantly to refill the glass and then move quickly away where he could watch and be ready to serve the needs of the three men without hearing any of their conversation.

Since the men had killed his father a quarter of a century ago, cut him open and thrown him into the sea, the waiter might not be blamed if he poisoned the trio. But he had only once considered such an action. Years earlier, when he had thought about such an act of retribution, his bowels had given way and he had sat in his small room shaking for most of a day. Through the window of his room that looked out at the ocean, he had considered what might happen to him whether he succeeded or failed in such an enterprise. No, he would never act, just as he had gradually realized that he would never marry, never have a family beyond his sister and her children in La Chapelle. He had little to lose but his life, should he decide to kill the men, but his life was still precious. They, or their survivors, might simply, or complexly, mutilate the waiter. He had heard tales. No, fear had kept him from action and now it was far too late.

Besides, the three gangsters tipped very well and the waiter had a reputation because of his almost nightly service to the three men and others they occasionally brought with them. The three men were talking business. The waiter could tell by the slightest signs of animation on their craggy faces.

"*Très bien,*" said the oldest man finally. "We go to Moscow."

Chapter One

The young man and woman sat eating porterhouse steaks at a table in the restaurant of the Radisson Slavyanskaya Hotel and Business Center at Bereszhkovskaya Naberezhnaya 2. The restaurant's meat was reputed to be the best in Moscow. The hotel, on the other hand, though it had once been the most popular in the city, had been quickly overtaken and passed in size, quality, and service by more than a dozen new capitalist hotels within walking distance of the Radisson.

Originally the hotel had been one of the many Soviet Intourist tombs of dark rooms and darker hallways. For about two years, it had been the headquarters for business travelers. Americans still accounted for a large number of its guests. Indeed, President Clinton had stayed here on one visit, eating the famous meat and watching CNN in his room with his shoes off.

Gradually the hotel had become a hangout for members of the various Mafias. The coffee shop, in fact, was a meeting place for Moscow's hit men, or *keellery*, who argued, drank, ate, and bragged to impress each other and the women who hung on their every word. The coffee shop was known as Café Killer to those who knew its reputation, which was much of the population of Moscow.

This young man who sat in the restaurant eating steak with his companion was dressed in designer clothes from Italy. His hair was brushed back. His face, though young, resonated with experience. He drank, ate, looked around, and minded his own business. The young woman was pretty, slightly plump, and dressed in an expensive green Parisian frock. The two talked quietly, neither smiling nor seeming to savor the expensive food brought to their table.

There were others watching the two. Since they were new to the restaurant, the regulars naturally wondered who the newcomers were and whether they were tourists or potential regulars. The regulars were curious, but they minded their business. Two of those examining the pair were Illya Skatesholkov and Boris Osipov, who had already discovered that the young man and woman were registered in the hotel, that they were Ukrainian, that his name was Dmitri Kolk and hers Lyuba Polikarpova, and that he had asked a bellboy, whom he had slipped a twenty-dollar American bill, if he knew who he might contact about attending a dogfight.

Packs of hungry dogs roamed Moscow. They had been pets, or attempts at protection from the soaring rate of personal crimes in the city. Most of the dogs were rottweilers, which cost as much as five hundred American dollars. Licensing was optional. Many of the dogs had been released by owners who could no longer feed themselves adequately, and certainly could not afford to feed a dog. They had been replaced by guns. Russians can own rifles, shotguns, and tear-gas pistols, and the number of registered weapons in Moscow, whose population hovers at nine million, was over three hundred thousand. Adding in the nonregistered weapons, the police estimated that there was one gun for every three Moscow residents, including babies and *babushkas.*

So, the dogs had formed into packs that came out at night, scavenging, attacking lone dogs, and, ever more frequently, humans. Recently, the packs had started to emerge during daylight hours. Food was scarce. Almost forty thousand dog attacks had been reported by Muscovites over the past year. Two-thirds of those had resulted in hospitalization of the victim.

Crews of uniformed policemen had begun combing the streets and dark corners of the city, shooting strays. Five policemen had been among those hospitalized with bites. One of the policemen had lost an eye. Another had lost the use of his left arm.

It was inevitable that enterprising criminals would find a way to reap profits from the wild dogs. First, some small-time dealers in stolen goods had captured the fiercest of the wild dogs and had organized dogfights, fights to the death in garages where men stood betting, shouting, smoking, and drinking from bottles sold them by their hosts. The enterprise was an immediate success. The newly rich, government bureaucrats, and a rabid assortment of bored tourists and Muscovites came to the illegal fights and wagered huge sums.

It was only a matter of time before the Mafias took an interest in the dogfights. The Armenian Mafia took over the original enterprise after persuading the four leading arrangers of such fights to sell out for a very reasonable price. One of the enterprising promoters had required a square carved in his back before becoming reasonable.

The Armenians, in turn, had made a quick profit in weapons by selling out to a group of Muscovites reported to be heavily financed by international investors.

Now, the dogfights were turning into big dollars in the early-morning hours of darkness. Now, there were private arenas, some with padded seats. Now, one could win or lose thousands of American dollars or millions of rubles.

The bellhop had told the young man in the silk suit that he would see what he could do. Dmitri Kolk had nodded, saying, "Tonight, if possible."

The bellboy had told the bell captain, who had told a contact he knew was into illegal dogfights, and the contact had gone to Illya and Boris.

The restaurant was abustle with hurrying waiters, table-hoppers, and busboys. Dmitri Kolk sat passively looking around the room. He made no eye contact and drank slowly.

Illya called a waiter, who came immediately to the table. "That man," Illya said, looking at Dmitri. "Give him this address and tell him to be there at midnight to get what he is looking for."

Illya wrote an address on a napkin with a felt-tip pen and handed it to the waiter, who immediately took it to Dmitri Kolk, who listened, glanced at the napkin, and tucked it into his inside jacket pocket. Kolk did not look around to see who might be watching him.

Sasha Tkach and Elena Timofeyeva had been assigned to track down those who were running the illegal fights. This was not considered a choice assignment and neither of the two deputy inspectors from the Office of Special Investigation had any idea of why the Yak, Director Igor Yaklovev, had taken on the dogfight problem. There had to be some political gain to be had, but neither officer could come up with an idea of what that gain might be. They had dutifully taken on the identities of Kolk and Lyuba, and for several days Sasha had enjoyed the rich life and the four-hundred-dollar-a-night room. Elena would have preferred her own identity.

Sasha was just past thirty but looked at least five years younger, in spite of his growing problems with his wife, Maya, and the prisonlike condition of living in a tiny two-room apartment with two children. Making the situation worse was the neurotic intrusion of his mother, Lydia, who appeared whenever she wished, shouted her directives for proper living and child rearing, and was constantly on the verge of battle with Maya. Younger men were being promoted ahead of Sasha, who was considered part of the old guard in spite of his age. Sasha was seldom in a good mood, but he was feeling rather content tonight.

Elena, on the other hand, was a few years older than Sasha. She was being pursued by Iosef Rostnikov, Inspector Rostnikov's son, who had recently joined the Office of Special Investigation. Iosef was smart, handsome, and, in spite of being considered Jewish, looking toward a promising future. Iosef had proposed marriage to Elena three times in the last few months. She had turned him down each time. She had a career and ambition, and she did not want to come home each night to anything but the emotions she had earned during the day. Still, Iosef was wearing her down, which was not entirely an unpleasant experience.

When they got the assignment from Chief Inspector Porfiry Petrovich Rostnikov, with a warning to be especially careful, Sasha had told Maya that he would be away for several days on a dangerous assignment. Maya didn't look convinced, but she accepted the situation after getting a call from Porfiry Petrovich telling her that, indeed, her husband had been selected by Yaklovev himself for the job, a job he was not at liberty to discuss.

Elena, on the other hand, had had little trouble after telling her aunt Anna that she would be away on assignment for a while. Elena lived in a small, one-bedroom apartment with her aunt, who'd been a state procurator until a series of heart attacks had sent her into retirement. Recently, Anna and her niece had been finding it difficult to make ends meet. Anna's pension money had not come in for months, and Elena's salary, not particularly high, had arrived later and later each month. The two women had lived increasingly on Anna's small savings.

It was the Yak's idea that Sasha and Elena engage in this role playing. It was the Yak who had arranged for Sasha to have both a pocket full of American dollars and two credit cards in the name of Dmitri Kolk. The investment seemed out of proportion to the crime, but the Yak was not to be questioned. Besides, Sasha thought, it was a respite, a small if possibly dangerous vacation with enormous benefits.

"How do I look?" Sasha asked Elena when they were back in the hotel room and he had changed clothes.

Elena examined him. Sasha had daubed more hair cream into his hair and combed it straight back. He had changed out of his designer suit and was now wearing gray slacks, a blue button-down shirt, and a gray silk zipper jacket.

"Fine," she said. "You saw the dog?"

"A pit bull," he said. "Kennel has several of them. This one is supposedly particularly mean, but he looked quite benign to me. I hate dogs. My aunt had a dog. He growled and snapped at me and my cousins. Twice he bit me. I dreaded visiting my aunt. When the dog, Osip, died, my cousins and I celebrated. This pit bull is named Tchaikovsky. He was shipped to Kiev and then shipped here to me. He's in a private, very expensive kennel. You should have come to see him."

"I prefer cats," said Elena, more than a bit irked but not showing it. She had never been offered the opportunity to examine the animal upon whose performance their safety and the success of their assignment depended. "It's almost midnight."

Sasha nodded, adjusted his shirt and sleeves, and checked his hair with the palm of his right hand. "I'd better hurry," he said.

"I still think I should go with you," she said.

"The invitation was for me," he said.

"I can follow, watch," she said.

"Unnecessarily dangerous," he said.

"You look pleased. You've looked pleased about this whole assignment."

"Perhaps, a little," he said.

"You're not curious about why so much money is being spent to put on a front for us—hotel, clothes, shipping a dog to Kiev and back, bets you'll have to make?" she asked.

"No," he said. "That is the concern of Director Yaklovev."

"Be careful," she said.

"Of course," he said, checking himself again in the mirror.

Elena wasn't so sure.

"You have the address where they told me to come," he said, adjusting his hair. "If I am not back by morning . . ."

"Then I'll know you are really enjoying yourself," she said.

The naked, rather hairy body of a large man floated facedown in the Moscow River. His massive buttocks rose and bobbed like twin pale balloons. The body was corpse white and bore a tattoo on the left arm which, like the right, drifted outward from the dead man.

The tattoo, Rostnikov could see from the police boat, was of a knife with a snake twisted around the blade and handle.

"Shall we pull him out?" asked a uniformed officer.

"No, not yet," said Rostnikov. "We'll wait. You have coffee?"

The uniformed officer, a very young man with a cap that looked a bit large for his narrow face, said yes.

"Please," said Rostnikov, sitting on the wooden seat at the rear of the boat. "What is your name?"

"Igor Druzhnin."

"Bring a cup for yourself, too, Igor Druzhnin," said Rostnikov. "We can talk while we wait."

The young officer left.

An excursion boat, filled no doubt with tourists, chugged past. One or two people on board saw the body and began to take pictures. Others joined them.

In English, one of the tourists said, "Can't we get a little closer?"

The boat cruised on down the river.

Once, the river had been relatively clean, a wide, dark, flowing, meandering path which Muscovites liked to watch from the banks while fishing, eating lunch, or simply thinking. But that was gradually changing. There had always been those who under cover of night dumped their garbage in the dark water. Now, though such dumping was illegal, it had grown less covert. And garbage was only part of the problem. Far north, factories poured liquid waste into the river. Much of it was filtered out by natural processes. Much of it was not.

"Others do it. So, I do it too," was the often-spoken excuse of those who lived near enough to the river to defile it.

It had grown worse with the fall of the Soviet Union and the chaos that had overrun the city. The police, in the days before the new democracy, would from time to time arrest people who spread filth in the waters. Now no one seemed to care.

There were those who said the river had taken on a new and not pleasant smell.

"It has the stink of freedom," Lydia Tkach had said.

Porfiry Petrovich Rostnikov was the senior investigator in the Office of Special Investigation. This office had been started as a dumping ground for politically touchy cases and cases the MVD and even State Security, the old KGB, wanted no part of because they promised nothing but failure and a threat to those who might pursue them.

Rostnikov and his staff had been brought to the Office of Special Investigation by the pompous Colonel Snitkonoy, the Gray Wolfhound, who was considered a fine figure of a fool on whom could be dumped disastrous cases without the possibility of furthering his ambition.

They had been wrong. When Rostnikov had been transferred from the Moscow Procurator's Office after one confrontation too many with people in power—the KGB and the chief procurator himself—he had taken with him his small staff. The sensitive crimes that others had imposed upon the Wolfhound and his staff began to be brought to conclusions, and at one point the Office of Special Investigation had even stopped an attempted assassination of Mikhail Gorbachev, who was then president of the Soviet Union. There were those later who said that it would have been better had Rostnikov failed, but at the time it had brought grudging respect for Snitkonoy and his men.

So successful was the office that the Gray Wolfhound was transferred and promoted to head the security service at the Hermitage Museum in St. Petersburg. He was a perfect choice in his neat, bemedaled uniform, a relic standing tall with flowing silver hair, an exhibit worthy of placement next to a Rublyov icon.

The Office of Special Investigation had recently been taken over by Igor Yaklovev. The Yak was about fifty, lean, with hair cut short and the bushiest eyebrows Porfiry Petrovich had ever seen, with the possible exception of Leonid Brezhnev. The Yak, a former KGB officer, was given to dark, uneventful suits and suspenders. His hair was receding and his glasses had thick lenses. He was ambitious, Rostnikov knew, and was using the office to further that ambition. Information gathered in the course of investigations could and well might be used by the Yak to put pressure on those above him, or traded to them to aid his ascension of the ladder of political power.

But to give the man his due, Yaklovev had promoted Rostnikov, given him a free hand, and pledged his support if one or more of the varied criminal organizations and the confused state bureaucracy attempted to impede the performance of his duties. Up to now, the Yak had been as good as his word and had successfully bought the loyalty of Rostnikov and his staff.

The wake of the passing excursion boat, now about a half mile down the river, had lifted the corpse and set his right hand moving in what looked like a wave to a school of small fish below him.

The boat was on the northern bank of the meandering river, directly across from the Hotel Baltschug Kempinski Moskau. An elegant hotel built in 1898 and reopened in 1992 after a complete renovation by a German-Russian group, the hotel boasted 234 luxury rooms. Rostnikov knew that on the other side of the hotel was St. Basil's Cathedral, Red Square, and the Kremlin.

Rostnikov shifted his weight as the young uniformed officer came back on deck and offered the detective a blue mug. Officer Druzhnin had a gray cup. Rostnikov took the cup, thanked the man who looked out at the corpse, and began to drink. The coffee was tepid and awful, but it was coffee.

As he drank, the two men watched the naked corpse.

"Are you married, Igor?"

"Yes."

"Children?"

"Not yet."

"You want children?"

"Yes, but we can't afford even to feed ourselves. I haven't been paid for two months. Fortunately, my wife works. She sells papers and sweets at the Kazan train station."

Rostnikov could never quite get comfortable. He was a man of average size but built like the German tank that had crippled his left leg when he was a boy soldier. For almost half a century, Rostnikov had dragged the leg painfully, had listened to its complaints like those of an aged parent for whom one is responsible. Then, one day, the pain had gotten worse and a doctor he trusted, his wife Sarah's cousin, Leon Moiseyevitch, had told him that the leg should go. Rostnikov had agreed with regret, and now he had a prosthesis that allowed him to walk almost normally. Rostnikov missed his withered leg and knew that Paulinin, the half-mad scientific technician whose laboratory was two levels below the Petrovka Police Headquarters, had kept that leg somewhere among the hundreds of specimens that cluttered his laboratory.

Rostnikov had sent for Paulinin. Paulinin would certainly grumble and complain. He didn't like leaving his laboratory. If there was a corpse to be examined, he wanted it brought to him. If there was evidence to be pieced together, Paulinin wanted it laid out at his convenience among the retorts, burners, and tools, many of which were his own inventions.

Rostnikov, from the time he was a boy, had been an avid lifter of weights. He kept a set of barbells and a bench at home and from time to time entered park and district competitions, which he invariably won. Now that he was placed in the senior bracket of such competition, he won even more regularly and thus competed less.

"How did you get here, huh?" asked Rostnikov.

"Well, my father . . ."

"No, Igor. I was talking to our floating friend."

"He is dead," said the young officer.

"If not, we are witnessing a miracle," said Rostnikov. "I was told once by a Inuit shaman in Siberia that it is a comfort to the souls of the dead to talk to them before they are taken by the spirits."

"You believe that?" asked Druzhnin. "I'm sorry. It's not my business to question . . ."

"No, that is fine," said Rostnikov, taking another sip of the coffee. "I don't believe either, but I find it helpful to speak to the dead even if they do not answer. If the Hindus are correct, our floating friend has already been reincarnated, perhaps as a very small ant in a forest where he will not know he had once been human and might never, in his life as an ant, see a human being."

"Perhaps," said Druzhnin, adjusting his cap and trying not to look directly at the chief inspector, who seemed, to give him the benefit of the doubt, a bit odd.

A group of four men was coming down the embankment not far from the boat.

"Forensics," one of the men called to Rostnikov.

"I know," said Rostnikov.

"We'll pull in the body," the man on the shore said. "Can you give us a hand?"

"No," said Rostnikov. "It stays where it is."

The man onshore, who was no more than forty, looked at his colleagues, one of whom said something Rostnikov could not hear. Then the man spoke again. "We have to do our job," the man said. "My name is Penzurov. We have met before."

"I recognize you."

"Porfiry Petrovich, we have to do our job," Penzurov repeated.

"No, you do not," said Rostnikov. "The job must be done. But you do not have to be the ones who do it. Would you like to come aboard and have some coffee?"

"We were sent to retrieve and examine the body," Penzurov said in confusion.

"Then return to whoever sent you and inform them that Inspector Rostnikov of the Office of Special Investigation told you that your outstanding services would not be required."

"Why?" asked the man.

"Because," said Rostnikov. "And I mean no offense, you have a less than outstanding record of examination of bodies, crime scenes, and collected evidence. The responsibility is mine. Technician Paulinin of Petrovka will conduct the examination of the body."

The four men conferred. Rostnikov sipped his coffee and looked across the river at the massive Hotel Baltschug Kempinski towering over the smaller, ancient decaying buildings and churches.

"I believe we have jurisdiction," said the man as firmly as he could.

"I believe you do not," said Rostnikov. "Do not try to pull the corpse in or I shall come ashore in a black mood and be forced to embarrass you into departure."

"We shall report this immediately," said the man.

"That is a very good idea," said Rostnikov.

The four men made their way back up the embankment. One of the men, the oldest, slid and slipped on the dewy grass of late spring. No one helped him up. He scrambled to the top of the incline and looked down at his dirty hands before joining the others.

Rostnikov handed his empty mug to Officer Druzhnin, who said, "Would you like more?"

"No, thank you," said Rostnikov.

The officer nodded and headed for the door to the cabin, the two mugs clinking together as he moved.

Rostnikov turned awkwardly to the bobbing corpse and said, "What are you doing here? What happened to your clothes? Who are you?"

A small undulation raised the body slightly.

"Well, I'm sure you'll talk to Paulinin," said Rostnikov. "I'm comfortable talking to the dead, but *he* gets answers. Let us both be patient. It's not a bad day. The sky is clear. There is a breeze and the river doesn't smell as bad as it often does lately."

Now two men appeared at the top of the embankment. Rostnikov turned again, giving his artificial leg a hitch.

The two men who stood looking down at the inspector and the

floating corpse were an incongruous pair. One was tall, very pale, and dressed completely in black—shoes, socks, slacks, turtleneck sweater, and jacket. His dark, receding hair was brushed straight back. Rostnikov looked at Detective Emil Karpo who returned the look without emotion. Karpo was known as "the Vampire" or "the Tatar" by criminals and law-enforcement officers. Karpo had been a completely dedicated Communist who had not overlooked the political system's many shortcomings but who believed that eventually the system would succeed. It was not Communism that was the problem but the men who seemed determined to corrupt it.

The sudden transition from corrupt Communism to corrupt democracy had been difficult for Karpo, but he had been helped through the change by Mathilde Verson, a redheaded part-time prostitute who had grown quite close to him. And then Mathilde had been killed in the crossfire between two Mafias. Karpo had survived by throwing himself into his work even more than was usual. In fact, Emil Karpo spent all of his waking hours relentlessly pursuing criminals from both the past and the present. Karpo's small room was dominated by shelves filled with notebooks on past unsolved and solved crimes. The rest of the space in which he lived was little more than a cell, with a small dresser, cot, and closet. Since he spent little, Karpo had money to buy the computer that sat on the desk in his room. The computer was devoted to storing Emil Karpo's vast files and running cross-checks which might link anyone to any crime.

The man at his side, Paulinin, was shorter, disheveled, clad in a stained white laboratory coat, and decidedly uncomfortable. He seemed to be talking to himself.

Rostnikov waved for the two men to come down and join him.

Officer Druzhnin appeared on deck, looked at Rostnikov, who nodded, and let down a plank for the two men to board the small boat.

"Thank you for coming," said Rostnikov to Paulinin. "I'm sorry to bring you out so early, but you are the only one I trust to give me a meaningful report about our floating friend."

Paulinin grunted, adjusted his glasses, and stood at the rear of the boat next to Rostnikov, looking down at the dead man. Behind Paulinin, Karpo said, "He's a member of the Tatar Mafia. The tattoo is theirs."

"A start," said Rostnikov. "Paulinin?"

"By the condition of the corpse, I would say he has been in the water less than a day, perhaps much less. My guess? He died last night. But . . ."

Paulinin looked around, found a grappling pole, and awkwardly but carefully nudged the corpse toward the boat. He used the flat side of the pole to keep from damaging the bloating corpse.

"Hold this," Paulinin said, handing the pole to Karpo, who took it and firmly pulled the body closer to the boat.

"We must turn him over," said Paulinin.

"Officer Druzhnin, please," said Rostnikov.

The young officer climbed over the rear railing, feet on a narrow platform near the water level and one hand on the railing. He reached down and tried to turn the naked corpse over on its back, but the man was too heavy and slippery. Karpo moved forward and joined the young officer. Together, they managed to turn the corpse. Druzhnin held the body awkwardly to keep it from turning facedown again.

Paulinin looked down at the corpse.

The dead man was thick necked and had a well-trimmed short beard. A dark hole burrowed into his forehead just above the bridge of his nose. He also had three dark spots in his hairy chest and stomach.

"Pull him up here, carefully," said Paulinin.

Karpo and the young police officer tried to lift the waterlogged dead man into the boat.

"Careful," said Paulinin. "No new bruises or cuts."

The dead man easily weighed two hundred fifty pounds.

Rostnikov rose, turned, knelt on the wooden bench, and reached down for the dead man's arm. The arm was cold and the flesh soft. Rostnikov motioned for the police officer and Karpo to back away as he lifted the body. Rostnikov managed to grab the dead man under each arm. He took a deep breath and lifted the naked corpse from the water.

"Take his feet," Rostnikov said.

Karpo and Druzhnin reached down for the corpse's legs.

The three men lifted the dead man over the side of the boat and placed him, faceup, on the deck.

Paulinin knelt next to the dead man and leaned over to examine him.

Rostnikov knew better than to ask the scientist any questions. He simply watched and waited.

"Yes," said Paulinin, touching the man's chest. "He is talking to me already. He will tell me much more in my laboratory. Porfiry Petrovich, I don't see why I had to come here. I have work piling up back home."

"I thought you might see something here that I have not seen," said Rostnikov, who was using a small soiled towel Druzhnin had handed him to wipe away some of the touch of death.

Paulinin sighed and adjusted his glasses. "I suggest you search the opposite shore," he said. "An elusive combination of wake, flow, and current. I think the body came from over there."

Rostnikov looked at where Paulinin was pointing.

"That is providing I am correct about the approximate time of death. I'll be more specific later. Now, bring the corpse to my laboratory."

"I'll take care of it," said Karpo.

Chapter Two

As Porfiry Petrovich Rostnikov talked to the nude, bloated corpse, Sasha Tkach woke to summer sunlight streaming through the window of his hotel room. The sun was painful and so was the construction noise outside, which was barely muted by the closed windows. Sasha had a hangover from the night before.

"Get up," Elena said. She wore a blue dress with red stripes running down at an angle.

Sasha tried twice to sit up before he succeeded. Elena handed him a cup of coffee, which he took gratefully. He vaguely remembered coming back to the room and throwing his clothes on the floor till he was down to his undershorts. Elena, who had slept on the pull-out bed in the living room of the suite, had watched Sasha weave into the room at four in the morning. She had taken a look at him and realized that there would be no point in asking him any questions. And so he had barely made it to the bed, where he collapsed, felt a wave of nausea and dizziness, and was almost instantly asleep.

Now Elena stood over him, waiting as patiently as she could and drinking her own coffee.

Sasha needed a shave, and the hair he had slicked back the night before was a wild mess. There were circles of darkness under his red eyes and, all in all, he looked terrible.

"Tell me what happened," Elena said. "I'll write the report."

"Thank you," Sasha said, finishing his coffee. It helped his head a bit but gave him a slight taste of nausea.

Elena sat in a soft armchair near the window, put down her cup, and took a small tape recorder from her pocket. She placed the recorder on the table near her armchair and waited for Sasha to speak. Had he been thinking less of his head and of the events of the morning, Sasha might have noted that Elena wore a look of irritation that contained no sympathy for her partner.

"You checked the room for . . . ?" he began.

"There are no listening devices," she said. "I have had a great deal of time to check carefully. You can speak. But I would not trust the phone."

He nodded, blinked his eyes against the pain of the morning light, and began to speak as Elena turned on the recorder.

"I took a cab to a house, a private home with an iron gate, on Mira Prospekt beyond the Outer Ring Circle near the Botanical Garden. There were only a few cars parked in the driveway beyond the gate, which was opened for the cab by two big men who wore weapons under their jackets, after I showed the napkin with the address on it.

"I paid the cab driver, who tried to cheat me because he thought I was a Ukrainian. I haggled and paid more than I had to but less than he asked for. I got out of the cab, and the two armed men let the cab back out through the gate. The parked cars were expensive; there was even a Rolls-Royce. The door to the house opened as I walked toward it, and a slim, well-dressed blond man greeted me and let me pass.

"I entered the house, heard noises from somewhere inside. The blond man told me that I was a little late and led me to a door, which he opened, increasing the noise. We went down a flight of stairs and I found myself in a big, high-ceilinged room with a wire-fenced square in the middle surrounded by about forty people, all men, standing. Two dogs were inside the wire fence.

"The spectators placed bets with men who walked among them. The men who took the bets all wore blue blazers with a golden bear emblazoned on the breast pocket. The fight that was going on was almost over. A big black-and-white mongrel was bleeding but about to triumph over an equally large white German shepherd, which had lost its right ear in the battle and had lost a great deal of blood from numerous bites. It was disgusting. It was fascinating. The shepherd stood bravely on wobbling legs, showing its teeth in a final brave stance. The mongrel attacked with a growl and the fight was over.

"A man appeared at my side. We had seen him in the restaurant earlier. He said his name was Boris Osipov. He is tall, wears good clothes, well built, dark hair, false smile and, I think, false teeth, though he can't be more than my age or a little older."

"I'll see what I can find out about him," Elena said. "Go on."

Sasha touched his stubbly morning beard with the back of his hand and with the same hand attempted to tame his hair. His hair refused to cooperate.

"Over the noise of bettors arguing with each other about the merits of the dogs in the next fight, Boris explained that bets could be made only with the house men in the blue blazers. Side and private bets were not permitted. Drinks were available at slightly more than a reasonable price. I asked for a Scotch on the rocks. It was the first of several. Boris raised a hand. A waiter appeared, took the drink order. He was back with it almost immediately. I reached for my wallet. Boris stopped me and said the first one was on him. I thanked him. Two men in jeans and black shirts removed the dying German shepherd and led the victor off to have his wounds tended.

" 'You know dogs?' asked Boris.

" 'A bit,' I said.

" 'What do you say about these two?' Two fresh dogs were led into the fenced square. One, tall, black and brown, a Doberman, was straining toward the other dog, growling, showing its teeth. The other dog regarded the Doberman, showing no reaction. The second dog, smaller than the Doberman, was, by his look, part terrier, part wolfhound, an odd-looking creature who seemed neither thirsting for blood nor afraid. He showed dignity.

" 'I'll take that one,' I said, pointing at the part wolfhound as the Doberman strained at the short leash and began to bark.

" 'How much?' asked Boris, motioning for one of the men in a blue blazer, who came immediately.

" 'Two hundred American dollars,' I said. I got out my wallet and gave the man two hundred dollars.'"

"You bet two hundred dollars?" Elena said incredulously.

"What choice did I have? I did bet more as the evening progressed. Sometimes odds were given. Sometimes there were no odds. Sometimes I won. Sometimes I lost. You needn't worry. I wound up six hundred dollars ahead for the night."

"Go on," Elena said with a sigh.

"The Doberman was killed, quickly. After two more fights, the main event of the night was a pit bull and a rottweiler. I bet and lost. The noise in the room was worse than a soccer match. I drank. Boris asked me questions. I told him I had a fighting pit bull back in Kiev, that I had my own growing dogfighting business. He pumped me and I dropped the name of Alexander Chernov. He said he knew Chernov. I shrugged. I'm sure he has called Chernov by now to check on me."

Alexander Chernov had been a wheeler-dealer in the black market in Kiev during the days of the Soviet Union. When the Union ended and the underground black market became an overground but still illegal market for goods, food, and services, Chernov had made even more money. He had, however, made the mistake of bribing a Kiev police officer, only to discover—to his amazement—that the officer was completely honest and incorruptible. Chernov had not believed such a creature existed. The officer had taped their conversations, arrested Chernov with plenty of evidence, and brought him in to face a great deal of prison time. The officer's superior, who was not quite as honest as the man who had trapped Chernov, had struck a deal with Chernov. Chernov could continue to operate in exchange for a regular payment to the official. In addition, Chernov might be called upon to perform certain acts, tell certain lies, betray certain friends. Chernov had readily agreed. This time his assignment had been simple. If called by anyone in Moscow about a certain Dmitri Kolk, he was to say that Kolk was well known in Kiev for his dogs, and that the young man had made a great deal of money in a variety of ventures, including illegal passports and drugs. Even if Sasha were found out, Chernov could claim to have been duped.

"And?" Elena prompted.

"Not much more to tell," said Sasha, swinging his legs over the side of the bed and feeling quite dizzy from the effort. "I bet, watched, talked to Boris, was introduced to some of his associates. I told Boris and his friends that I had a dog I was interested in having fight in Moscow. I told him I had other dogs, all great fighters, in Kiev and that I could send for them. Perhaps we could arrange a cooperative venture. Boris said he would call me here. We drank. I watched animals maimed and killed. I pretended to be excited by it, to enjoy it."

"And did you?" asked Elena.

"Did I?"

"Enjoy it," she said. "Were you excited by it?"

"Is this relevant to your report?"

"No," she said. "I was just curious."

"Perhaps I did, a bit. I had more to drink than I ever had, but I was careful to keep alert and perhaps the drink made me . . . I don't know."

Sasha tried to stand and with one hand on the bed managed to do so. He stood on unsteady feet, wearing nothing but his underpants. Even had he shaved and had no hangover, Elena knew she would not be moved sexually by the sight of her partner. Sasha was not her type, and she knew too much about him to be interested.

She reached over and turned off the tape recorder, watching Sasha stagger toward the bathroom.

"You have anything else to add about your adventure, either on or off the record?" she asked.

"No," he said, taking another slow step toward the bathroom.

"I picked up your clothes and hung them in the closet," she went on.

"Thank you," he said, one hand on the wall next to the bathroom to steady himself.

"Your clothes reek of perfume and the smell of a woman," she said. "Your jacket has red marks, lipstick."

"You sound like a wife," he said, holding his head.

"When you look in the mirror," Elena said, "you'll see more lipstick marks on your neck and chest."

Sasha turned to look at Elena, who sat looking up at him expressionlessly. It had been nearly two in the morning. He had downed several drinks. Boris had taken him to a private room upstairs, a living room, and introduced him to the woman. He couldn't even remember her name at the moment, but he did remember that she was young, had very short dark hair and clear white skin, smelled wonderful, was slim but let her cleavage show, and that she had full, erect breasts. She had worn a red strapless dress and . . . it had happened. Boris disappeared. She had led him to a bedroom. His first thought when it was over was AIDS. Things like this had happened to him before, not often. Each time he had felt guilt and fear. He would have to be tested. The woman was either an expensive prostitute who could have any disease, or a *tyolki*, a gangster's woman, who could also have a disease.

Sasha looked at Elena.

"Don't worry," she said. "Your battle scars will not be in the report."

"Thank you," he said, moving into the bathroom and looking at himself in the mirror. It was a horrible sight.

"Why is it so *shoomeet*, so noisy?" he asked, closing his eyes.

"Did you expect the great Mayor Yuri Luzkov to stop billions of dollars of construction because one man wakes up with a headache?"

"It would be considerate," said Sasha.

Construction of a new Russia with money that had best not be questioned had begun two years earlier. The change was enormous. Supposedly, the construction had been for the celebration in September of Moscow's eight hundred fiftieth anniversary, a number in some dispute. The celebration had come and gone and the construction went on and on.

New ornate buildings with stucco facades; massive fake cathedrals; new wrought-iron lampposts that echoed those of a century ago; and two or three floors added to old buildings and the buildings themselves remodeled and sandblasted by workmen in orange overalls. The skyline had already changed and it was due to change even more.

It was not the first time in this century that the face of Moscow had undergone a major change. Lenin, who moved the capital from St. Petersburg to Moscow, had disdained the czarist past and brought on a new era of modern architecture that was supposed to reflect the new Russia. Lenin's Moscow was a hodgepodge of styles, and the construction was often subpar and crumbling almost before it was completed.

Stalin in the 1930s had a new vision of elaborate and impressive metro stations underground, and imposing and threatening skyscrapers and great statues aboveground. The seven skyscrapers that still tower in the skyline were a Stalin contribution. Monuments to who-knew-what. But Mayor Luzkov was planning what he called the "eighth tower," a pink monster on the grounds of Moscow State University.

Then the Krushchev 1950s brought the construction that resulted in blocks of huge gray apartment buildings.

And now, not the leader of Russia or the Soviet Union, but the mayor of the city, who wanted to replace Yeltsin, had unveiled great plans, none of which would do much to change the housing

problem. He planned a third ring circle; more underground park-
ing—though only twenty percent of the people of Moscow have
cars; a railroad running alongside the new ring road; at least two
new subway stations; American-style shopping malls; a new business district called Moskva-Siti, at a cost of over eight billion in
American dollars; and the world's tallest building, the Tower of
Russia, which would reach 1,950 feet into the sky.

Little if any of this construction promised much to the vast
majority of Muscovites, who still lived in crumbling, poorly constructed housing. But the people of Moscow loved their mayor,
and ninety percent of those who voted, voted for him.

Sasha, even through the hangover, had to admit that since the
rise of the new mayor, his salary and that of city workers, and of
those employees of the government who worked in the city, had
come regularly. There had even been a small raise at the start of
the year.

But the noise. Just a moment of respite. A brief pause. A
blessed silence.

The phone rang.

"So many places," said the woman sitting on the spotless white
sofa.

She shook her head and looked down at her folded hands. At
her side, a lean young man put his arm around her and said,
"Mama, he is not worth it."

The woman was Olga Pleshkov. She was fifty-two years old,
well groomed, with stylishly cut, short gray-black hair. A dozen
years earlier she had been acknowledged to be one of Moscow's
great beauties and that beauty, it was generally agreed, had been
more than slightly instrumental in her husband's political rise, a
rise that came in spite of the fact that he was less than sympathetic
to the existing government and had only reluctantly joined the
Party, an affiliation he had been one of the first to denounce when
Yeltsin mounted the steps.

Knowing the police were coming, Olga Pleshkov had worn a conservative blue summer dress instead of the jeans and cotton shirt she usually wore to work in her garden. The young man at her side was Ivan Pleshkov, thirty-one, who had taken no pains to dress for the visit. He wore a wrinkled pair of tan chinos and a loose-fitting, pullover Chicago Bulls sweatshirt with cut-off arms.

They were at the Pleshkov family dacha in Manikhino, thirty miles west of Moscow. In the 1950s, small garden plots had been given to employees at the nearby MIG fighter-plane factory. With the coming of the new Russia, those with money earned through enterprise, corruption, and bribery had begun to buy these plots, tear down the small cottages, and build large homes, which brought on the envy and anger of their far less affluent neighbors.

Olga Pleshkov's statement, "so many places," had been in answer to the question from the young policeman who sat across from her. A decade ago and with nothing on her mind, Olga Pleshkov would have attempted to "cultivate" a powerfully built and good-looking blond like this. She might still be able to accomplish it, but it would be more for the challenge than the pleasure. Now, now there was Yevgeny, his ambition—and hers—and his not-very-strange disappearance.

The question had been, "Where does your husband go when he . . . ?"

The unfinished question from Iosef Rostnikov was, "Where does your husband go when he goes on an alcoholic bender?"

At Iosef's side, sitting awkwardly erect and not knowing what the proper behavior was in this situation, was Akardy Zelach, a hulking, stoop-shouldered, and not terribly bright member of the Office of Special Investigation. Zelach's primary virtues were his loyalty to whomever he was assigned to work with and his willingness to do whatever was asked of him, regardless of how difficult or dangerous it might be. That willingness had, on more than one occasion, almost cost him his life. Zelach's silent hope was that he would not be asked to do anything that required great initiative, creativity, or intelligence. Zelach knew his limits, and there was no question about who was in charge of this case, though Akardy Zelach had been a policeman for almost two decades and Iosef had been one for about a year. The simple truth was that Zelach did not wish to be in charge of anything and he dreaded even the very distant possibility that he might be promoted to a position of greater responsibility.

The missing Yevgeny Pleshkov was an elected member of the Russian Congress. He was one of the most articulate and outspoken defenders of Boris Yeltsin and his policies and principles. Pleshkov was not afraid of confrontation, verbal or physical, and generally his old-guard political enemies backed away from the huge bass-voiced man with the wild gray hair. Pleshkov was a perfect spokesman and was in great demand for television interviews and public appearances and debates.

From time to time, however, like now, Pleshkov disappeared for days or weeks, even if an important debate or vote was coming in the congress.

When the other agencies of criminal investigation had made it clear that they had pursued Pleshkov in the past and emerged with neither thanks nor great success, the Yak had instantly volunteered the Office of Special Investigation to find and deliver Pleshkov before a crucial issue on the rights of foreign investment was to be voted upon. That vote was three days from now.

Rostnikov had given the job to his son and Zelach. Though he knew of the periodic flights of the bombastic member of congress, finding him didn't appear to be a particularly difficult assignment, though it could be a delicate one. In spite of the fact that Iosef had been a policeman for so short a time, aside from his father he was the member of the office capable of projecting the most empathy for a victim or even a criminal suspect. Part of this skill was inherited. Part of it came from Iosef's several years as an actor after coming out of the army. None of the empathy he displayed came from the hard lessons he'd learned from being a soldier in Afghanistan, a soldier labeled a Jew and subject to the most dangerous patrols and vindictive abuse from his superiors, who knew they were losing a senseless war fought in a terrain of rocks and soil incapable of supporting even the most simple crops.

"A list of places would be helpful," Iosef prompted. He nodded at Zelach, who pulled out his notebook and pen, ready to take down a list.

"Places," Olga Pleshkov repeated. "I don't know. He could be in a hotel room. He could be . . . I don't know."

"If someone else is paying," Ivan said, "my father would be at any of the new bars or casinos. Jacko's, Casino Royal, Casino Metropole, the Golden Palace, B.B. King's, Rosie O'Grady's, the Sports Bar, or the Up & Down Club. He gets there after midnight and stays till dawn. Because of who he is, someone usually takes him to a room to sleep it off during the day. My father," Ivan went on with obvious disgust, "does not become boisterous when he drinks. If you didn't know him, he would appear to be a quiet, dignified businessman, even a respected judge, holding court with tourists, prostitutes, and Mafia bosses who have something to gain from him. My father, in short, is a disgusting drunk."

"Ivan," Olga Pleshkov commanded.

"How often does this happen?" asked Iosef.

"Once or twice a year," said Olga Pleshkov.

Her son shook his head, folded his arms, and said nothing. Iosef addressed him. "More often?"

"Increasingly," said Ivan, ignoring the warning looks of his mother. "Perhaps four times a year, and for longer periods. My father's liver is a miracle of heredity and evolution. It should, by all reason, be the size of a soccer ball. And yet after each bender he manages to return to his old abusive self."

"Your father is not abusive," Olga Pleshkov said. "He has never laid a hand on either of us."

"There are many ways to be abusive," said Ivan.

Iosef didn't bother to ask for a photograph of Yevgeny Pleshkov; his picture was frequently in the newspapers and on television. In fact, Iosef had seen the large man on a news interview television show only a week ago, and had been impressed by his ability to express himself and the apparent sincerity of his words. Depending on how the political winds blew, Pleshkov might well have a bright future in Russian politics.

"Valentin Itchak said this would be handled with suitable discretion," Olga Pleshkov said.

"And it will be," said Iosef, having not the slightest idea of who Valentin Itchak might be. "We will locate your husband and return him to you."

"You won't hurt him?" she asked.

"Hurt father?" Ivan said. "They'll be lucky to bring him here screaming and luckier still if they don't lose a tooth or an eye in the process."

Akardy Zelach, who had lost much of the sight in his left eye two years earlier after being attacked from behind by a thief, winced at the prospect of a further attack.

"We won't hurt him," said Iosef. "I must ask one more question. Yevgeny Pleshkov is an important man. Is it possible that there may be some reason for his disappearance other than his . . . problem?"

"Like what?" asked Olga Pleshkov.

"Like he was kidnapped and possibly murdered by political enemies," said Ivan.

His mother turned to the young man with horror in her eyes. "No!"

"Why not?" asked Ivan with a shrug. "These are dangerous times and my father is a loud, popular man, hated and feared by many. But if you ask me, he is simply drunk somewhere."

Though he did not particularly care for the young man in the cut-off sweatshirt, Iosef's inclination was to agree. Gorbachev had, before his fall, cracked down on alcoholism with little success. Now it was back and more open than ever. Russians had drunk before because it was part of their heritage, and to escape the burdens of Communist rule. Now they drank to escape the chaos of unregulated freedom. It was estimated, Iosef knew, that two hundred fifty thousand Russians were dying each year from alcohol-related causes. Yeltsin drank. Pleshkov drank and might well be dead this time or the next.

Olga Pleshkov rose, erect, handsome, clasping her hands to indicate that the policemen were excused and she would not be shaking their hands. "Please excuse me. If you have any more questions, you can ask my son. He seems to have all the answers."

She left the room quickly and her son said, "You will have to forgive my mother. She didn't even offer you tea or coffee. But I will do so."

"*Nyet, spahssebah,*" said Iosef.

Zelach would have liked some tea and perhaps a biscuit, but he also said, "No, thank you."

"You have more you can tell us about where we might find your father? His friends? People he drinks with, anything that might help?"

Ivan Pleshkov did not hesitate.

"There is a woman he goes to when he decides to lose a few days, a week or two. Her name is Yulia. I think her last name is Yalutshkin or Valushkin, something like that. He spends the days sleeping it off in her apartment. Also, there is an old childhood friend, Oleg Kisolev. He's a coach of the Dynamo soccer team, used to be a player. I remember watching him. Even as a child I could tell when he visited my father that Kisolev was a pandering fool, with a good but not great kick."

Zelach was writing carefully.

"Any address for Kisolev?" asked Iosef.

"I don't have one. You can look in my father's desk in there."

"Thank you," said Iosef. "You've been very helpful. Are you interested in politics too?"

"You mean," said Ivan, "do I have a job? The answer is yes. I am a computer-program designer for the power company. I make more money than my father. I have my own apartment in Moscow. I like girls. I do not drink and I have no political ambition. Any other questions?"

"Not now," said Iosef, rising.

Zelach put away his notebook.

"My mother will want me to watch you go through my father's things. We have been through this before, as you might have guessed. My mother is afraid that the police might steal something of value. I have no desire to offend you, but I hope you understand."

"You don't know us," said Iosef. "No offense has been taken."

The search of Yevgeny Pleshkov's office yielded little of any possible use—not even a hidden bottle of vodka, not a personal telephone book, no letters. The office hardly seemed used. The search was quick, made quicker by the hovering of Ivan Pleshkov.

"You are a basketball fan?" asked Iosef, giving up on his search and looking at the young man's shirt with a cartoonlike design of the head of an angry bull.

"Yes," said Ivan. "It is my goal to move to Chicago and buy season tickets to all the Bulls games. It is my hope that I can do this before Michael Jordan retires. Getting work as a computer-program designer will be no problem."

"Might it not affect your father's political ambitions were his son to move to the United States?" asked Iosef.

"I'm sure it would," said Ivan. "I do not hate my father, but he has taught me to care little about what happens to him. I hope you find him alive, but if you don't, my mother will cope and I will move to America that much sooner."

Ivan walked out the door to the office, with Zelach and Iosef behind.

"Thank you for your help," Iosef said. "We will contact your mother as soon as we find him."

When the two detectives were outside in the morning sun, Iosef took a deep breath.

"Well, Akardy?"

"I don't like him," said Zelach, who did not look forward to the half-mile walk and the train ride back to Moscow.

"The father or the son?" asked Iosef.

"Neither," said Zelach.

"Understandable," said Iosef, starting to walk down the road. "I think it might be reasonable to add the mother to a list of the unlikable."

"Ah, look, they have a car," said Zelach. "He could have offered us a ride."

"That would have been polite," said Iosef with a smile. "But it is a nice day and this promises to be a relatively easy assignment."

"Perhaps," said Zelach, slouching along at the younger man's side, "but this morning my mother got out of bed and accidentally touched her left foot to the floor instead of her right. She says I will have bad luck and should be careful."

"You believe that?"

"Of course not," said Zelach without conviction. "We shall find Deputy Pleshkov."

"With luck we will find him during the day," said Iosef. "If not, prepare yourself for little sleep tonight."

When they were a few hundred yards down the road and had passed both newly constructed large dachas and crumbling little cottages, a Mercedes-Benz pulled up next to them and Ivan Pleshkov, who had changed into a plain white shirt with short sleeves, said through the open window, "You don't have a car?"

"No," said Iosef.

"I'll give you a ride to Moscow," he said. "I'm going there anyway. Get in."

"Maybe your mother was wrong about which foot she touched to the floor first," said Iosef, opening the back door.

Zelach didn't think so.

Chapter Three

Rostnikov had returned to Petrovka and immediately reported to Yaklovev.

Pankov, the sweating dwarfish secretary who had survived Colonel Snitkonoy's promotion and now served as secretary to the Yak, had ushered Rostnikov into the director's office, as was his standing order. The only requirement was that the director was alone and that Pankov announced that Rostnikov was there to see him.

Pankov lived in constant fear of his superior. The slightest sign of disapproval or possible problems sent the clean-shaven little man of indeterminate age into a sweat, regardless of the heat or lack of it in Petrovka.

The meeting had been relatively brief, with Rostnikov standing in front of the desk of the Yak, who listened carefully to the early report on the new cases.

"Another report by the end of the day, or earlier if there are changes," said the Yak, sitting erect. "I want the names of those involved in the dogfights, and I want Congress Member Pleshkov found as soon as possible—and I would like it done quietly."

"I understand," said Rostnikov, noting that the Yak did not seem particularly interested in the naked mobster found in the river.

"I'm sure you do," said the Yak, looking up. "If you have more to report, you may sit. If not . . ."

"The director of the forensics laboratory may be coming to you with a complaint about my turning his men away from a crime scene this morning," said Rostnikov.

"The corpse in the river?"

"Yes," said Rostnikov. "I have Paulinin examining the body."

"Good," said Yaklovev. "I will take care of it with an apology and by being my usual charming self. Anything else?"

"No," said Rostnikov, and the Yak resumed the reading of a thick report before him, a clear sign of dismissal.

Rostnikov left the office, nodded at Pankov, and went to the stairs.

The relationship between Porfiry Petrovich and Director Yaklovev was completely symbiotic and beneficial to both men, though the Yak did not like Rostnikov and Rostnikov did not like the Yak. However, both men trusted each other and knew that, to a great degree, their futures depended on that trust. The Yak was corrupt but he was a man of his word, and Rostnikov was reasonably confident that when the time inevitably came that the director felt he had to betray his chief inspector, the Yak would inform Rostnikov that it was coming.

Instead of going back to his office, Rostnikov went down four flights. The last two flights were underground. There was no one in the corridor, so Rostnikov leaned against the wall, taking all of his weight on his good leg. Four flights down had resulted in a slight soreness where the artificial leg connected to Rostnikov's leg just below the knee.

"Leg," he said. "We have been through far worse. It is time to stop grieving over the loss of an old friend who had to be dragged around like a child's wagon. Ah, that's better."

Rostnikov opened the door to Paulinin's laboratory and entered to find Emil Karpo watching Paulinin carefully examine the white body, which lay upon the table. The body had been cut from neck to groin and peeled open, exposing the organs, only one of which Paulinin had yet removed. The scientist was slicing the corpse's liver on what looked like a restaurant meat slicer.

"*Kofyeh*, coffee?" asked Paulinin, white surgical gloves reddened with blood.

"I thank you, but I have just had several cups," said Rostnikov.

"*Nyet spahssebah*, no, thank you," said Karpo.

Paulinin's eyes didn't leave the mechanism, which slid back and forth with a smooth metallic sound. Rostnikov and Karpo stood silently watching till Paulinin had had enough and turned off the machine. He turned to Rostnikov, eyes wide, smile small, and said, "New toy, the slicer. You know what a pathology slicer costs? Never mind. You can't get one even if you have the money. But this is better. I got it for some of those new rubles. I can't be bothered keeping up with what they are worth. At least the new ones are bright. Where was . . . oh, the slicer was purchased from a restaurant, the Cosmos on Gorky Street. It was cheap and it works better than the surgical ones I've seen. It slices just as thin and if you keep the blade sharp, as I do, there is no tissue and little cell damage."

"Interesting," said Karpo.

"Yes, and had you given the corpse to the bumblers who pass themselves off as pathologists, they would have concluded that our dead friend was told to strip, shot to death in the middle of the night on the riverbank, and shoved into the water."

"He wasn't?" asked Rostnikov, knowing that the man wanted, needed appreciation.

"He was not," said Paulinin, rising and putting his right hand on the shoulder of the corpse. "Our friend drowned. He is a quite amazing creature. He was shot three times, any wound of which would have caused his death in a short time, except the wound to the head. That went around the cranium and lodged at the back of his brain. Relatively little damage. His lungs were filled with water, but not water from the Moscow River. No, the water in his lungs is clean and filled with chlorine. He died in a swimming pool after he was shot. See these bruises on his rear and back? Whoever did this was very strong, or it was more than one person. Our friend here weighed about two hundred and forty-eight pounds. He was dead weight and in a pool would be even more of a dead load."

Paulinin raised the body so that the two detectives could see. "Those occurred after death. Whoever pulled him from the pool put him in some kind of vehicle—a cart, a wheelbarrow—something wooden and painted white. There are splinters, small but detectable. The bruises came during transport of our friend. And though the traces are almost infinitesimally small, when he was transported he was covered by something made of blue terry cloth, probably an oversized bath towel. Pieces of the material are in the blood and around the edges of the gunshot wounds. There was probably a lot more, but the corpse was in the river for seven or eight hours before we pulled him out. He died last night, probably late. Next . . ."

Paulinin released the corpse, which slumped back with a thump, removed his gloves with a snap and threw them into an almost full garbage can.

"Next," he said, "the bullets. Perhaps the most interesting part of what appears to be a puzzle. They are forty-four caliber, fired from a well-preserved but very old weapon, which suggests . . . ?"

"That he was probably not shot by a Mafia member, or that, if he was, the use of such a weapon carries some specific meaning," said Rostnikov.

"Precisely," said Paulinin, looking down at the face of the corpse. "Now you must leave. I have to talk with our friend's liver and other organs. I'll tell you more soon."

Rostnikov and Karpo went into the empty corridor and let the heavy door to Paulinin's laboratory slam shut.

"The dead man is Valentin Lashkovich," said Karpo. "He is known as Shtopahr—'Corkscrew'—a simple-minded killer for the Tatar Mafia. He is suspected of at least nine murders, but has been arrested for only one and released when the judge said there wasn't sufficient evidence."

"But there was?"

"Yes," said Karpo.

"So, many people may have wanted Lashkovich dead?"

"Many," said Karpo. "The obvious conclusion, were it not for the bullets used to kill him, is that he was killed as part of an on-going war between the Tatars and the Chechins. Three others, two Chechins and one Tatar, one shot in a hotel health club, one in a hotel exercise room, and one in a hotel swimming pool."

Rostnikov knew this but listened attentively and then said, "And the weapon used?"

"The bullets were neither examined nor kept," said Karpo. "The deaths were ruled as casualties of a Mafia dispute—a dispute, I wish to add, that may well grow larger when the Tatars learn of this murder. If they do not already know."

"So, Lashkovich was murdered in a swimming pool," said Rost-nikov. "But why was his body thrown in the river?"

"To disassociate the crime from yet another hotel health facil-ity," said Karpo.

"Yes," said Rostnikov. "Which suggests?"

"That the killer is somehow associated with hotel health clubs."

"Or that such a location has special meaning."

"And then there is the question of why such an old weapon was used. Definitely not a Mafia gun of choice."

"It is intriguing, Emil Karpo."

"The Tatars will ask for the body," said Karpo.

"And when Paulinin is finished with it, they will have it. And you and I, Emil, will attend the funeral."

Karpo nodded.

"Meanwhile, find out where Lashkovich lived, and swam," said Rostnikov. "You know what to do. I'll talk to . . . who is the leader of the Tatars?"

"Casmir Chenko," said Karpo. "He is known as the Glahz—the Eye. He wears a patch to cover the open socket where a rival gang leader destroyed the eye with his thumb when Chenko was still a young man. The rival is now blind and hiding in Estonia."

"Perhaps you should see Chenko and I should find out about Lashkovich?"

"I believe you would deal with Chenko much more professionally than I," said Karpo.

Rostnikov nodded. Since the death of Mathilde Verson, shot to
pieces in the crossfire of two Mafias, Karpo had found a new mission in his life: the eventual destruction of all the Mafias in Russia. It was a task he well knew might not be accomplished till years
after he was dead, if ever.

"Where do you suggest I look for Casmir Chenko?" asked Rostnikov.

"The Leningradskaya Hotel," said Karpo. "Leave a message at
the desk. I do not know where he actually resides, but many of his
people live there and go to the hotel casino. If you wish, I will discover where he lives. It may take me several days."

"That won't be necessary. At least not yet. Find the hotel or
health club, Emil Karpo."

There was nothing more to say. Both men were well aware that
finding a solution to the murders was crucial to the avoidance of a
bloody war on the streets of Moscow. Of course, they might well
discover that these murders were but the first step before the coming battle. As much as such a battle might make a slight dent in the
gang population of Moscow, it might take a few, or perhaps more
than a few, innocents in addition.

Rostnikov made his way slowly back to his office while Karpo
went in search of Lashkovich. When he got to the office, Rostnikov
removed his leg, put it on his desk, and reached for his phone.

"My twelve-year-old daughter can make a better corner kick
than that," Oleg Kisolev shouted.

Kisolev was a compact man wearing a gray sweatshirt and gray
shorts. Kisolev had powerful legs and thighs and a look on his flat
face, dominated by an often-broken nose, that suggested he was
not a particularly brilliant human specimen. It was an unfair conclusion, only partially supported by the conversation that was taking place.

"Scheplev," Kisolev shouted. "Go on the other field and kick one hundred corner kicks. Pushnik, go with him in the goal."

The other players paid little attention when Scheplev and Pushnik walked off toward the other field. Two other players sitting on the sideline put on blue shirts and replaced the departing players.

"Play," shouted Kisolev, blowing his whistle.

The red-shirted team took the ball downfield.

Iosef Rostnikov and Akardy Zelach had introduced themselves and stood watching and waiting while Kisolev ignored them.

"Coach Kisolev," Iosef said gently to the coach, who was concentrating on the weaknesses of his players.

"Menchelev," he shouted in exasperation, "you're too far upfield. Their line will run right past you. Back up." Kisolev shook his head. "Menchelev is a great fullback, but he thinks he can run like a track star. I—"

"We must talk to you now," said Iosef.

Kisolev motioned Menchelev back even farther. Iosef reached over and grabbed the whistle Kisolev was about to blow. The whistle was on a cord around the coach's neck. Iosef tugged at the whistle and Kisolev turned.

"What the hell you think you're doing, you son-of-a-bitch bastard?" said Kisolev, pulling the whistle from Iosef's hand. Red faced, he clenched his fists and looked into Iosef's eyes.

Iosef smiled and said, "I suggest you smile and we talk, or you might well be spending a few days in a local police lockup. Do you know what they are like? No? Well, you don't want to know."

Kisolev looked at Zelach, who had no expression on his face, though his left eye seemed to be slightly glazed over.

"I have important friends," said Kisolev.

"You have one important friend," said Iosef. "And we're looking for him. Yevgeny Pleshkov."

Kisolev turned to the field, blew his whistle, and shouted, "Break. Get some *vahdi*, water. Don't leave the area."

"Thank you," said Iosef.

"If you weren't a policeman, I'd . . ."

"After we talk," Iosef said, "I'll be happy to go behind the stands and give you the opportunity."

Kisolev looked at the young man, who was only slightly taller than he, and saw a new smile that made it quite clear that the good-looking policeman was not only unafraid but actually welcomed a chance at him. Kisolev caved.

"What do you want?"

"Yevgeny Pleshkov."

"I don't know where he is if not at home. He might be at his dacha."

"He is neither there nor at his apartment in the city," said Iosef.

"Then I can be of no help to you," said Kisolev.

Zelach had wandered over to a cluster of four soccer balls a few feet away and had begun dribbling while Iosef and the coach continued to talk.

"Think. Where might we find him? Where might he be? Where does he go?"

"Who knows?" said Kisolev with a shrug and a scratching of his head of ample dark hair.

"You know," said Iosef. "Where does he go when he drinks? How do we locate Yulia Yalutsak?"

"Yalutshkin," Kisolev corrected.

"And where might we find her? It would be in your best interest for us to find him. He needs to be found soon."

Kisolev looked down in thought and then said, "Why soon?"

"His political presence is needed," said Iosef. "An important vote is coming up in the congress and he is needed for that and the debate that precedes it. His future may depend upon appearing, taking positions, and voting on several crucial issues."

"Yevgeny, Yevgeny," Kisolev said, sighing as he looked across the soccer field at his players who were lounging on the grass. "I love Yevgeny and we have been friends since we were children and I take great pride in that friendship, but no one can stop these . . . these benders. These lost weekends."

"Can you help us find him?" asked Iosef, trying not to sound impatient.

"He hasn't come to me," said Kisolev, "but I can tell you where to find Yulia Yalutshkin. Almost every night at the Casino Royal. When he is like this, you are right, he goes to her. I don't like her. I've told Yevgeny to stay away from her. She's a whore. She gets picked up by Chinese, Mafia, sometimes Americans and Germans, mostly Germans. She probably has diseases."

"The Casino Royal," Iosef repeated patiently.

"Yes, a gambling palace now, but it was once a real palace where the czar stayed when he went to the horse races. I'm not a royalist. I'm not a Communist and I don't like this new democracy and I don't care if you know it. There were times and there are places that are part of our history."

"History changes," said Iosef.

Kisolev shook his head and looked at his whistle for an answer. "History changes," he agreed. "Don't go to the Royal before midnight. She won't be there."

"Thanks," said Iosef.

"As I said, Yevgeny is my friend. I don't have many friends. I'm a tyrant as a coach and it carries over into my private life. I get paid to win. It is simple. To win I must be a tyrant. Tyrants have few friends and—"

The solid impact of a shoe against a soccer ball made both men turn and look at Zelach, whose left foot was still out following his kick. The ball was sailing high into the air and across the width of the field. It came down in the arms of one of the lounging players. The players looked across at Zelach and applauded.

"Can you kick like that often?" asked Kisolev.

Zelach nodded.

"Can you corner kick?"

Zelach shrugged and looked at Iosef, who shrugged back.

"Take a ball," said Kisolev. "Go . . . you prefer the right or left?"

"Doesn't matter," said Zelach.

"You kick like that with either foot?" asked Kisolev.

"Yes," said Zelach, looking across at the players sitting on the grass.

"Please, go take a corner kick."

"It's all right," said Iosef, interested by this unforeseen side of the man known derisively at Petrovka as "the Slouch."

Zelach dribbled a ball slowly to the nearest corner of the field and placed the ball in the small chalked-in space for the corner kick. He stepped back five or six paces and took three long strides to the ball. He kicked the ball, which went soaring up in the air about twenty feet from the ground and came down about five yards in front of the goal. Again the lounging players applauded.

"Who do you play for?" asked Kisolev.

"No one," said Zelach. "I'm a police officer."

"I know that, but don't you play for some club?"

"No."

"Where did you learn to kick like that?"

"I don't . . . when I was a boy, I practiced, alone. Many hours. I still go out in the park and kick. It makes me feel . . . I don't know."

"Would you like to play, professionally?" asked Kisolev. "I mean have a tryout, maybe play for one of our park teams for a while. You could do it and be a police officer. We have firemen, police, even one of the mayor's staff."

Zelach shook his head.

"Why?" asked Kisolev. "You'll be paid."

"I don't play," said Zelach. "I just kick the ball alone. And I have a bad back and my left eye is . . . *spahssebah*, thank you, no."

The bad back and permanently injured left eye were the result of the attack on Zelach during a stakeout with Sasha Tkach. While Sasha was being seduced by a female member of the gang, Zelach had been beaten by three of the gang of computer thieves. Zelach had spent weeks in the hospital, and months recuperating.

"Well," said Kisolev. "I guess you're a little old for this anyway, but your kick is powerful, beautiful."

"Thank you," said Akardy Zelach sheepishly.

Iosef motioned for Zelach to follow him and the two men started to move away. Kisolev blew his whistle and the team members began to make their way back onto the field.

"If Pleshkov contacts you," said Iosef, "call me at Petrovka. Office of Special Investigation. Iosef Rostnikov."

"No," said Kisolev. "I will talk to Yevgeny, try to get him sober, try to get him home, ask him to call you, but I cannot afford to lose my best friend by betraying him."

"I'm sorry about—" Iosef began, but Kisolev waved him off.

"I probably deserved it," he said. With that, Kisolev trotted onto the field toward his waiting team.

"You have hidden talents," said Iosef as the two investigators walked out of the stadium. "Are there other things you can do, about which I know nothing? Throw a javelin, wrestle?"

"No," said Zelach.

"Would you mind sometime if I made a wager on your kicking skills?"

"I don't know," said Zelach uncomfortably.

"We'll talk about it. We have to be at the Casino Royal at midnight. You might want to go home and take a nap later this afternoon."

"I cannot nap," said Zelach as they reached the street where a kiosk stood selling American hot dogs. There was a small line.

Iosef got in the line and Akardy Zelach joined him. "You kicked that first ball fifty yards," said Iosef.

"Perhaps," said Zelach.

Iosef stood silently considering some way of capitalizing on the talent of the man at his side.

Sasha's head was a hot balloon of searing hangover pain. His stomach threatened nausea. There was no place he wanted to be.

He didn't want to be lying down in the hotel room, where the ceiling insisted on going back and forth like a light boat on the water. Even if he could, he didn't want to go home to his wife, children, and mother, where he would get no rest. And, besides, he had been ordered not to go home. He didn't want a hot shower. He didn't want to eat. All he wanted to do was sit alone in a darkened room and moan.

Instead, he leaned back confidently in the antique wooden-armed chair and accepted a cup of strong coffee from Illya Skatesholkov.

They were in a large, expensive, and tastefully decorated office in Zjuzino on Khaovka not far from the Church of Boris and Gleb. The office was on the second floor of a line of high rises built in the 1950s. This series of high rises was better maintained than most.

Sasha had been called and then picked up at the hotel by a white American Lincoln limousine. The driver had not spoken, and Sasha, who was supposed to be a Ukrainian, looked out at the miles of apartments, wasteland, and remaining memories of small villages. Down many of the roads, Sasha knew, were communities of dachas, many old and crumbling, some being renovated right down to Jacuzzis and swimming pools, which their owners could use only a month or two each year.

More than ninety percent of the people of Moscow live beyond the Outer Ring Circle. Tourists and visiting businessmen seldom go beyond the Ring, and even those who come frequently have no idea of how most Muscovites live. They live not well. Amid oases of parks, athletic stadiums, restored churches, and even a steeplechase race course are miles of apartment buildings from whose windows hang laundry and in whose corridors children steal from children, adults fight over water and inches of space, and families depressed by lack of food and money battle over meaningless slights.

Sometimes these conflicts led to serious injury or even death.

On more than one occasion, if the identity of the one who committed the crime was not immediately obvious to the uniformed police who were first on the scene, Sasha had been part of an investigation.

A moment of near panic. What if someone in this building recognized him, approached him? This fear was a familiar one, one that came whenever Sasha went undercover, which was frequently. He had nightmares about being exposed, pointed at by a child or a woman carrying a baby, or by an old man. The person pointed to him and screamed his name and he tried to run, with some deadly presence close behind. He would pass people, young, old, and they would point at him and scream. Once, he had been pointed out in a dream by an obviously blind young man.

Sasha came out of the state of panic, hoping it had not been noticed. The pain of the hangover, that was what caused this weakness, that and . . . He turned his attention back to the bleak miles of apartment buildings.

Some of these complexes were in decay. Some were reasonably well maintained by residents determined to retain dignity if not great hope. Sasha had been in buildings like this. He knew.

And now he sat in a ground-floor apartment which had been converted into period luxury, right down to expensive wallpaper. Sasha felt as if he had walked through a door into another century. He sat with Illya Skatesholkov and Boris Osipov drinking coffee and discussing the events of the previous night. Both Boris and Illya, though they tried not to show it, were noticeably nervous.

"So," said Boris, "what did you think of our little arena?"

Sasha looked around and said, "Impressive."

Boris let out a mirthless laugh and said, "Not the office. The dog ring. Last night."

"Impressive also," said Sasha, drinking some coffee. The pain in his head was nearly unbearable, and he feared his nausea would force him to ask for the rest room. He fought the nausea and affected a small, knowing smile. The Yak had approved the purchase of three suits, complete with silk shirts, ties, and shoes. He was wearing the second of the suits. Elena was taking care of having the one he wore yesterday cleaned, a task she clearly felt should be his, but when the call had come she accepted the responsibility with minimal reluctance.

"And Tatyana?" asked Illya.

"Impressive," Sasha repeated, taking another sip of his very good coffee.

So that was her name. Oh, he had been drunk. As his mother, Lydia, would say, remembering her long-dead husband, he had been "drunk as a cross-eyed cossack." It had been Sasha's impression since first hearing the expression that he had seen few cossacks and none that he could recall having crossed eyes.

"Versatile," said Illya.

"Yes," Sasha agreed, preferring not to discuss the woman who had led him off to a room after the dogfight. He had been drunk, but she had been beautiful and talented. She enjoyed her work and so had Sasha.

His two hosts smiled.

"We have made some inquiries about you and your Kiev operation," said Boris.

Sasha noted that neither of the two men moved behind the huge cherrywood desk, impressive due to its size and ornate legs and because there was nothing on its polished surface, not even a telephone. Both of his escorts sat in chairs identical to the one in which Sasha sat back with his legs folded. The chair behind the desk, Sasha assumed, was reserved for the person for whom his hosts worked. "Chair" was hardly the word for it. It, like the desk, was of another century. The very high-backed chair, with each dark wood arm coming forward to clasp a wooden ball, looked as if it belonged in a museum.

"And?" asked Sasha, sipping carefully to avoid spilling on his perfectly pressed suit.

"We are informed that you have a growing operation," said Boris, "not equal to ours, but growing rapidly."

Sasha nodded.

"From what I have seen of your operation," said Sasha, "I would say that mine is already equal to yours."

"Let's not bicker about size," said Illya. "It is sufficient that you have a prospering operation. We would like to discuss a proposal, a proposal that would make your operation part of our operation, a proposal that would certainly double or even triple your earnings, a proposal that would make you part of an international syndicate growing each week. We would bring some of our dogs to Kiev. You would bring some of your dogs to Moscow. We would provide advice from our dog trainers. We would locate and draw bettors, high-stakes bettors, to your operation."

"I am doing well on my own," said Sasha.

"You could be doing better with us," said Boris.

"I'll consider it," said Sasha. "I'll have to talk to some of my people."

"Of course," said Boris. "We believe our arguments can be very persuasive."

Boris spoke with a friendly smile but Sasha recognized the threat, as he was intended to do. "I'm sure," Sasha said. "I have some questions about the details of this merger."

"Ask your questions and we will come back to you with answers," said Illya, leaning forward, hands clasped together.

"I would prefer to ask my questions and get my answers from your boss," Sasha said, trying to duplicate the way Jean Paul Belmondo had said nearly the same thing in an old French movie Sasha had recently seen on the television.

"Perhaps," said Boris. "We will see. Meanwhile, you have a dog you wish to enter into our fights to show us the quality of your kennel?"

"A pit bull," said Sasha. "If the effort proves profitable, he can fight again and we can begin our negotiations with my bringing more dogs."

"Your animal is good?" asked Illya.

"My dog will win," said Sasha with a smile and a tone of confidence he did not feel. He was speaking from information provided by an older uniformed MVD officer named Mishka, who had tended and overseen the training of the dogs of Petrovka for a quarter of a century. Mishka had dogs that could locate drugs, seek out hiding fugitives, and attack when signaled to do so. Mishka had assured Elena and Sasha that Tchaikovsky, the pit bull, would kill any human or animal on command. Mishka was particularly proud of Tchaikovsky, who had been named thus because the famous composer had lived in Mishka's hometown of Klin, an hour northwest of Moscow on the old Leningrad Highway.

The beagle-faced Mishka had warned the two young officers that they were to be very careful with Tchaikovsky.

The white pit bull with black spots had seemed docile enough when Mishka had taken him from his pen, petting him and talking softly to the dog, even nuzzling the animal with his head. Tchaikovsky had wagged his tail.

"Don't be deceived," Mishka had said as he petted the animal. "Our Tchaikovsky can, on command or on his own if provoked, or even for no reason, attack and sink his teeth into an antagonist with deadly and determined ferocity. Getting Tchaikovsky to release his grip can be very difficult, and if it is a death grip, it can be nearly impossible until the victim is dead."

"That is very reassuring," Sasha had said, and Mishka, recognizing no irony in the comment, had responded:

"Yes."

Sasha was not particularly confident about placing his safety in the jaws of a pit bull. These were dangerous men. If the pit bull didn't do well, Sasha might be in very serious trouble.

Illya and Boris, a bit clumsily, questioned Sasha, whom they knew as Dmitri Kolk, about Kiev. Sasha had casually responded using his wife, Maya's, history in Kiev as his own. In spite of the desire to get back to the hotel room, turn off the lights, and close the drapes, he chatted, drank, accepted some Italian biscotti, which he normally liked but which now caused a renewed wave of queasiness, and made himself as amiable as possible.

"It is getting a bit late and you will want to prepare your dog," said Boris, standing.

"Yes," said Sasha, taking a final bite of biscotti and saying, "delicious."

"Thank you," said Illya. "Our driver will take you back to the hotel."

"Good," said Sasha, straightening his slacks and adjusting his blue silk paisley tie. "And tomorrow I would like to discuss the proposed operational merger with your boss."

"I think that can be arranged," said Boris. "But tonight, your dog fights. He has a name?"

"Tchaikovsky," said Sasha.

Boris and Illya smiled.

"Amusing," said Boris.

"Disarming," said Sasha.

The two men ushered Sasha to the entrance to the building. Two women in their forties, carrying shopping bags, stepped aside to let the three men pass. The Lincoln was waiting and the driver was behind the wheel. There was no doubt that someone had been listening to the conversation in the office, that someone had probably been watching; otherwise, what was the point of driving all the way out here?

"One last question," said Boris. "How well do you know the woman you are with?"

"Lyuba Polikarpova?" asked Sasha.

"Yes," said Boris.

"She's Russian," Sasha said casually, though he was sensing warning signals. "I picked her up last time I came to Moscow for some fun and called her when I returned here on Tuesday. She's a whore, but an educated one who asks no questions, looks good, and is very accommodating. Why do you ask?"

"Caution," said Boris with a smile Sasha did not like. "Just being careful."

"Good," said Sasha. "I like working with people who are careful."

The three men shook hands and Sasha got into the Lincoln, which drove off. Boris and Illya went back into the building to the office. Behind the desk sat a young man, younger than Sasha. He was dressed in dark slacks, a fresh white dress shirt, and a pullover black cashmere sweater. The young man had a round, pink face with a thin white scar about two inches long running in a straight line directly under his nose. His hair was dark and recently cut, and if one was close enough, the musky smell of expensive aftershave was faint but evident.

His name was Peter Nimitsov. His nickname, never spoken in his company if one wanted to survive the encounter intact, was "Baby Face." He was twenty-seven years old and had been born in the apartment building in which he now sat. He had formed a gang in the complex of crumbling concrete high rises when he was fourteen and the Soviet Union and Communism had begun to die. When he was seventeen, the gang had taken over these apartment buildings and extended their influence to other complexes, eliminating competition and making deals with other gangs. When he was strong enough, Peter Nimitsov had begun to move his operation inside the Outer Ring Circle. In the course of his rise, Nimitsov had murdered, suffered his white scar, and grown powerful enough to have his Zjuzino Mafia feared or respected by even the largest and most ruthless of the other Mafias of Moscow.

Peter kept a very low profile. His goal was power and wealth, not infamy, but power and wealth were a means to an end. He maintained a large suite at the National Hotel, but he lived in a luxurious apartment adjoining the office in which he now sat. The apartment, like the office, was decorated in antiques of the Russian czars. Some had cost Nimitsov a great deal of money. Others had cost people their health or, in the case of one stubborn thief, a life. Peter Nimitsov shared his wealth with his mother, father, sister, various relatives, and the initial members of his teenage gang, who formed the inner circle of those loyal to him.

Boris and Illya were front men, inner-circle Muscovites, hired bureaucrats who had held middle-level government jobs and lived on their meager salaries, bribes, and corruption before the fall of the system. The two men had connections, knew where skeletons were buried, and were invaluable to Peter. Both men were old enough to be their boss's father, though neither had paternal feelings for the young baby-faced man behind the desk. They had seen him suddenly explode because of a lie told, a remark made. They had seen him draw a gun and begin to fire wildly at a member of his gang who had told a minor lie: Peter had begun to shoot, missing the man who had lied but killing another who had gone flat on the floor and taken a ricocheting bullet to the head. Peter had fired till he ran out of bullets. In addition to the dead man on the floor, Peter had shot one of his own cousins in the arm. The man who had lied had stood with his back to the door, hyperventilating, waiting for Peter to reload or order his death.

Instead, Peter Nimitsov had said, "Don't lie to me again," and let the man live.

Peter's mother had told her friends that her son had always been a bit "emotional." She did not share their belief that her son was quite mad, had inherited some disease of the mind from her father and grandfather, both of whom had died young with "brain illness." Peter's mother was very proud of her son. Her father had swept up scraps of imitation leather in a shoe factory. Her grandfather had been a very unsuccessful thief who, till the day he died, bragged about his one supposed triumph, the stealing of a not-very-young horse from the Moscow stable of Czar Nicholas II.

Peter had listened to the conversation with Sasha from the next room. Now he sat thinking about it, running a finger gently over the ridge of his scar and biting his lower lip, deep in thought. "I don't like him," Peter finally said to the two men who stood before his desk.

This surprised neither Boris nor Illya, since Peter Nimitsov liked practically no one. Peter was into a wide variety of criminal activity centered mostly within twenty miles of where he now sat. But an increasing portion of his income was now coming from inside the Outer Ring Circle. Gambling, drugs, extortion, car theft were all sources of income—the dogfights were but a small part of Nimitsov's enterprise. But dogs were Peter's passion. All the czars had owned dogs, regal dogs, dogs bred especially for the czar. But Peter was interested not in how his dogs looked but how efficiently and with what style they killed.

Now, international expansion was a distinct possibility, and with it might well come the next step in his ambition. He had witnessed the deaths of many dogs, had begun as a boy, while engaging in his other criminal activities, to stage fights between stray dogs, taking bets, making money. But it was the fights themselves that excited the young man with the baby face. Women, drugs, gun battles did not mean anything to Peter, but the sight of two dogs trying to kill each other aroused his passion and even gave him erections that had to be satisfied immediately after the battle, with the closest prostitute in his employ.

"You think he is all right?" asked Peter, looking at the two men. Peter's eyes were blue, very blue.

Neither man wanted to commit himself, especially since their leader had expressed a reservation about the cocky young Ukrainian. If Boris or Illya proved to be wrong in their assessment, there was a good chance they would be found with their throats cut in a park or on a dark street, or in this very office. Peter was brilliant. Peter was bold. Peter was leading them to great wealth, but Peter was clearly growing more mad each day. Neither man wanted to commit himself, but Peter was giving them no choice.

"I think he should be watched carefully," said Illya.

"Watched carefully," said Nimitsov, shaking his head. "I have already seen to that, but that wasn't what I asked you. What did I ask you?"

"If Dmitri Kolk could be trusted," said Illya, looking for help to Boris, who gave him none. Illya would have dearly loved to say that he did not know if the Ukrainian could be trusted, but Peter definitely did not want evasion. "I don't trust him," said Illya.

"Boris?"

"I don't trust him either."

"So," said Peter. "We watch him. We do not let him out of sight. He could be the police or State Security. He could simply be someone dishonest who plans to betray us. The czars lived on constant alert, except for the last Nicholas. That state of alert kept them alive, and those who would betray them dead. The woman?" Peter asked.

"Morishkov is almost certain that he has seen her before," said Illya, on safer ground. "He still thinks she may be a police officer."

"And Kolk doesn't know it?" asked Peter, looking at Boris.

"I don't think so," said Boris. "I think she approached him, that—if she is a police officer—she wanted to get close to him to penetrate his operation."

Peter thought for a while and then said, "If she is a spy, it troubles me that this Kolk from Kiev doesn't know it. Follow her. Find what you can about her. Take her picture and show it around. Show it to our people in State Security. Show Kolk's picture too. Meanwhile, we watch and we see how good a dog his Tchaikovsky is. I want Kolk's dog to fight Bronson tomorrow if he wins tonight."

"We won't get any odds with Bronson fighting an unknown dog," said Boris.

Bronson, a massive, shaggy, uncontrollable street stray, had killed nine opponents with a mad fury and a bloodthirst. After each battle, Bronson, who Peter had named for the American film star, had to be pulled off the dead dog he continued to bite. On more than one occasion, Bronson had turned on those trying to pull him off. One man had lost a finger. Several others had needed medical attention and numerous stitches.

"If Kolk's dog wins tonight, I want to see Bronson tear this Kolk's animal to pieces tomorrow," said Peter. "I want Kolk humbled and manageable, very manageable."

Chapter Four

"Is your word no good?" came the unmistakable voice of Lydia Tkach over the phone.

There had been no hello, no identification, no small talk.

Rostnikov was sitting at his desk, drinking a cup of abysmal coffee after having just called the Leningradskaya Hotel and leaving a message for Casmir Chenko, Glahz, the one-eyed Tatar. He had no idea how long it would take to hear back from Chenko. In fact, he had no idea whether he would ever hear from him, which would mean the usual legwork.

And now, Lydia Tkach.

Sasha's mother had been enough trouble when she was working at the Ministry of Information, but since her retirement, Rostnikov was convinced, Lydia had a daily checklist of those who required her scolding, which reminded all who knew her of the angry cawing of one of the big gray-and-white crows that ruled the bird world of Moscow.

The list of those most in need of scolding began with her own son and daughter-in-law. Lydia no longer lived with Maya, Sasha, and their two children, but she sat with the children while Maya and Sasha worked. This gave her certain privileges, such as camping rights in the small apartment and the right to complain about child rearing, the dangers of her son's job, and the temptations that faced her daughter-in-law in the workplace. But Lydia was an enigma, a hard-of-hearing enigma. Her grandchildren loved her, and Lydia had begun supplementing her son's income.

Lydia had saved her money and her dead husband's pension.

Through bits of information picked up in the ministry when she worked, she had invested in a variety of borderline legal activities and made a great deal of money, though she told no one how much she had.

Within days of the end of the Soviet Union, Lydia had bought a state bakery on the Arbat. She had hired a Turkish baker to provide not only bread, which she sold at a reasonable price, but also inexpensive and simple pastries and cookies. Business had boomed. Lydia had hired, at Rostnikov's suggestion, Galina Panishkoya, who had just been released from prison, a woman whose grandchildren Rostnikov and his wife had taken in. The woman and the grandchildren were living with the Rostnikovs until suitable arrangements could be made, a dim prospect. Rostnikov knew that he would be paying, in some way, for Lydia's generosity. It was a price he was willing to pay, though there were moments when he wondered if he had made a pact with a dark angel.

However, the major mistake in the Lydia Tkach saga had been made by Anna Timofeyeva, Rostnikov's former chief in the Office of the Moscow Procurator. Anna had been forced to retire after a series of heart attacks and now lived in a one-story concrete-block apartment with her niece Elena. Anna had made the mistake of finding an apartment in the building for Lydia after Maya had issued an ultimatum that her mother-in-law move out. Anna had laid down rules when Lydia moved into her apartment down the hall. No unannounced visits to Anna and Elena. No complaints about her daughter-in-law. No complaints about the dangers of Sasha's job. No complaints about how her two grandchildren were being raised. And Lydia had to wear her hearing aid when she visited.

Lydia had violated all these rules and several others within hours of moving in.

Very close to the top of Lydia Tkach's list was Porfiry Petrovich Rostnikov, who was to be hounded into getting her son a safe office job in Petrovka or State Security or the Ministry of the Interior or anywhere else.

"Good morning, Lydia Tkach," said Rostnikov, deciding that with his new position he could probably have someone screen his calls. It would keep Lydia at bay but it would mean that someone else, possibly Pankov, would know everyone who called him. Pankov and the Yak probably knew anyway, however, so screening might . . .

"All right then, good morning," Lydia said impatiently. "You promised."

"I did not," Rostnikov said loudly, knowing his caller was not wearing her hearing device. "I said I would talk to Sasha. I talked to him. I told you that. He does not want to sit in an office, at a desk. He says it would drive him mad. He is a young man. He doesn't want to sit at a desk preparing reports and answering phones for the next thirty years."

"He would be alive those thirty years," she said. "You have the power to have it done even if he doesn't want it."

"Again, I have told you that perhaps I could get him reassigned over his objections. He would blame you. He would blame me. He would hate going to work each morning. He has enough things to be depressed about without adding that."

"What has he to be depressed about?" asked Lydia.

"Beyond the fact that he is Russian and part of our proud heritage of depression," said Rostnikov, "I can't think of a thing."

"You are being ironic," she said. "I hate ironic. I have trouble understanding it. I have one son. If he is hurt or dies, it will be on your head. I'll never let you forget it."

"I am confident of that, Lydia Tkach."

"Talk to him again," she said. "Persuade him."

"I'll talk to him again," said Rostnikov, who would indeed do so, though he would not try to persuade Sasha to his mother's cause. If Sasha could control his moods and depressions, he still had a promising future, promotion would come quickly. But time was running out on Sasha. If he did not come around in the next year or two, he would be a lower-level investigator for the rest of his career. It could be worse. He might not have a career.

"Report to me," she said and hung up.

"Yes, Comrade Stalin," he said to the dead phone, and he too hung up.

The moment the phone hit the cradle, it rang.

"Rostnikov," he said.

"Pushkin Square in front of the statue in thirty minutes," said a heavily accented voice which Rostnikov thought was probably Tatar. "Not a second later. Wait there."

The man hung up, and Rostnikov, who desperately wanted to finish the last four pages of his dearly purchased copy of Ed McBain's *Sadie When She Died*, put on his artificial leg, adjusted it, and rose with the aid of his desk. He checked his watch and calculated that he would have ample time to get to Pushkin Square by metro. He could, in his new capacity, he reminded himself, requisition a car and finish his book in the backseat, but it would take time to get an approval signed by the Yak and a car waiting downstairs.

No, the metro would be faster.

In fact, Rostnikov made it in less than twenty minutes. He emerged from the Pushkin Square metro station in the old Izvestia Building, looked across the Boulevard Ring and down Gorky Street. He surveyed the Square and glanced at the Rossia Cinema.

The dark clouds rumbled but it was not yet raining. This had been going on for several days, and Rostnikov imagined that the skies were waiting for something before they began to cry. There was plenty to cry about already, but using that logic it should be raining constantly throughout Russia.

The square was crowded with people hurrying by but there was no one standing in front of Pushkin, who looked down at the policeman in front of him. Pushkin's hat was in his left hand at his side and the poet's right hand rested inside his vest in a Napoleonic pose popular in the 1880s when the statue was completed.

Occasionally, a visitor or a Muscovite would place a flower or two at the foot of the statue, but it was nothing like the wreaths that used to be found here. It was said that when Dostoevsky was presented with a wreath of flowers for his achievements, he carried the heavy wreath and placed it at the foot of this very statue.

Cars bustled, honked, and speeded past the square. People hurried by. Behind Porfiry Petrovich and over the sound of the traffic, a man spoke. Rostnikov did not turn.

> " 'How oft in grief, from thee long parted
> Throughout my vagrant destiny
> Moscow my thoughts have turned to thee.' "

Rostnikov continued with:

> " 'Moscow . . . what thoughts in each true-hearted
> Russian come flooding at that word.
> How deep an echo there is heard.' "

Rostnikov turned to face the dark young man in black slacks and a black zipper jacket. The young man was handsome and slender. He looked up at Pushkin.

"He wrote that a long time ago, when times were different," said the young man.

"But you know the words," said Rostnikov.

"Once I believed them. Once I wanted to be a poet. But there is no market for poets."

"There never has been," said Rostnikov, "yet they strive, survive, and breed. Perhaps they are born with a deviant gene."

"Perhaps," said the young man. "When we get in the car, you will be searched. If you are wearing a listening device or recorder, we will find it. If you are carrying a weapon, it will be taken, you will be asked to get out, and we will be gone."

"I carry no weapon. I carry no electronic or recording device," said Rostnikov.

The man nodded, looked around, lifted his right hand to his head as if to smooth back his hair. No more than five seconds later, a modest black Zil pulled up, stopping traffic behind it. The windows of the car were tinted. The young man led the way to the car and opened the back door. Rostnikov slipped in awkwardly, pulling in his prosthetic leg a fraction of a second before the young man closed the door.

The car started. The young man remained behind on the street.

At Rostnikov's left was a pale, thin, young, and quite ugly man with large teeth and a matching nose. The man wore a black zipper jacket exactly like the one worn by the man Rostnikov had spoken to moments earlier.

The driver didn't turn around. All that Rostnikov could see of him was his recently cut dark hair and his bull neck.

The thin young man said nothing and showed no emotion as he patted Rostnikov down, checking his wallet and even the paperback novel in the inspector's pocket. He went so far as to examine Porfiry Petrovich's artificial leg for secret compartments or listening devices. Satisfied, the ugly man reached over and touched the shoulder of the driver, who turned right at the next corner. Halfway down the narrow street the car stopped and the ugly man reached over to open Rostnikov's door. Rostnikov obliged by stepping out, which, given his leg, took a bit of time.

As soon as he had cleared the door, it closed and Porfiry Petrovich found himself on an empty street of houses and shops with boarded-up windows. There was another car, black, tinted windows, not large, parked directly across the street. The rear door to the car opened and Rostnikov proceeded to the car and climbed in. He closed his door himself and looked over at the man at his side, as the car started and moved at a reasonable pace up the street.

"You wish to talk to me," the man said.

He was about Rostnikov's height but much lighter. He was also about Rostnikov's age but looked much older. His hair was thin and straight. His skin, already dark, was weathered and wrinkled by the sun. The face, however, was dominated by a black patch that covered the man's right eye. All these things Rostnikov had known about Casmir Chenko, Glahz, the Tatar.

"Valentin Lashkovich," said Rostnikov, trying to find a comfortable position and keep his eyes on Chenko. "You know he is dead."

"I know," said Chenko.

"Do you also know who killed him?"

"The Chechin," said Chenko.

"Shatalov?" asked Rostnikov.

"Shatalov," said Chenko. "He uses no other name, so one of my men called him Irving. We all call him that now. Shatalov knows and it displeases him. We have reason to believe he is a Jew. So you see, Chief Inspector, we Tatars do have a sense of humor, perhaps not a profound one, but a sense of humor nonetheless. And we are not stupid, or foul-smelling, or particularly sullen."

"I never thought you were," said Rostnikov.

Chenko, who had sat forward when he spoke, now leaned back. "What do you want, policeman?"

"You are going to kill one of Shatalov's men in retaliation," said Rostnikov as the car drove past the old Tretyakov Art Gallery.

"And you don't want me to do it?" said Chenko.

"That is right," said Rostnikov.

"This began when Shatalov killed one of my men two months ago," said Chenko calmly. "Shot him in a hotel sauna. You knew that?"

"I knew that," said Rostnikov. "I mean I knew that one of your men was murdered. I do not know that Shatalov did it. I have some reason to believe that it may indeed be someone else."

"Who else?" asked Chenko.

"Another Mafia that wants you two to kill each other off so they can move in on your territories when you are both weak," said

Rostnikov. "A lone man, perhaps a member of one of your organizations, who sees an opportunity for advancement if a war breaks
out between you. Perhaps . . ."

"You are groping for diamonds in the Siberian tundra," said
Chenko. "Shatalov did it."

"And you did it back and he did it back. And now it will continue."

"I have not yet answered his affront. If someone has killed one
or more of his people, let him look to his own organization. For
the last time, policeman, what do you want?"

"A meeting between you and Shatalov."

"I do not think that a good idea," said Chenko.

"All right then, a promise from you that there will be no violence, no retaliation for Laskovich's murder, not till my office has
time to investigate."

"That might be possible," said Chenko, "if no more of my people are attacked by the Chechins, though I see no good that can
come from a one-sided truce."

"I will try to arrange a truce with a time limit," said Rostnikov.
"You want something in return. You would not have agreed to see
me if you didn't want something."

"The body of Valentin Lashkovich," said Chenko. "Tonight. To
be delivered to this location."

Chenko handed Rostnikov a card. It contained a name and address of a well-known mortuary known to be used by criminals at
all levels. It was more than suspected that the mortuary did more
than handle the internment of the publicly dead. A large number
of people who had unfortunately displeased criminals had disappeared, supposedly into unmarked graves far outside the city. Dis-
posing of the dead was now big business in Moscow.

"It shall be," said Rostnikov. "I have your word?"

"Under the conditions and if the Chechin agrees to the same
terms," said Chenko. "You are going to meet with Shatalov?"

"Yes," said Rostnikov.

Chenko opened a small zipper bag on the floor, took out a cell phone, dialed, and handed it to Rostnikov.

"A woman will answer," said Chenko. "Tell her who you are. Tell her you have a message that must be delivered in person."

Chenko handed the phone to Rostnikov. A woman's voice said, "Yes?" Rostnikov said what Chenko had told him to say and gave his office phone number. "I do not know any Shatalov," the woman said.

"The message remains," said Rostnikov.

Chenko reached over and took the phone from Porfiry Petrovich. "Natalya, daughter of a snake," he said. "Tell Irving I will hang his head over my desk."

Chenko pressed a button on the phone and put it back in the zipper bag.

"You think that will make it more likely that Shatalov will call me?" asked Rostnikov.

"It will make your request undeniable," said Chenko. "Shatalov will be angry. Shatalov will want to save face. Shatalov will call you, meet with you, and give you a message for me. It will be a warning. I will laugh at it."

Rostnikov could not imagine Chenko laughing.

"There is no more to discuss," said Chenko.

"I may wish to talk to you again when more is known," said Rostnikov.

"If there is something to discuss," said Chenko, "you know how to get a message to me. Final question, policeman."

"Ask."

"Why do you want us to stop killing each other? Why do you want to prevent a war?"

"Innocent people die in wars," said Rostnikov. "Besides, it is an assignment that has been given to me by my superiors."

Chenko made a sound. He may have been clearing his throat. It may have been his version of a laugh.

"Let me tell you something, Russian policeman," said Chenko, cocking his head to one side to see Rostnikov. "We care nothing for your wars. We are Tatars. Until 1552 we were an independent state, and then Ivan the Terrible conquered us. In Kazan, the town where I was born, on a tiny island where the Volga and Kamra rivers meet, is a white pavilion built one hundred years ago in tribute to Ivan the Terrible. My mission in life is to return to Kazan and blow up that pavilion. Meanwhile, the self-declared Republic of Tatarstan flies only the red and green flag of ancient Tataria, and we have recently withheld tax payments from your corrupt government. When you people attacked Chechnya, Shatalov sat back in Moscow and let his people be murdered and crushed. If Russia attacks Tataria, we will wage a guerrilla war that will put Shatalov and the Irish Republican Army to shame."

The car stopped. Chenko folded his arms and looked forward with his remaining eye. "If you give me Lashkovich's body and the Chechin agrees, you will have your short truce. If you promise the prompt turning over of any of our people killed in battle in these streets, I will meet with Shatalov, but expect little from such a meeting."

Rostnikov got out. The door closed and the car drove off. Rostnikov was, once again, standing before the statue of Pushkin.

Emil Karpo stood looking at the panorama before him—the Kremlin in the distance across from the river, the tarnished onion-like balls atop the churches along the river, the streets jammed with cars. The day was overcast, threatening. There was also the ever-present haze of pollution that seemed to grow worse by the week. What interested Karpo most about the view through the huge window, however, was the river. Getting the nude body of Valentin Lashkovich from the swimming pool behind Karpo to the river would have been a difficult task. Getting the body out of the hotel would have been more difficult. Yet Karpo was certain this was the place where the Mafia enforcer had been murdered.

His reasons for coming to the conclusion were simple.

Lashkovich lived in the hotel. That had been easily discovered.
Also, Lashkovich took postmidnight swims by himself almost
every night. These things were not proof and Emil Karpo did not
jump to conclusions. No, the evidence which a disinterested child
could see was in the water itself. The water was slightly pink.

"Inspector," came the voice of the day manager of the hotel who
stood behind Emil Karpo, waiting for him to move or say something. The pale policeman in black had been standing at the window twelve floors above the street, hands at his sides, simply
staring. Even at the sound of the manager's voice. Karpo did not
turn.

"Inspector," the day manager, Carl Swartz repeated, "I have to
get back to my office. We have almost one hundred Japanese businessmen staying with us, not to mention . . ."

"Why didn't you call the police?" Karpo asked, without turning
to look at Swartz.

Swartz was Danish. His Russian was extremely good. He wore a
sad, understanding smile that said to all that he understood their
problems, sympathized with them, and would do what he could to
help. His suits were light gray, his ties stylish but not flashy, and
his sparse, faded-yellow hair was brushed straight back. Swartz was
lean, tall, and always calm.

"When I was informed about the condition of the pool,"
Swartz said, "I came up and looked. Neither the pool-and-spa
night manager nor the cleaning woman assigned here had the
slightest idea why the pool looks like this. And I do not understand
why you . . ."

"You have called them both and told them to come here?"
Karpo asked.

"I had my assistant do so as soon as you requested their presence. I warn you. They have had little sleep. Both are on the night
shift, five P.M. till one in the morning."

Karpo said nothing. He watched a flat garbage boat slowly wind
down the river. The two employees had probably gotten home

around two in the morning. It was now almost nine. That was seven
hours of sleep. Karpo never slept for more than five hours a night.

"You didn't call the police," Karpo said.

"I did not know what had happened," said Swartz calmly. "I still
do not. The day pool manager informed the desk of the problem.
The desk told me. I came up and looked. The water is pink. It
could be anything. Mischief by a drunk. Who knows? If the police
had bothered to come, what would they have seen, done?"

Karpo turned, his hands at his sides, to face the manager. Swartz
could not keep from taking a step back, though he was already a
dozen feet away from the policeman. The manager's helpful sad
smile did not flicker.

"Unless you have some reason why we should not drain the pool
and clean it, I'd like to get my people started. We're not letting any
of the guests in yet, but . . ."

"Did Lashkovich have his own locker?" asked Karpo.

"Lashkovich?"

Their eyes met. Karpo did not blink.

"The dead man," said the police inspector when Swartz turned
his eyes for an instant. "I believe you know who and what we are
discussing. If you wish to discuss this elsewhere . . ."

"No," said the hotel manager. "That won't be necessary. Let's
see. Lashkovich. Yes, I think he had a locker. I will ask the daytime-
shift pool and spa manager."

"Have him see me, and keep the guests out," said Karpo. "Tell
me when the night manager and the cleaning woman arrive."

Karpo walked past Swartz, heading for the door marked Men's
Shower in Russian, English, German, and Japanese.

"If you need help . . ." Swartz said, but Karpo was already
through the door to the showers.

Swartz stood still waiting till the shower room door slowly
closed. Only then did the helpful smile fade. He ran his open palm
over his lips nervously and wondered what the hotel owners and the
Mafia leaders would say or do when they discovered that

Lashkovich had been murdered right in the hotel. He managed to restore his usual calm facade as the shower room door came open again.

"How many people are on your night staff?

"Sixty-four to seventy-one, depending on various factors."

"Another officer will return tonight to talk to them," said Karpo.

"All of them?" asked Swartz.

"Yes," said Karpo, disappearing into the shower room again.

This time Swartz moved quickly. He wanted to spend as little time as he could with this ghostly figure. He preferred to take his chances with his superiors and the Mafia leaders. Swartz moved through the door to the carpeted reception area where a short, muscular man in dark slacks and a white T-shirt looked at him from behind the reception desk.

"How many guests have you had to turn away?"

"Fourteen."

Swartz nodded as if filing the information for appropriate future action. The short man with the muscles looked relieved as his employer started to open the outer door.

"The policeman wants to see you," said Swartz. "Cooperate. We must get him out as soon as possible. Be ready to drain the pool and have a crew come in to clean it. Tell Mitavonova to send at least five women for the job."

The muscular man nodded. His boss left. The muscular man was named Kolya Ivanov. He was a body builder and had won the Mister Moscow competition five times in ten years. He was strong. He was confident, but he wished he did not have to deal with the pale policeman.

Kolya found the policeman in the men's shower, where he was kneeling, one knee on the tiles.

"I was told you wanted to see me," said Kolya.

"Wait," said Karpo, examining the blue and white tiled wall under one of the showerheads.

The policeman looked at each square of tile and ran his hand gently over every inch. He was at the third showerhead. He rose slowly, feeling his way up the wall. Kolya was fascinated, but not so fascinated that he did not want to leave.

The policeman took a clear plastic bag from his pocket and removed something from the eye-level tile on which his hand had paused.

"How long has this tile been cracked?" asked Karpo, putting something Kolya did not see into the plastic bag.

"Cracked? I inspect every foot of the space here every evening when I leave. There was no crack last night."

Kolya moved forward for a better look, which required him to get nearer the policeman than he liked. Kolya's eyesight was not perfect, but he could see well enough so that he didn't have to wear his glasses to work. He had to get to within a yard of the tile before he saw it: a very thin, almost imperceptible crack.

"Lashkovich's locker," said the policeman.

"This way."

The locker room was carpeted, an indoor-outdoor brown carpeting. The lockers were in three rows with padded benches for guests. The lockers were tall, polished oak, and quite elegant. Lashkovich's locker was at the beginning of one row. Kolya opened it with his master key. It was empty.

"How did Lashkovich dress when he came up here?"

"Dress? Clothes?"

"Yes."

"I've only seen him up here a few times," said Kolya. "The night manager would know."

"No one is to touch this locker, come in this room, come through your doors."

"But our guests are . . ."

"No one," Karpo repeated. "Not you. Not Swartz. Not the cleaning lady. No one."

"No one," Kolya said in resignation, dreading the rest of the day.

"The workout room," the policeman said, facing Kolya.

"Through that door," said Kolya, pointing to a door at the far end of the locker room.

"Inform me as soon as the night manager and the cleaning woman who was on duty last night arrive," said Karpo, moving toward the door to the weight room.

"Immediately," said Kolya.

The policeman entered the weight room, and Kolya quickly escaped to the relative safety of his reception room and the anticipation of angry guests who paid an average of three hundred dollars a night to stay in this hotel, which boasted all the amenities of the finest hotels in the world.

Except today they would not be able to use the health center.

Chapter Five

Elena was sure she was being followed almost as soon as she stepped out of the hotel. The young couple behind her, arm in arm, moved past her, laughing. The woman had long dark hair. The man was slender, equally dark, and handsome. They were poor actors. Their mirth was quite false. Neither one of them looked at her as they passed. And then Elena caught sight of the couple pausing half a block in front of her when she stopped to look in the window of a clothing store. Nothing was certain, however, till she had gone four more blocks, meandering through the streets, catching glimpses of the couple who now kept their distance and no longer smiled.

The relative incompetence of the couple did not keep Elena from remaining alert. She had planned to see her aunt, Anna Timofeyeva. Normally, she would not have considered such a visit while undercover, but her aunt had shown small signs of distress over the past few weeks, including one moment at dinner when Anna gasped, started to reach for her chest, and brought herself under control, saying, "Gas."

Anna Timofeyeva had been a Soviet procurator, a very successful, workaholic procurator whose chief investigator had been Porfiry Petrovich Rostnikov. A heart attack had ended Anna's career and forced her into one-bedroom retirement, looking into a cement courtyard watching mothers and small children, waiting for visits, which she dreaded, from Lydia Tkach. Anna would never speak up if she was not feeling well. Elena knew her aunt would prefer to die in the chair at the window with her cat, Baku, in her lap than admit weakness.

But Elena was worried and had decided that she had to talk to her aunt, had to convince her to see a doctor, preferably Sarah Rostnikov's cousin, Leon.

Had she told Porfiry Petrovich, he would have understood, probably would have volunteered to visit Anna himself, though he would certainly have little hope of success. But to tell Rostnikov would have put him in an awkward position. Elena was supposed to be undercover, contacts made in only one way and only if necessary. If Porfiry Petrovich sanctioned her visit home and did not tell the Yak, it was possible that something could go wrong and Rostnikov's position as chief investigator, not to mention Elena's safety, would be compromised.

No, Elena had decided to do it on her own and to be very careful. Sasha was back in the hotel waiting to be picked up that evening by Boris Osipov; taken to the small arena where he was to bring Tchaikovsky to do battle against one of the dogs that Illya and Boris's boss had chosen. Sasha suspected that the dog Tchaikovsky would be fighting would be a particularly vicious one with an excellent survival record.

Elena walked down Kalinin Street to Vorovsky Street and paused in front of the small old Church of St. Simon the Stylite. The church, during the generations of Soviet Communism, had been the exhibition hall of the All-Russian Society for the Preservation of Nature. She didn't know what it was used for now. She looked at her watch and caught a glimpse of the couple standing in the doorway of one of the twenty-four-story blocks of flats ahead. There were five blocks of flats on her right, built in the 1960s, each containing 280 apartments.

Elena looked impatiently at her watch and moved to the jewelry shop, past the couple who had entered the building before which they had stood. They did not appear again till she entered the pedestrian underpass in front of the Moscow Book House. They continued to remain far behind, but not so far that they would lose sight of her.

Elena had walked slowly, going up the stairs at the end of the tunnel, moving past a sudden rush of a dozen or so people coming down. As soon as she reached the broad sidewalk, she did her best to act as if she had forgotten something. Turning, she started back across the street, dodging cars, moving quickly. She managed to enter the bookshop and close the door in time to look back and see the couple emerge from the tunnel on the other side of the street. Elena stood back as the couple looked in all directions, had a quick discussion, and headed for the nearest shop.

As soon as they disappeared inside, Elena moved back to the street and went quickly to her left, away from them. The couple was now lost behind her, searching shops and cafés.

But Elena knew that one of two things had happened. Either the people who wanted her watched were incompetent, or she was meant to spot the couple, lose them, and feel free. That would mean someone far more able was somewhere nearby watching her. She decided on caution and was rewarded when she turned her head suddenly and found her eyes meeting those of a rotund man with pink cheeks, carrying an American shopping bag. The bag was black. So were the man's eyes, even at a distance of a dozen paces.

The man was good. He did not look away. Instead, he walked directly up to Elena and said, "You dropped this." He held up the black shopping bag. A white art-deco figure of a woman decorated the back.

"No," she said politely.

"No?" he said, apparently puzzled. "I could have sworn . . ."

"*Prastee't'e*, excuse me."

"Two honest people," the round man said with a smile. "I find a bag and try to return it, and you, who could take it and whatever it contains, reject the offer of that which is not yours. It seems to be from a very expensive shop, too."

"Your good fortune," Elena said with a smile of her own, and turned away.

The man was indeed remarkably good, and Elena knew she had a problem. She could lose the man, but that would bring suspicion upon her. Her evasion of the couple, crude though their methods had been, might well raise questions, but to lose this man would have been very dangerous. Elena abandoned the idea of visiting her aunt and headed slowly back to the hotel, pretending to look in the shop windows.

The rotund man moved slowly, smiling, having a good idea now that she had been frightened into heading back to the hotel. He had watched her elude the incompetent couple. The woman known as Lyuba had been very skillful in her evasion of the couple. It certainly looked like a professional effort. The rotund man, who was Peter Nimitsov's uncle, continued down the street.

It took Iosef Rostnikov and Zelach only two hours to find Yulia Yalutshkin, the sometime mistress of Yevgeny Pleshkov, the missing member of parliament.

The soccer coach, Oleg Kisolev, had told them where they might find her at midnight. *Midnight* and *might* were not enough reason for Iosef to delay his search. Kisolev might possibly know where to reach his friend, or the Yalutshkin woman, and might warn them that the police were looking, and where they might be looking.

The computer center at Petrovka was desperately in need of updating, new programs and people to feed data into the system's memory, not to mention one full-time technician to service the existing system until he or she went mad.

Iosef was well aware that there were stacks of arrest-and-questioning reports that had never been fed in. Such stacks reportedly were several feet high and filled an entire office, from which two computer programmers had been ejected to make room. It was rumored that the central computer staff, badly undermanned, had reached an unspoken agreement to simply throw out or shred huge piles of reports when no one was looking. These legendary stacks supposedly dated back at least four years.

Still, it was a place to begin. He got an order from the Yak and was given a computer next to a woman of about forty with a very sour look on her face. The woman was built like a small automobile and squirmed in her chair, muttering to herself and cursing the computer. Iosef was usually able to charm even the most lemonlike of faces with his smile of even, white teeth. This woman was not to be charmed. He gave up the effort and began his search.

Meanwhile, Zelach, who did not know how to use a computer, was in the file room on the far side of the building, searching through written reports for anything on Yulia Yalutshkin or Yevgeny Pleshkov. It would have seemed logical to an outsider for the file room and computer room to be next to or near each other, but, in fact, given Russian thinking, the distance kept the computer people from simply piling the files in that secret office or destroying them. The computer staff was young. The file-room staff was old and did their job—slowly, but they did their job.

The search lasted much of the afternoon, with Iosef finding very little. The Yalutshkin woman had been questioned for a variety of incidents, all dating back several years. There were probably many more incidents that he could not find. She had witnessed a murder, been present at the suicide of a young woman who jumped through a window at a party, reported the theft of a number of possessions taken from her apartment when she was out "with a friend" all night. It was all petty, and as with most high-class prostitutes, she was never arrested for streetwalking or in connection with any drug offenses. What Iosef did walk away from the computer with was an address where Yulia lived four years earlier and a very bad headache.

As he rose, the sour-faced muttering woman, whose fingers had been dancing on the keyboard in front of her while she looked down at a pile of documents through the lenses of her half-glasses, paused. "I have American aspirin," she said, stopping her typing and glancing up at Iosef.

"How do you know I have a headache?"

"That screen," she said. "There's something wrong with it. Everyone who uses it gets a headache. Maybe it's too bright. And I eat a handful of aspirin three times a day. I think I am addicted. I know I need them."

"American aspirin would be very helpful," he said.

The woman reached under her desk, lifted up a large black bag with a large black zipper, and fished out a white plastic bottle. She handed it to Iosef.

"Thank you," he said, starting to open it.

"Keep it," she said, "I have many. You're Porfiry Petrovich's son."

"I am."

"He is a good man in a world of filth."

Iosef didn't know what to say. So he nodded.

"I may be overstating the condition of the world in general and Moscow in particular," she said, removing her glasses and placing them next to her computer. "Sitting here for eleven years, reading what I read . . . it may give me a distorted picture of the world, but I don't think so."

"Thank you for the aspirin," Iosef said.

The woman nodded, put her half-glasses back on, and went back to racing her fingers over the keyboard.

Zelach had turned up several things, including another address where Yulia Yalutshkin had lived.

The two detectives, after Iosef had taken four aspirin, were on their way to the most recent address they had found. When they got to the building on Monet Street just off Ostrov, Iosef had the feeling that they would not find Yulia Yalutshkin here. In the past several years, assuming her record was reasonably accurate, she had almost certainly moved beyond this neighborhood.

The five-story apartment building was run down, its white concrete facade a dirt-covered and splotchy gray. Inside the doorway, the hall needed sweeping and the inner door, which supposedly required a key, was opened by Iosef with his police identification card. There really wasn't an inner lobby, just a stairwell of concrete. The detectives moved upward, following the light from a window on the first landing.

The apartment was on the second floor. Iosef and Zelach walked down the narrow corridor lit only by a window on each end. It was early in the afternoon but there was noise coming out of many of the apartments, the noise of loud television, louder arguing voices, children laughing and crying. There were also smells, not exactly good ones, but definitely strong and cabbage-sweet. The walls were painted something that used to be yellow.

Iosef was accustomed to such places, though the soft little ball of depression still came to life inside his chest. Zelach, on the other hand, did not seem to notice.

"Here," said Zelach, stopping in front of one of the doors on his right.

Iosef nodded at the shadow of the Slouch, and Zelach knocked firmly. There was a sound of music, soft and classical, beyond the door. Iosef guessed that it was Mendelssohn. There was no answer. Zelach knocked again as Iosef moved to his side so that both men were facing the door when it opened.

"*Kto tahm*, who is it?" came a woman's voice.

"Police. Office of Special Investigation. I am Inspector Rostnikov. I am here with Inspector Zelach."

"I cannot talk," the woman said. "I'm going out and I am late."

"This will be very brief," said Iosef.

"I don't . . ."

"Then," said Iosef with a tone of regret, "this may not be so brief."

"Identification. Under the door."

Iosef and Zelach knew this routine. They removed their identification cards and slipped them under the door. In truth, the cards proved nothing. They could be purchased for a few thousand rubles, maybe much less with the new currency.

The door opened and a petite, beautiful woman with short blond hair stood before them, one hand holding out the cards to the two men, the other behind her back. She was obviously dressed for the evening in a black tight-fitting dress and costume-jewelry pearls and earrings. Her makeup was minimal and carefully applied. Iosef's less-than-successful year as an actor and playwright had taught him about makeup and costumes. This lovely woman was ready for a show.

"Yes?" she asked.

"Police," said Iosef. "We have a few questions about Yulia Yalutshkin. May we come in?"

"*Vighdyeetyee,* come in," she said, stepping aside, her hand still behind her back.

They walked in, leaving the door open.

"I have no answers," the woman said. "I don't know her."

"How long have you lived here?" asked Iosef pleasantly.

"Three years."

"Yulia Yalutshkin gave this as her address two years ago."

"We shared the apartment briefly. I haven't seen her in . . ."

"You can put the gun down," Iosef said.

The woman looked at the faces of the two detectives, shrugged, and took her hand from behind her back. Both detectives recognized the .22 North American Mini-Revolver. She put the weapon in a small black purse on a nearby coffee table and closed the door.

"This is a dangerous building," she said.

"It is a dangerous world," said Iosef.

"I have had to show it more than once," she said, turning to them and folding her arms, defiant. "I have had to fire it twice. I think I shot one of the three men on the stairs whose unspoken but clear intentions were rape or theft, quite possibly both."

The apartment was clean, neat, and inexpensively but, to Iosef, tastefully furnished with slightly out of date modern chrome and vinyl furniture. It was a typical Moscow apartment. Small everything. Small living room with an attached little kitchen area. The kitchen was barely big enough to hold a metal-legged table with four chairs around it. The music came from a CD player.

"I don't have much time," the woman said, looking at her watch, unfolding her arms, and lighting a cigarette. "So . . ." She didn't offer the two men a seat.

"Yulia Yalutshkin," said Iosef. "The reputation of an important man, perhaps the life of an important man is in danger, Miss? . . ."

"Katerina Bolkonov," she said. "I really must go soon. There's a tea dance for Russian women to meet American businessmen looking for wives. If I'm late, I may not be noticed again."

"We'll be brief," said Iosef. Zelach stood at his side, hands folded in front of him. "Does someone else live with you here?"

"My son," she said. "He's twelve. He's at school. If a rich American picks me, my son can move with me to the U.S. and become an American. We can escape this existence."

"Yes," said Iosef.

Zelach was silent and impassive. The idea of living anywhere but Moscow seemed vaguely frightening to him. To go to a place where people spoke another language, had strange thoughts and expectations, was almost a nightmare. Torture for Zelach would be telling him he and his mother had to move to someplace like Paris, London, or Boston.

The woman, whose pale skin was smooth, almost perfect, paced the small living room, still smoking, one hand clutching her arm just below the shoulder, kneading it nervously. The woman's fingernails were red, long, and probably artificial. She wanted desperately to catch an American.

"I want no trouble," she said. "I have a job in a magazine publishing office. We publish engineering magazines. I'm just a receptionist-typist, but . . ."

"We are not here to give trouble," Iosef said, assuming from her having shared an apartment with Yulia Yalutshkin that she was also a part-time prostitute. Iosef dreaded going back to the computers and files to check on her background. He hoped it wouldn't be necessary. "We are just here to ask some simple questions."

"No questions are simple," she said suddenly, stopping and facing him. "If I get into trouble, the matchmaking service will drop me. We have to be clean. No drugs. I will have to stop smoking even. These Americans have fantasies. My hair isn't blond, but that's what they want, so if I am lucky enough to get an American he will never know."

"Yulia," Iosef said. "No one will ever know where the information came from."

The woman gave a slight laugh, shook her head, took a deep drag of her cigarette, and watched the smoke float lazily from her mouth.

"I knew this would happen someday, something like this. Trouble from you if I don't tell you. Trouble from them if I do."

"No one will know who told us whatever you have to tell us," Iosef repeated. "There are always many sources for information."

"All right," Katerina said with a sigh. "Yulia had a friend. Yulia's friend was a foreigner, a German, I think. She never gave his name and I stayed away when he came. He always wore black leather and a false smile. He wanted people to think he was Mafia. Maybe he was. I didn't like him. Once he tried to proposition me. I told Yulia. She didn't seem to care. Then one day he came to the door. She was packed. Off they went."

"Where?"

"Oh, God," Katerina said. "An apartment on Kalinin. One of those with a doorman. I heard them talking. I heard them talking about how Yulia was going to be some kind of Marta Herring."

"Mata Hari," Iosef corrected.

"Yes. She would be a spy. She would seduce secrets from Russians. She would be rich. I heard these things through the door. I did not let them know what I heard. I like Yulia. She was protective, as if I were her sister, and she had lived a difficult life, even more difficult than my own. As beautiful as she was, it was not enough to protect her from the streets. I didn't like the German. I was afraid for her, but she seemed so excited and she kissed my cheek, hugged me, gave me some money, and promised to stay in touch. I never heard from her again, and when they left, the German stepped back inside this room to put a finger to his lips to let me know that I should be quiet. I have been quiet. It's getting late. I can't be late."

"You have a photograph of Yulia?" asked Iosef.

Another sigh. Katerina put her cigarette out in a small ashtray on a good-sized glass-top coffee table with chrome legs. "Yes," she said and moved into the other room of the small apartment.

Iosef looked around and then at Zelach, who had his head down in thought. Iosef wondered what kind of thoughts the man beside him had.

"Here," Katerina said, hurrying out of the other room.

She handed Iosef a small photograph.

"This was taken just before she left," said Katerina. "She was all made up for a party. She forgot to take it with her when she left. I meant to give it back when she called, but . . ."

Iosef looked at the color photograph, a waist-up picture of a slender, beautiful woman with long dark hair brushed straight back. She wore a dress that revealed her shoulders and a knowing smile that revealed even, white teeth.

"Even when she had little money, Yulia took care of her teeth," said Katerina. "She always said, 'As long as I have good teeth and take care of my face and body, I have a chance to escape from this life.' She escaped. Keep the photograph. I must leave."

"You have the address of the apartment building on Kalinin?" asked Iosef.

"I've written it on the back of the photograph," Katerina said. "Yulia also spends time at the bar in the Metropole and at the Café Royale. The German likes it there."

Katerina held up her hand to show them the door. She plucked a lightweight coat from a rack in a corner. Iosef pocketed the photo and went through the door with Zelach.

"Please do not come back," she said softly. "I am afraid of the German; afraid for my son, afraid for me."

"We won't come back," said Iosef, reaching into his pocket, taking out his wallet and removing several bills, which he handed to Katerina. "Take a cab."

She gave him a long look to determine if he thought this entitled him to a return, unofficial visit. She was a good judge of such things. This time she was almost certain that she saw nothing but sympathy in his eyes.

She stuffed the money into her purse and hurried ahead of them, closing the door and putting on the coat. Without glancing back she entered the dark stairwell and went down. The policeman could hear her shoes clapping against the concrete.

"Kalinin Prospekt?" asked Zelach.

"Kalinin," Iosef answered.

Fifteen minutes later they were at the address of the apartment on Kalinin. The building was tall, relatively new, and sported a uniformed doorman, who was large, pleasant looking, and carrying a weapon which bulged under his gold-buttoned coat.

Iosef and Zelach showed their identification. The man examined the cards carefully and handed them back.

"This woman," Iosef said, showing him the photograph.

The doorman nodded.

"Miss Yalutshkin," he said. "She's not in now. She left less than ten minutes ago."

"Does she have a guest staying with her now?" asked Iosef. "A man?"

"Miss Yalutshkin entertains a great deal. She also tips well," said the doorman. "It is my belief that she tips well to insure privacy. However, if you are asking if anyone is in her apartment now, the answer is no."

"Do you know this man?" asked Iosef, taking out a photograph of Yevgeny Pleshkov.

The doorman took the picture, looked at it, and said, "Yes, I've seen him on the television."

"Has he ever visited Miss Yalutshkin?" asked Iosef.

"Perhaps," said the doorman. "I try to mind my own business."

"So you wouldn't remember a German who visited her?"

"A German? So many people," said the doorman. "So many people and such long days. You know it can be very boring being a doorman? I'm not complaining. Except for buying my own uniform, the money and tips are good. But people, tenants, want privacy."

"Don't tell her we were looking for her," said Iosef pleasantly.

"I won't," said the doorman.

Another ten minutes later Iosef and Zelach were at the Metropole Hotel directly across from the Bolshoi Theater.

The Metropole was designed in 1898 by an English architect. Its reputation for elegance has been maintained for a century, and shortly after the revolution, Lenin and his top lieutenants moved into apartments in the one-block-square, four-story stone edifice with its stained-glass windows and marble fountains.

Today the Metropole is part of the Russian-Finnish Inter-Continental Hotels and Resorts. The large rooms were renovated in 1991, but the workmanship and materials were cheap and the rooms are already looking a bit shabby. The suites, however, are well maintained for rich Russians and visiting foreigners drawn by the hotel's reputation. The suites feature genuine antiques and Oriental carpets.

Iosef was well acquainted with the Metropole. He had attended endless rounds of discussions and parties in the Artists Bar, downstairs off of Teatralny Proyezd. The purpose of one of these discussions was to convince a rich Englishman to produce one of Iosef's plays in London. Iosef found the bar dismal and the food mediocre even in the hotel's main restaurant, the Boyarsky Zal.

Nothing had come of the meetings. The Englishman had simply disappeared one day, and Iosef was left with memories of the stuffed bear in the hotel restaurant.

The desk man to whom they spoke did not seem to be the least impressed by Iosef's and Zelach's police identification cards, but, on the other hand, he was not uncooperative. What he was, was busy—sorting registration forms, credit-card receipt copies, and bills charged to the rooms.

"Yes, I know Miss Yalutshkin," the frail man said. He wore a neatly cut French suit and a very sedate blue tie in addition to a look of harassed distress.

"Do you know if she has been in the hotel today?" asked Iosef.

The man shrugged, examining what appeared to be a barely legible signature on a small yellow sheet.

"Can you read this?" he asked in exasperation, handing the sheet to Zelach, who took it and frowned.

"It says 'Fuad Ali Ben Mohammed, room three forty-three,'" said Zelach, looking at the sheet.

"The amount?" the clerk asked hopefully.

"Two million and sixty rubles," said Zelach, handing the yellow sheet back to the clerk.

"Thank you," the clerk said gratefully. "I saw her going into the bar about an hour ago. I don't know if she is still there. I would prefer if you did not mention that I told you her location."

"We will not mention," said Iosef, moving in the direction of the bar with Zelach at his side.

"Zelach," Iosef said, "your skills are a constant source of surprise to me. First you kick a ball like a professional, and now I discover you can decipher obscure handwriting."

"I have always been able to read poor handwriting," said Zelach. "I don't know why. That bill I just looked at, I think the writer purposely made it difficult to read."

"I would guess that was not his only bill," said Iosef, opening the door to the darkness of the bar.

There were only a handful of people at this hour. A CD unit in the corner with two dark square speaker boxes was playing Louis Armstrong, singing "Wonderful World."

"There," said Iosef, looking at Yulia Yalutshkin alone at a table against the wall.

There was no doubt even at this distance that she was a very rare, pale beauty, far too thin, however, for Iosef's taste. Elena would never be a model, but she had a solid beauty that Iosef far preferred to the butterfly appearance of the Yulia Yalutshkins of modern Russia.

She saw them coming, hesitated for only a fraction of an instant, and went on slowly drinking.

"Yulia Yalutshkin?" Iosef asked.

The woman didn't answer.

"May we sit?" asked Iosef.

The woman shrugged her slight shoulders. The two policemen sat.

She had still not looked at them. She seemed to be fascinated or hypnotized by something beyond the far wall.

"We are the police," Iosef said.

A smile touched Yulia's perfect, full red lips.

"You couldn't be anything else," she said in a throaty voice that reminded Iosef of the American actress—Zelach would know her name. Yes, Lauren Bacall.

"I used to be a soldier," said Iosef.

"Now," she said taking another sip from the glass of amber liquid before her, "you look like a policeman, and your partner could be nothing but a policeman. It is the curse of being a policeman."

Zelach shifted uncomfortably. He slouched.

"Do you know what we want?" asked Iosef.

"No," she said. "How much do you weigh? In pounds."

"Slightly over two hundred," said Iosef.

"You work out?"

"My father has passed on his passion for lifting weights."

"I am very light," she said. "And I like being picked up gently. Especially by big men."

"Yevgeny Pleshkov," said Iosef.

Yulia didn't respond.

"We can continue this discussion at Petrovka, if you would find it more comfortable," said Iosef.

Yulia sighed. "What do you want?"

"We want to know where Yevgeny Pleshkov is," said Iosef, wanting to order a drink but certain that he could not afford one, especially after having given Katerina taxi fare.

"I don't know where he is," she said. "Would you like a drink? My treat. It won't compromise you."

Iosef nodded and Yulia lifted one thin hand with long dark fingernails and a waiter appeared.

"I'll have a beer," said Iosef. "Dutch, if you have it."

"We have it," said the very ancient, jowly waiter whose thin white hair was brushed and gelled straight back.

"Pepsi-Cola," said Zelach.

"Coca-Cola?" asked the waiter.

"Coca-Cola," Zelach agreed.

"Thank you," said Iosef.

"Yes," said Zelach, definitely uncomfortable in the presence of this distant, beautiful woman.

"We must find Yevgeny Pleshkov," Iosef said when the waiter had shuffled away.

Yulia looked at her drink. "I don't know where he is," she said. "I saw him yesterday. He was drunk. Yevgeny is usually drunk when he sees me. He is also usually very generous. When he is drunk he is absolutely incapable of having an erection, no matter what I do. He was gone this morning when I woke up."

Zelach was definitely uncomfortable now.

"It doesn't matter," she went on. "His interest in me is always how I look and carry myself. He wants me at his side, holding his arm, smiling as I look into his eyes. He has always paid well for this service. Other male friends pay well for other services. Is that what you wanted to know?"

"Where is Yevgeny Pleshkov?" Iosef repeated as the waiter brought drinks for all three of them, though the woman had not ordered for herself.

"I have no idea," she said with a casual wave of her hand. "He will turn up again. Maybe tonight. Maybe weeks from now. I have no idea."

They drank. Iosef questioned and Zelach watched and listened. Yulia Yalutshkin revealed nothing more.

"Well," said Iosef with a sigh as he finished his beer and stood, "I would suggest that you call me if he turns up. It could mean his career. Our job is to help him."

"To help him get sober and go home?" she asked.

"Yes."

"And if he does not wish to get sober and go home?"

"Then he may become a very minor footnote in Russian history when he could be a significant figure," said Iosef.

"You sound like an amateur playwright," Yulia said.

"Very insightful. But I was a poor one. That is why I'm a policeman. Here is a card. Call our office, ask for me."

"It wasn't insight," she said. "Half the young men who approach me have written a play. The older ones claim to be wealthy or powerful. I can tell which ones are."

Iosef wrote his name on the back of the card and handed it to the woman, who placed it on the table without looking at it. Then he and Zelach left.

Outside the Metropole, rain was still threatening. A warm breeze blew and the two detectives walked.

"She was lying," Iosef said. "She knows where Pleshkov is."

Zelach grunted. He had no idea the woman might have been lying. "She bears watching?"

"And looking at," said Iosef with a smile.

Zelach blushed. He had done his best at the table not to reveal that he could not keep his eyes from Yulia Yalutshkin. She was the most beautiful woman he had ever been this close to. Zelach hoped that Iosef would assign him to be not only one who looks but one who watches.

Chapter Six

The room off the entrance to the health club was small, a cubby-hole passing as an office. On the walls were signed black-and-white photographs of athletes. Emil Karpo stood behind the desk, hands together in front of him. He was almost at attention, a fact which disconcerted the night health club clerk, Sergei Boxinov.

Sergei, at Karpo's insistence, had sat in the chair on the other side of the desk. Sergei was a former Mr. Universe contender. He had never finished among the top five, but once, in Helsinki, he had finished sixth. That was where a Danish businessman had seen him and offered him the job he now held, night manager of the hotel health club. The Danish businessman had been gay, but not obviously so. He had let Sergei know his preference for men during their conversation. Sergei was not gay, but Sergei had a family and needed a good job. The experience with the Danish man had not been at all as unpleasant as Sergei had expected. Now, all that Sergei wanted to do was cooperate with the pale unsmiling police-man in black and get back home for a few hours' sleep.

"What happened last night?" asked Karpo.

"Happened? Nothing unusual. I left about one in the morning. Mr. Lashkovich was here. And the other man."

"Other man?"

"He came in when I was adjusting the weight machines. I check them every night before I leave. I heard the door open and heard Lashkovich's voice. He was not a quiet man. I never really got a good look at the other man. But Raisa did."

"The cleaning woman," said Karpo.

"Yes, she got a good look, I think."

"You left at one."

"About one," Sergei said. "Lashkovich and the man were still here. It wasn't unusual for him to be here alone and lock the door when he left. He was a very influential man and I was told to do what he wanted done."

"So Raisa and the two men were here alone for a while?"

"Yes, but Raisa was almost finished and probably left shortly after I did. Am I going to lose my job?"

"No," said Karpo. "Unless you have done something wrong. Have you done something wrong?"

"I don't know. I don't think so."

"In that case, you may leave. Send in Raisa."

Sergei rose quickly, almost tipping the wooden chair over. He was out of the office in seconds.

The door opened again but it wasn't the cleaning woman. It was Paulinin, distraught, his hair Einsteinian wild, his glasses slipping dangerously. He had come to the hotel at Karpo's request to examine the pool and the shower and anyplace else where he might find even a trace of evidence.

Though he far preferred to work in his subbasement in Petrovka, the challenge of a crime scene intrigued him almost as much as the viscera of a corpse.

"I just called Petrovka," Paulinin said, breathing quickly. "They've taken the body, Lashkovich, turned it over to the . . . the Tatar gang. I wasn't finished with it. They're going to bury him tomorrow. How can I check the evidence I gather here against the corpse if I have no corpse?"

"Who ordered the release of the corpse?" asked Karpo.

"Rostnikov, Porfiry Petrovich himself," said Paulinin. "Is he mad? How can he take my corpse before I'm finished with it? There was so much more to learn. I was just getting to know him. He was just really beginning to speak to me."

"Learn what you can here," said Karpo. "Then we will take time for tea and biscuits. If Chief Inspector Rostnikov gave them the body, I am sure he had good reason."

Paulinin calmed a bit, brushed back his hair, and adjusted his glasses. Tea and biscuits with the man he considered his only friend was calming, but not quite enough. "Porfiry Petrovich has gone mad," Paulinin said, leaving the room with a shake of his head. "That is the only explanation."

There were many other explanations, as Karpo well knew. Rostnikov could have been threatened, bribed, ordered by a superior. None of these possibilities was the least bit likely except the last.

Emil Karpo had no time for further speculation. Raisa Munyakinova had entered the small office and said, "Should I close the door?"

"Yes," said Karpo, pointing to the chair from which Sergei had fled.

The woman closed the door and sat, looking up at the ghostly policeman, who now stood looking down at her from the other side of the desk she had dusted the night before.

Raisa Munyakinova could have been any age from forty to sixty. She had the stoop-shouldered stance, the haggard and weathered face of the women who cleaned, baked, swept the streets, controlled crowds at theaters. They appeared interchangeable. Raisa was built like a block of concrete, generations of peasant stock, solid, reliable but eroding.

"Tell me about last night," said Karpo.

"Mr. Lashkovich was killed," she said softly, avoiding the policeman's dark eyes.

"You saw him killed?"

"No. I was told this morning by Mr. Swartz, the hotel manager, who told me to come right away. I was asleep. I don't get much sleep. I have many jobs."

"You don't work here full time?"

"No, I wish they would hire me. It would be so much easier than . . ."

She trailed off and felt compelled to look at the somber white face above her.

"He was alive when you left?"

"Yes," she said. "Sergei had already gone. I had done the shower floor and walls. They were mildewed, but I know how."

"There was a man here with Lashkovich when you left."

"Yes," she said, nodding her head for emphasis.

"What did he look like? What did you hear?"

"The man was big, dark. He wore one of those light coats, tan. He kept his hands in his pockets. He and Mr. Lashkovich argued while Mr. Lashkovich swam."

"What did they argue about?"

"I'm not sure," she said. "I couldn't hear much in the shower and I tried to stay away from the pool. Mr. Lashkovich swam without any clothes on. He did not care if I saw him. Their voices were angry. The man in the tan coat was particularly loud and angry."

"Would you recognize this man in the tan coat?" asked Karpo.

"I . . . I don't want to get in trouble," she said. "I am frightened."

"The man in the tan coat is almost certainly the one who killed Lashkovich. Don't you want him caught?"

"I don't care if he is caught," she said sadly. "Mr. Lashkovich was good to me, left me tips, but I know he was in a Mafia, that he was a murderer. Let Sergei identify the man."

"Sergei did not get a good look at him, or at least that is what he says."

"I don't know," said Raisa, her eyes growing moist. "Whoever the man was, he might kill me if I identify him."

"He may decide to kill you and Sergei anyway, to keep you from identifying him. Your best hope for safety is to identify him so we can arrest him. We have photographs you can look at."

"I don't know," the woman said again. "I'm all alone. I work hard. I don't want trouble."

"What we want and what we must do are often quite different," said Karpo.

The woman sat silently, looking at her thick hands and shaking her head. "All right," she said finally with a huge sigh. "I'll identify him if I can. When, where?"

"At Petrovka," Karpo said. "We have photographs of members of various Mafias. We will start there."

"We will start there," Raisa repeated. "They will kill me. I know they will."

"They will not," said Karpo.

Something about the certainty with which the ghostly detective spoke made Raisa look up at him. What she saw and felt was a man who kept his word. She was a woman who also kept her word. She had little else left to her.

Night was falling. In the small café on Gorky Street, a young man with a baby face fingered the white scar on his nose, drank coffee very slowly, and spoke even more slowly. The two men with him, both considerably older, listened carefully, showing their full attention.

There was something both comic and frightening about the scene, but other patrons did their best not to pay attention or at least to disguise the fact that they were paying attention. It was something all Russians, particularly those who lived in Moscow, learned how to do at a very early age.

"Suspicious behavior," said Illya.

"Very," added Boris.

"I want the woman eliminated," said Peter Nimitsov calmly.

"She may be innocent," said Boris.

"I want her dead," Nimitsov said.

"The Ukrainian will be upset," said Illya.

"Do you want to argue with me, Illya Skatesholkov?" asked the young man with the baby face.

"No," Illya responded immediately. "She will die. I just . . ."

"Make it an accident," said Nimitsov. "And if the Ukrainian protests, then he will also have an accident."

"He could bring us a new market for the dogs," said Boris.

"Then let us hope we do not have to kill him," said Peter Nim-itsov.

And so the fate of Elena Timofeyeva, known to those at this table as Lyuba Polikarpova, was determined.

Porfiry Petrovich was tired. His day had been long, and for one of the few times in his adult life he did not look forward to the weights and he hoped that no neighbors were waiting for him with problems concerning their plumbing. Usually, lifting weights and fixing the neighbors' plumbing were respites from his days of confronting increasingly random violence, stupidity, lies, and the deep Russian sadness of the lives of those who either chose to or felt they had to engage in criminal activity. And then there were the insane, who were often cunning, often operating with little motive that made sense. But worst of all were the victims. His nightmares, when he had them, were not of grisly murder scenes and wild or cringing killers, but of the blank, confused faces of the victims, at least those who managed to survive.

But what now troubled Rostnikov most—besides the corruption that had not ceased with the end of Communism—was the rise of the gangs, the Mafias. Their power had increased. Their battles for territory and profits from prostitution, drugs, extortion, and gambling had moved to the streets. It was not, as so many of the Moscow news media were fond of saying, like Chicago in the 1920s. Rostnikov knew about Chicago. These gangs were animal survivalists, and the worst of them were the ones whose leaders conducted themselves like princes. Casmir Chenko, Glahz, the one-eyed Tatar, was like that. But the man he had met with earlier that evening had been a very different prince from the cautious Tatar.

Unlike Chenko, the Chechin Shatalov had made no elaborate plans involving car switching and public places. He had simply called Rostnikov and told him to meet him at the Pizza Hut on what was once Leningradskaya, the name with which Shatalov, himself, referred to the location. The Pizza Hut was one of the first American fast-food restaurants in Moscow. It had come well before the collapse of Communism and had been a success from its first opening.

Rostnikov had taken a red bus from Petrovka. He found it faster, though he had increasing difficulty keeping up with the hurrying and not even slightly considerate crowds. His useless leg had slowed him in the past, and now his artificial one was a problem. Though he was slow, Rostnikov's solid muscular body and arms opened holes in the crowds where none existed. He always moved firmly and resolutely, trying to keep from causing injury to his de-termined fellow passengers.

Squeezed between a fat woman with a grocery bag and a wiry man with a scowl and a cap, Rostnikov had managed to read his American paperback while holding a metal pole. Carella would fig-ure it all out. There would be a reason behind the deaths in the book he held—greed, jealousy, love, loyalty, pure evil. There would be closure and a reason.

The Pizza Hut had been crowded, but a well-built young man with a well-trimmed slight beard, wearing a tan leather jacket and brown shirt, had been waiting.

"This way," the young man had said, and Rostnikov had done his best to keep up with the man who led him to a table in the rear of the restaurant. Three men sat at the table. One, also wearing a brown leather jacket but older and with close-cropped white hair, continued eating a slice of pizza as Rostnikov and the young man with the beard approached the table.

Rostnikov did not look directly, but he was well aware of other leather-jacketed men at nearby tables. When they had reached the table, one of the three seated men, who looked no more than twenty and had the blank look of death in his eyes, stood up so Rostnikov could sit, which he did.

The white-haired man ignored Rostnikov and continued to eat.

"You'd like some pizza?" asked the other man at the table, a very big man, clean shaven, with neatly cut dark hair and a complexion that bespoke childhood disease.

Rostnikov reached for a slice of pizza with some kind of meat on it. The pizza was still warm but not hot.

"What do you want from me, policeman?" asked the big man with the poor complexion.

"Good pizza," said Rostnikov. "When I was a young man, we never even heard the word 'pizza.' Now . . . I want nothing from you. I want something from Shatalov."

"I am Shatalov," said the big man.

"And I am Spartacus," said Rostnikov.

The white-haired man laughed and spat out a piece of his pizza, an act that took Porfiry Petrovich's appetite.

"That's funny," the white-haired man said, wiping his mouth with a napkin. "I've seen the movie. I love American movies. Spartacus, I am Shatalov, the one the one-eyed Tatar dog of a bastard calls 'Irving.' Some day I will make him swallow his own tongue, or maybe someone else's, for that matter. Maybe I'll have him eat his own eye and wander blindly through what remains of his life. Or maybe I'll just kill him after he eats his eye."

"Would you like this civilized or with the grinding of warnings like sand on the teeth?" said Rostnikov.

"I don't care for civilized," said Shatalov.

"Very well. I want it to stop. I want the killing to stop," said Rostnikov. "If it does not stop, my office and I will devote all our waking hours to seeing that you and the Tatar either spend your lives in prison or die."

"You'd murder us?" asked Shatalov, obviously amused. "Not you, Rostnikov. I know too much about you, Washtub. Besides, I have many friends in the government, many who owe me more than just favors. Listen, policeman, do you think that confused old drunk Yeltsin simply decided to pull out of Chechnya? Do you think he really gained politically by doing so? Do you think he doesn't have his own small elite army of well-paid, battle-experienced soldiers who could have marched in and ended the life of every Chechin? Soldiers who are rewarded with apartments for their deeds, not medals. No, Chief Inspector, the drunk's people have made a deal with me, the devil, just as Russian leaders have for almost seven centuries. Money changes hands. Deeds are done. We give our support to important politicians as long as they hold their jobs, and Chenko gives his support to others. We cancel each other out. And you sit there threatening me?"

"Warning," Rostnikov amended.

"Then I consider myself warned. Now, please get on with whatever you have come to say, unless you have already said it."

"Do you dream, Shatalov?" Rostnikov asked, adjusting his leg under the table. He longed to remove the prosthesis.

"Dream?" Shatalov looked at the big man with the bad complexion as if to confirm that this was a strange policeman.

"Do you dream?"

"Everyone dreams," said Shatalov, running a hand over the bristle of white hair on his head.

"But not everyone remembers what he dreams," said Rostnikov.

"Your point?" asked Shatalov, now motioning for the young man with the neat beard to remove his plate, which he did. Shatalov folded his hands on the table. Two knuckles were badly contorted by arthritis.

"Do you ever dream that you are driving down the street in a car and you feel that something terrible will happen? Then your car grows smaller and smaller and a giant foot comes from the sky and you look up and it is about to crush you in your car. You can't escape. You wake up in fear."

"Not quite like that," said Shatalov, seriously. "Different, but close enough. How do you know this? I don't tell anyone my dreams."

"It is a variation of the dream others like you, other Mafia leaders, the older ones, have."

"The Tatar?"

"I haven't asked him yet," said Rostnikov. "He wouldn't tell me if I did."

"But you knew I would?"

"The moment I saw you eating your pizza," said Rostnikov.

The eyes of the mobster and the policeman met. Shatalov shook his head.

"I think I like you, policeman. I've heard much about you, but I didn't expect a dream-reading madman."

"The trick of surviving is not to expect but to anticipate," said Rostnikov.

"Speak on. I cannot stay here too long."

"You had Lashkovich murdered," said Rostnikov.

"Lashkovich? Is that the name of the dead Tatar? Is he related to our beloved mayor?"

"Yes, that was his name. No, he is not related to the mayor."

"I didn't have him killed," said Shatalov, sitting back. "If I did have him killed, I would tell you. Maybe not directly, but I would let you know, take credit."

Rostnikov believed him. He was sure that if he had killed the Tatar, the Chechin would have said so or made it clear.

"I have ordered the body of Lashkovich be turned over to Chenko," said Rostnikov. "He will be buried tomorrow morning. In return, Chenko has agreed that he will not seek retribution against you for seven days."

"That is sweet of him," said Shatalov with a smile.

"I ask that you too engage in no acts of violence against Chenko's people," said Rostnikov. "At least for one week."

"And why should I do this?"

"Three reasons," said Rostnikov, resisting the urge to reach for another piece of pizza, which was undoubtably cold by now. "First, because I ask you and would view your pledge as an act of good will that I would remember. Second, since you did not kill Lashkovich, and Chenko, I believe, did not kill your men, someone is trying to start a war between you. Personally, and I hope you will not forgive my saying so, I would normally not find it upsetting for such a war to break out except that innocent lives would be lost."

"There are no innocent lives," said Shatalov.

"That is a statement which you can make to a philosopher or a drunk if you wish a discussion," said Rostnikov. "I wish to save lives."

"And third?" asked Shatalov as a waiter brought a fresh pizza and took the old one's remains away.

"If you do not agree, if you kill, as I have told you, I will devote myself to the destruction of both you and Chenko."

"You are already devoted to that, aren't you?"

"No," said Rostnikov, unable to resist a slice of the fresh pizza, which seemed to be covered with mushrooms. Rostnikov had a passion for mushrooms, peaches, and his wife's cooking. "Your destruction is the province of the organized-gang division of the Ministry of the Interior. I have been given an assignment. I intend to fulfill that assignment."

"Tell me, Inspector," said Shatalov, handing a slice of pizza to the big man with the bad complexion and taking one for himself. "How would you like to make a great deal of money?"

"I think not," said Rostnikov. "It would change lifelong habits and disorient me. It might also, depending on the source of such sums, result in compromising me in the performance of my duties, duties that form the meaning of my life as a police officer."

"Impressive," said Shatalov. "Did you just think up that little speech?"

"Read it in an American novel, Ed McBain. It is a paraphrase but essentially accurate."

"Ed McBain?"

"I will be happy to let you borrow a copy of one of his books on the condition that you kill no one for a week. Do you read English?"

"A bit," said Shatalov with a mouthful of pizza, a string of cheese dangling from the corner of his mouth.

"It will be worth the effort. You agree to my conditions?"

Shatalov wiped the dangling cheese from his mouth, shrugged, and then nodded.

"If none of my people is attacked, I'll consider your seven-day truce," he said, putting down his napkin. "I'll do better. I'll do nothing for two weeks unless the one-eyed son-of-a-syphilitic-goat does something first."

It was Rostnikov's turn to nod.

"You want to hear a joke?" asked Shatalov, his mouth full of pizza.

"I can think of nothing I would like more," said Rostnikov.

"Your wife is a Jew. It will help you to appreciate it more."

Rostnikov said nothing. Shatalov, though he acted the fool, had subtly informed the inspector that he knew a great deal about him.

"Well," said Shatalov. "There were these two cows about to be slaughtered kosher. The first cow asked the other one, 'What's cooking?' The second cow said, 'Don't ask.'"

Shatalov laughed again. So did the big man with the bad complexion. Rostnikov did not laugh. He stood with some difficulty, pushing back the chair and working his artificial leg under him.

"You want to take the rest of this pizza?" Shatalov said. "We've had enough."

"Why not?" said Rostnikov after a very brief pause. "I do not think my superior would consider half a large mushroom pizza a compromise of my principles."

Shatalov laughed and pointed at the detective. The restaurant went silent. "I have a last question," said the Chechin. "Did the Tatar hen dipped in sheep shit call me 'Irving'?"

"I would prefer not to recall," said Rostnikov.

"I think I'll be seeing you soon," said Shatalov, motioning to the waiting waiter, who hurried over and packaged the remaining half-pizza for the rumpled man with the bad leg who looked like a re-frigerator.

And so it was that a weary Rostnikov entered his apartment on

Krasikov Street with a treat for two little girls, their grandmother, and Sarah Rostnikov.

"Why are you not in bed?" he asked, handing the box to Laura, the elder.

Both children were wearing nightshirts.

"Grandmother said we could stay up and watch you picking up the heavy things."

"We like to watch," said the younger girl.

"I know," said Rostnikov, taking off his jacket and hanging it on the rack near the front door.

Sarah got up and came to him, touching his face and looking at his eyes.

"Hungry?" she asked.

He shook his head. "Maybe later," he said. "Have a piece of pizza." The girls took the prize to their grandmother, who sat at the small table near the window.

"I've eaten," said Sarah.

"Are you all right today?" he asked, very softly, examining her face.

Sarah Rostnikov had undergone surgery to remove a benign growth from her brain more than two years ago. Since the operation, she had periods of dizziness and took pills her cousin, Leon the doctor, gave her. There were days when she could not go to work, and only the fact that Porfiry Petrovich was an important chief inspector saved her job.

"I'm fine," she said with a smile.

She had gained weight before her operation but had steadily grown more trim since. She looked, with her smooth pale skin and red hair, much as she had looked as a young woman. Illness had not aged her. On the contrary, it had, ironically, made her look younger.

There were no messages, no neighbors with toilet or sink problems, no urgent calls to contact his office.

The girls sat next to each other on the floor eating pizza while Rostnikov changed into his gray sweat suit, turned on a cassette of the American rock group Creedence Clearwater Revival. He had discovered the tape by accident, buying it for next to nothing at an outdoor market. Now it was one of his favorites. If he ever went to America, he would try to meet Ed McBain and John Fogarty, who sang and wrote most of the Creedence Clearwater songs. "Bad Moon Rising" began at the same moment Porfiry Petrovich lay back on the narrow bench he had pulled out from the cabinet against the wall. He lined up his weights and began. The women at the table talked softly, and the two little girls ate and watched the serious ritual that they knew was designed to make one stronger, only Rostnikov was already the strongest man in the world, they were certain. They had concluded some weeks ago that he simply enjoyed doing this, which struck them both as very strange, given the pain and grunting and sweat. Adults were very strange and unpredictable creatures.

Chapter Seven

That night in Moscow was a relatively quiet one.

A former farmer from a collective in Georgia, Anatoli Dudniki, weaved his way drunkenly down the middle of Kadashevskaya Prospekt, announcing to the hurtling taxis and cars that it was his sixty-fifth birthday. One driver, who had taken a few drinks himself, screeched to a halt directly in front of Anatoli, who leaned forward over the hood and laughed.

"Like a movie," Anatoli said. "My life is like a movie now. You hear that?"

The man in the car opened his window and shouted, "Get out of the street, you drunken old bum, before you get killed."

"You mean," said Anatoli, none too steady on his feet, "my head could be run over like a melon, a plum, a cabbage, a grape, something? Squish, skwush?"

The man in the car closed his window and drove on.

Anatoli made it to the curb and sat down. A few cars passed but there were no pedestrians. There was a feeling of rain in the air as there had been all day. There was no moon. Anatoli had learned to recognize the coming of rain from his years on that pitiful collective farm where his now-dead wife had learned two hundred ways to prepare potatoes. Oddly enough, Anatoli still loved potatoes, and when others on the collective had complained at the diet, he had nodded in agreement though he did not agree.

"I love potatoes," he shouted. "You hear that? I love them to little pieces. I could cry over them. I wish I had two potatoes now. You know what I would do? I would eat one and give one to someone else. That's the kind of man I am. That's the kind of man I am."

Now Anatoli worked in a bar, which was where he was coming from. He cleaned up after closing—sweeping, mopping, tending to the puke in the bathrooms, the sanitary napkins that blocked the toilets in the women's room, the stuff that stuck to the floor and to the small bandstand. The pay was poor but he got to work alone and drink as much as he wanted to when he finished his cleanup each night. The management never checked the stock. Anatoli drank only the best.

The alcohol compensated for the dirty job, and he could, because he came at closing time, avoid the loud music from the small band trying to sound like Americans, and avoid the young people in stupid crazy clothes who did something they called dancing and laughed at nothing.

"They laugh at nothing," Anatoli, sitting on the curb, said to no one. "At nothing. Not that there is anything to laugh at if you are not rich."

Anatoli shook his head. A little drink would be nice, but Anatoli knew better than to ever remove a bottle from the Albuquerque Bar. And so he sat, shoulders down, a huge burp and sigh escaping from him. He should go home, crawl into the narrow bed in the closet in his daughter and son-in-law's apartment, but he wasn't quite sure where the apartment was. Things seemed to be turned this way and that tonight. It had always been difficult for Anatoli, but since the revolution had ended and the street names had been changed, it had become worse.

He shifted his right foot, which was growing stiff, and kicked something hard, something in the street next to the curb. The streetlights were dim so Anatoli leaned over to look at the object.

"What's this? What's this?" he said, reaching over and picking up the object. "A gun. A weapon. A thing that shoots."

He held the gun in his hand. It was heavy. He had no idea what kind of gun it was or even, with certainty, that it was real.

"I found a *plotka*, a gun," he said aloud. "A weapon. Is this a thing or is this a thing? I could shoot it. I could sell it."

Anatoli looked at the black pistol in his hand and held it out. He had never held a gun in his hand. He pulled the trigger. The gun fired and sent him backward. He hit his head on the sidewalk and sat up quickly, at least as quickly as he could with the aid of gawky elbows and arthritic fingers.

He looked across the street. The gun had made a loud noise and the breaking of glass in a window across the street had created an almost musical follow-up.

"It's a real gun," Anatoli said, bracing himself with his left hand and firing again with his right hand.

This time the bullet hit brick or concrete and Anatoli saw a spark of light when it struck.

"I think I should get up and get the hell out of here before I am in big trouble," he said, still carrying on his conversation with the empty street. "I am a cowboy. I am a cowboy with a gun. All I need is a horse and one of those hats. I am going home."

The problem was that getting up from the curb was now a major chore that he could not accomplish. Oh, he was capable, but Moscow would not cooperate. It kept swaying. He placed the gun in his lap and began singing. The song he sang was "Baby Face." Anatoli didn't know it was an American song. He only knew the Russian words.

"You got the cutest little baby face," he bellowed hoarsely.

Across the street, three buildings down, Misha Vantolinkov had had enough. He had been awakened by gunfire on his street before. He had been awakened by gangs of kids shouting obscenities, but the loud croaking of the drunken Anatoli got to him. Besides, the drunk had the words to the song wrong.

Misha, who had to get up at six to get to his job at the reception desk of the Space Museum, turned on the lights and picked up his major luxury, the telephone. He called the police, giving the location but not his name, told them a lunatic drunk was shooting a gun in the street, and then he hung up.

Anatoli Dudniki was singing even more loudly, "I'm up in the sky when you give me a hug," when Misha got back in bed and covered his head with his pillow.

Ten minutes later a patrol car with two young policemen in it pulled up at the curb. The policemen got out, guns in hand, and ordered Anatoli to stop singing and put down the gun.

Anatoli complied and grinned, showing his few remaining teeth and a look of gratitude.

"I'm not at home," Anatoli said as he put the gun in the street. "I have a name, a medal, a daughter, a bed. That is where I would like you to take me, comrades. Oh, I forgot, no more 'comrades.' Citizen policemen. I am at your mercy. Get me home."

He staggered toward the policemen and fell into the arms of the younger one, almost knocking him over.

Eleven minutes beyond that, Anatoli was in a small damp cell in the nearest police lockup. The lockup was located next door to a paper-clip factory whose metal cutting machines throbbed all night and all day.

"This," he announced with confidence, "is not my bed. I want my bed. This is now a free country. I am a citizen."

"And," said the policeman, standing over him as Anatoli sat, "you have murdered a woman. One of those shots went through a window and killed a young mother."

"Killed?" said Anatoli, looking at the policeman.

Seconds later, he was asleep.

Raisa Munyakinova sat in the only reasonably comfortable chair in her minuscule apartment. They called it an apartment, but it was just a room. It was enough for her. She had work. She had a place to live. She would survive losing track of the days, having to carefully write her work schedule on the back of a flyer for Canadian cereal and place it under a glass on her tiny table.

The detective who looked like a ghost had not frightened her. It was not fear that now kept her awake. It was her decision to identify the man who had been with Valentin Lashkovich before he was murdered.

In a few hours, with the sky full dark, Raisa would get dressed and go to work and when she was finished take a bus to Petrovka to meet the ghost detective. She would look at photographs. She knew the face of the man she would be looking for. Would she have the strength to identify him? Or should she simply say, "He is not here," and go on with the life she had chosen and which had chosen her?

She had just returned from her night of work. She was tired, so tired that the idea of just rising from the chair to get to her bed was too much effort.

In the darkness, her head turned to the curtain in the corner. Behind the curtain was a cardboard box. It was not a particularly large box. From time to time she took the box out and removed items and memories, touched and examined them and put them back. It was her past and it was painful, but compelling. Whenever she went through the contents of the box, she smiled and wept.

She got up wearily, turned on the small sixty-watt table light and moved to the curtain. The meaning of her life was beyond that curtain in a cardboard box. She wondered how many others in Moscow kept their meaning in boxes behind the curtains.

Although Bronson was a dog, that did not mean he had no thoughts. On the contrary, he had many thoughts, but they were fleeting and he had almost no control over them.

Even now, as he lay in his large metal cage in the darkness, with only the dim night-light through the single small slit of a window, thoughts came racing through the head of the huge dark animal.

An image of a human bringing something heavy down on his back stirred the dog, but it was instantly gone, forgotten till the next time. A spark of a memory of looking into the eyes of another dog whose neck he had held with his best bloody grip rolled by on a wave. He felt the death of that other dog and it became part of the wave of death of many dogs. And that too passed. Memories did not linger consciously in Bronson. He felt, but did not think, that he would soon be facing another dog in the circle. Smelly, shouting humans would be there, some calling the name he had been given. His body would quiver with memories so deep that they went back to the wild free days of his ancestors in the forests. And then the thing would take over and he would attack. There was no plan, no thought. Bronson would give himself over to the ancient memory of survival, and it would either carry him through the triumph over the dead or dying other or leave him lying in the scent of his own death.

But none of this frightened the dog. Fear simply was not a part of his being. Nor did he think in terms of success or failure. He simply existed to live and fight and for the praise of the human who provided food and shelter.

The human had taught him two words that made Bronson's life simple—*vyshka*, death sentence, and *stop*, which was the same in Russian or English.

Bronson had attacked two humans in his five years of life. One of the two he had killed. The other, he did not know about. He did not particularly like attacking humans. They provided no meaningful battle that would leave the dog with a fast-beating heart of triumph. But, if ordered, he would attack and he would kill, and he would lose himself in the smell of fear and the taste of flesh and blood.

Bronson slept.

Oleg Kisolev, the soccer coach, lay in bed that evening next to his lover, Dmitri. Dmitri was a left-wing on Kisolev's team. Dmitri was, at one time, the fastest player in the league, a graceful, dodging flash who consistently led all others in assists. Oleg remembered the lean man with long dark hair and powerful legs running with the ball ahead of him, passing defense men, centering the ball in a perfect low arch in front of the goal for a header. Dmitri was almost thirty now and, while still fast and the best corner kicker in Moscow, he had lost as much as a quarter of his speed.

Oleg touched the head of the man beside him, who was exhausted from a long practice and who needed a shave. The light on Oleg's side of the bed was dim and he had to wear his glasses to read the book on his chest. Over the past two years or so Oleg had begun selecting books more for the size of their type than the content of their pages. Now he was reading a book on the history of the Soviet Union in the Olympic Games. The book was ten years old but full of things Oleg did not know.

The light did not bother Dmitri. When he was exhausted, not even the cry of *pazhahar*, fire, would awaken him.

Oleg thought about the two policemen who had come to see him about Yevgeny Pleshkov that afternoon. The policeman who slouched had kicked the ball farther and with more accuracy than anyone Oleg had ever seen, with the possible exception of Karishnikov. The policeman was a little old for the game but perhaps he could still play fullback. This speculation was only a game for Oleg, an exercise of his imagination. The policeman would never play. In addition to which Oleg really did not wish to see the man and his partner ever again. Oleg had good reason. Oleg preferred never to see any policemen again. He was sure he had done well, but the young one had smiled and made Oleg feel uncomfortable.

"I didn't betray Yevgeny," Oleg told himself. "Yevgeny went wild. It was when the German touched Yulia between her legs and Yulia bit her lower lip and tried to look as if she were thinking of somewhere else, another time."

It was in Yulia's apartment on Kalinin. Yevgeny was just a little drunk and he told Oleg they would surprise her. Surprise her they did. She answered the door wearing a pair of pink silk panties and a matching bra. She didn't try to keep the two men out of the room. On the contrary, she had opened the door for them to enter and they had immediately seen the German, Jurgen, sitting naked on the spindly legged sofa. His arms were outstretched and draped along the top of the sofa.

Oleg immediately noticed that the man was flaccid, though his penis was unusually thick and long, even longer and thicker than Dmitri's.

Yulia gave no explanation. She closed the door to the room and went to get herself a drink from the small wooden cabinet against one wall.

"An unexpected visit," the German had said. "And from such a distinguished member of the government. I've been hoping to meet you."

Neither Oleg nor Yevgeny had responded. The German had continued talking with only the slightest accent.

Oleg was well trained in his hatred of Germans. He and two generations before his were taught in school with graphic photographs of staggering numbers of dead Russian soldiers, women, and children. Those who had survived and helped repulse the obscene invasion of their country told tales of German atrocities and the horrors they had endured and witnessed. The teachers, the survivors, the books did not differentiate between Nazi soldiers and German citizens. They were all born with a madness to conquer. This one was no different.

"Yulia and I were waiting for the proper time to suggest a lucrative business proposal with you," the German said. "Your coming now is a fortunate act of fate."

Yulia had now put on a flimsy robe, a white one through which you could see. Oleg, though his sexual interests were with another gender, recognized the long-legged beauty of the woman and understood his friend Yevgeny's obsession with her.

She handed Yevgeny a drink: vodka, no ice. She offered Oleg nothing. In the several years his friend had been having binges with her at his side, Oleg had met Yulia only twice. Oleg did not drink. He did not carouse and so he seldom saw Yulia, though the two had formed an instant dislike of each other from the moment they had met. The source of their dislike was obviously Yevgeny, whom she quite successfully manipulated when he was drunk and whom Oleg tried, with almost no success, to wean back to sobriety and safety. Yevgeny was too prominent a man to continue to avoid being exposed by the press for his drunkenness, his gambling, his being seen around with a beautiful woman who was obviously his mistress. And Yevgeny was not one to fade into the shadows when he was on a drunken spree. Oh, no. He was loud, very loud. He practiced speeches in the streets and stopped individuals to tell them what had to be done to save Russia and return it to a power its people deserved. If anyone recognized him, they did not admit it. Most people simply walked by.

While Yulia and what little she wore had not disturbed Oleg, the German sitting naked on the sofa had disturbed him deeply. He was sitting there like an Aryan prince, smiling with perfect white teeth. He was enjoying the surprise visit and made no move to cover himself. In spite of his instant dislike of the man, Oleg had found himself engaged in a sexual fantasy. He had managed, however, to put it away, though he knew it would come back sometime in the future and he knew he wanted to remember.

"Please sit," the German had said, pointing to two chairs that matched the sofa from which he reigned.

Neither man sat, nor did the woman.

"As you wish," said the German, standing and smoothing back his hair. "Yulia."

The name had been spoken as a command, and the woman moved across the room, drink in hand, to the desk neatly tucked in a corner. She opened a drawer and removed a wooden box. She crossed the room again and handed the box to the German, who took hold of her arm and clearly ordered her to stand at his side, though he said not a word.

"In this box are items, not the originals but copies," the German said. "The originals are someplace safe. Open it. Gaze upon your fate. *Das ist dein Schicksal gaverin*, your fate."

The dazed Yevgeny had taken the box. He stepped back to Oleg's side and opened the box. Inside were small cassette tapes and photographs. Some of the photographs were of Yevgeny in bars, casinos, laughing, looking drunk and red-faced, Yulia at his side. Most of the photographs, however, were of Yevgeny and Yulia in sexual embrace. As Yevgeny went through each photo and Oleg watched, the soccer coach's initial response was that his friend had no sexual imagination. In all the photographs in which they were engaged, Yevgeny was in the traditional male position, face to face and on top. Oleg was more interested in the look on Yulia's face. It was almost identical in each picture in which her face could be seen. Her head was turned away. Her eyes were closed. There was no smile on her beautiful face. Apparently, the sexual performance of Yevgeny Pleshkov left a great deal to be desired.

"Those are yours," the German said. "Keep them. Destroy them. Listen to the tapes. Some of them are difficult to understand. Many of them are of indiscretions on your part, in which you reveal information of a highly sensitive nature about others in the government and secret actions, which I am sure were not meant to be revealed outside of a very small circle in the Kremlin. Some might even say that the sharing of such secret information with a woman would constitute treason."

"I don't have money," Yevgeny said, closing the box with a sudden snap and handing it to Oleg.

"Money," the German said, running a hand down Yulia's body. "No, I am not after money. I need your power, your influence. I need to be able to go to business and political sources in other countries and guarantee them certain things from Russian governmental agencies, things which you can arrange."

Yevgeny had swayed slightly, his eyes on the German. Oleg had no idea what his friend was thinking. Yevgeny cheated on his wife—which, considering his friend's wife, was completely understandable. Yevgeny was often away from his role in running the fragile government; he gambled away his money and was ever prepared to take offense at a look or a comment. He was easily swayed by a pretty face.

On the other hand, Yevgeny Pleshkov was an honest man who stubbornly held to his own principles in spite of pressure from his own party, from outside lobbies, and sometimes from the press. The people seemed to love him. An honest man in a dishonest world. A compassionate man who was frequently quoted. Once he had said, "To err is divine. To forgive is human." People who loved Yevgeny and did not know him smiled when they spoke these words. In the valley of the blind, the one-eyed man is king. Yevgeny might well become a political king. Oleg didn't always agree with what his friend said and stood for, but he admired and respected his courage in saying what he thought, doing what he believed was best for Russia.

Maybe he was thinking about such things as he looked down at the wooden box. And then he looked up and saw the German's hand move under Yulia's gown and between her legs. She neither protested, moved, nor indicated in any way that she welcomed being used.

Oleg knew what was coming. He had seen Yevgeny like this before when he had been drinking. Oleg wondered if Yulia had warned the German, and if the German knew some kind of martial art or had a gun, but he was stark naked. There was no place to hide a weapon.

The German stood, working his hand between Yulia's legs, under her open gown.

Oleg reached for his friend's arm as Yevgeny strode forward toward the couple and made a deep animal sound. The German spread his legs, amused for a moment, but only a moment. Oleg had no idea what the German had expected, but he certainly didn't expect to be hit in the face with the wooden box. The German staggered back in surprise and pain. Blood spurted from his nose. A purple welt like a fat worm streaked over his left eyebrow.

Yulia stepped away, watching, no sign of fear or a move to escape the room or step between her lovers. She was, Oleg thought as he rushed quickly forward to restrain his friend, indifferent. She takes drugs, Oleg had thought. A normal person wouldn't act like this.

Oleg put his arms around Yevgeny, but the drunken man of the people was beyond restraint. He shook Oleg off. The German, his left eye closing quickly, started toward a door that must have been the bedroom. He moved on legs far less steady than the drunken Pleshkov. The German got about five feet before Yevgeny caught him and with a two-handed grip slammed the wooden box against the side of the fleeing man's head.

The box splintered and came apart at the hinges. Photographs and cassettes sprayed around the room. The German was on his knees now, holding the side of his head. Yevgeny stood over him, breathing heavily, a piece of the shattered box in each hand. The piece in his right hand was a jagged splinter.

Oleg was afraid to tackle his friend again but he knew he had to try. But before he could do so, the German turned on his knees, a dazed look on his face, blood trickling down his lips and into his mouth.

Yevgeny plunged the splinter into the man's neck.

The German said something like "Ahhggg," and Yevgeny stepped away, watching the German fall to the floor on his back and attempt to remove the sharp broken wood from his neck. It was useless. He rolled over atop photos and cassettes and died trying to curl up into a ball to escape the pain.

Yevgeny was breathing hard. He looked around as if he did not know where he was. First he looked at the piece of the box in his hand. Then he looked at the German and at Oleg and finally he looked at Yulia, who walked over to the dead German and poured the remains of her drink on his body.

She placed her glass on a small table next to a lamp and took two steps to the bewildered Yevgeny Pleshkov.

"Sit, Yevi," she said, leading him by the arm to one of the chairs the German had offered him. Pleshkov sat and Yulia took the remains of the box from him and dropped them on the floor.

"Yevgeny," Oleg said, "let's get out of here."

Pleshkov looked at his friend as if surprised to see him there, wherever *there* might be. Yevgeny did not rise. In fact, he sat back and closed his eyes.

"Help me clean up," Yulia had said to Oleg.

"The body?" Oleg asked.

"We'll think of something when we come to that," she said. "I'll change into something that won't be ruined by the blood."

Oleg got on his knees and began picking up photographs, many of them splattered with blood, and cassettes, some of which had broken and flown across the room, leaving a brown vinyl trail of thin tape. And there were dozens of pieces of wood. In his hurry, Oleg picked up a splinter in the palm of his hand. There was enough visible to pull it out, though his hand was shaking.

Oleg found a wastebasket and was filling it when Yulia reappeared in faded blue jeans and a blue sweatshirt.

"No," she said, handing Oleg a large green plastic garbage bag. "Fill this. I can dump it in the trash. It will be picked up in the morning. Put in everything."

The man and woman worked together. Yulia produced a blanket to wrap the German's body, which they did with surprising ease, though Oleg did his best not to look at the grotesque naked man with the battered face and the sharp piece of wood buried in his neck. Without hesitation, Yulia pulled the wooden stake from the neck of the man who had humiliated her. She wiped it to remove any possible fingerprints and dropped it into the rapidly filling bag. Then she produced two electrical extension wires and used them to tie the top and bottom of the makeshift shroud in which what was once a man was wrapped.

The blood was the most difficult part of the operation. Yulia said, "I'll be right back. Try to rouse Yevi. We will need his help."

Oleg did as he was told and tried not to look at the bundle on the floor. Yevgeny Pleshkov did not respond to his entreaties, but he did look into Oleg's face as if trying to recognize him. Oleg gave up and resumed his cleanup, wondering if Yulia would suddenly appear with armed policemen and point her finger at the scene, denouncing Oleg and Yevgeny.

She did reappear with a bucket containing a variety of plastic cleaning items, a pair of brushes, and some towels.

"Took them from the storage closet on the next floor," she explained. "I will have to get them back soon. Let's put the body by the door. See if he is leaking through first."

Again, Oleg did as he was told. The blood did not seem to be spreading, at least not yet. Together they moved the wrapped corpse near the door.

Cleaning up the blood took almost half an hour and left the thin carpet wet.

"We can do no better," Yulia had announced, surveying the room. "I'll rearrange the furniture later to cover the spot. It will look fine. Now we get rid of the bag and the body."

"How?"

"I'll take the bag," she said. "I'll carry it to the park and drop it in the trash there."

"Burn it," Yevgeny suddenly said in a monotone, without looking at the others. "No one must find those photographs, those tapes."

"All right, I will burn the bag," she said.

"I want to watch," said Yevgeny.

"You don't trust me," Yulia said with a smile.

"No."

Yulia gave a raspy, deep laugh which sent an icicle down Oleg's back. "Then you shall watch," she said.

"The originals," said Yevgeny, slowly coming to life and rubbing his eyes.

Yulia shook her head. "I will protect you, Yevi. I will burn these photographs and tapes. I will help get rid of the body. The three of us, if the police get close, and they are looking for you, must never vary from the story that Jurgen was attacking me, that he had a gun, that you bravely overcame him and had to kill him to protect yourself. As for the body, you panicked and to protect me again wrapped him up, and we, you and I, took him to the place I have in mind. Your friend Oleg need not be involved."

Yevgeny nodded in agreement.

"I have the originals of the photos and the tapes safely hidden," she said. "And so they will stay. I ask you for nothing in exchange. They are my insurance that the two of you will not betray me. I like you, Yevi. You have never hurt me. You have been generous and undemanding. And now you've rid me of my beast. No, that is a cliché. You've rid me of something that looked like a human, something with an insatiable lust, who enjoyed the anguish of others. He is the only person I have ever known who simply enjoyed being evil. One time I asked him if he was the devil. He said he was."

Yevgeny finally stirred and stood. "Let us do it," he said.

The rest was a frightening nightmare for Oleg, who was grateful that Yulia was clearly in charge and knew what she was doing and that Yevgeny was participating. She carried the bulging garbage bag through which shards of wood from the broken box now jutted like angry little spikes, while Oleg and Yevgeny carried the awkward and heavy dead German. Yulia also held a two-liter plastic bottle. Yulia had surveyed the hallway and, assured that no one was in sight, led the two men carrying the body to the service steps. Oleg started to head down but Yulia said, "No. Up."

Oleg was in no state to challenge anything she said, and Yevgeny had lapsed back into a near-somnambulistic state.

They struggled up two flights, where Yulia opened the door to the roof and put down bottle and bag to open the door with a key.

"Jurgen had the key made," she explained. "I was never sure why. Now I have a reason."

They struggled onto the roof. Yulia led the way to a ribbed metal shed whose door was open.

There wasn't much inside the shed: a few paint cans, a pile of rags, something that looked like a radio with its electrical intestines showing. The shed was dark, and no light came from the moon and stars covered by clouds. But there was enough, just enough, light coming from Kalinin Street below so that Oleg saw where Yulia pointed. He guided Yevgeny and the body to the spot she had indicated and they put their burden down.

"Back," said Yulia, pouring the contents of the bottle she had been carrying over the body and the garbage bag she had placed atop it.

Oleg led Yevgeny several steps away from the shed. There was a sudden flare of flames as Yulia joined them.

"Someone will see," Oleg said. "Someone will report a fire on the roof. The police . . ."

Yulia stepped to Yevgeny's right and took his arm.

"No one will see. No one will report. No one will discover perhaps for days, and no one will be able to identify the corpse. The evidence will be gone. It will remain a mystery. I have seen such things happen. Yevi can stay with me tonight. Tomorrow . . . I don't know."

"It looks like rain," Oleg said as the sky rumbled above them.

"It has for days," she said, "but the shed will keep it from our work. Even a deluge won't stop that fire."

They stood watching for a few minutes, just to be sure the body and the bag were on fire and not likely to go out.

"Go home, Oleg," Yulia said.

Oleg was hypnotized by the flames, the smell of tape and flesh. He stood transfixed.

"Go home, Oleg Kisolev," she said firmly.

And, finally, he did.

Oleg had made his way home and now lay in his bed next to
Dmitri, trying to convince himself first that the whole thing had
not happened. He failed. Then he tried to convince himself that he
was safe, that the body of the German would burn beyond recognition, that the green garbage bag and its contents would also be
burned without leaving a trace, aside from ashes.

Oleg put the Olympic history book down and reached over to
turn off the light. His hand hesitated and he realized that he did
not want to be in darkness. He adjusted his pillow and slid down
under the covers, turning to put his arms around Dmitri, who
made a slight sound of childish pleasure,

Maybe, thought Oleg, maybe I can sleep like this. Maybe.

Sarah Rostnikov's cousin, Leon Moiseyevitch, the doctor, sat at
the piano beside the cellist and oboe player with whom he had performed for almost five years. They specialized in standard works,
Bach and Mozart particularly, and Leon found that he could lose
himself in the music, that rehearsal after rehearsal, concert after
concert, brought him closer to the magical state in which he could
simply let his fingers and body perform while he listened.

It was late, but the small hall which held seventy-five was full
and the trio had played for more than two hours.

Some nights Leon played with a jazz group at a nightclub called
Hot Apples, a short walk from the Kremlin walls.

It had been a nightmare of a day in his office, a nightmare from
which he tried to distance himself emotionally, and from which he
knew he could partially cleanse himself through music. When he
was finished, he would go home, kiss his sleeping son, and go to
his bedroom.

Leon was financially comfortable. His reputation was secure
among both the newly rich and the old powerful Communists who
had managed to make the transition to new power by renouncing
the crumbled party and embracing the sham of democracy. Leon
was secure.

To help cleanse his conscience, he put in a dozen hours a week at the public hospital, treating whoever came into the emergency room and charging nothing.

The past week had been typical. He had treated one woman who had been struck by a piece of falling concrete from a crumbling building. The woman had died from massive head wounds, as Leon had known she would when she was brought in. It was amazing that she had stayed alive long enough to be brought to the emergency room. About one hundred Muscovites died each year after being struck by falling bricks and concrete. Another dozen died annually after being crushed by huge icicles as they walked down the street. Leon had treated people who had stepped into holes in the sidewalk and suffered broken limbs, people who had drunk contaminated tap water, people who had received deadly shocks of electricity while riding trolley buses, people who had been poisoned by bootlegged vodka, people who had been struck by automobiles driven by motorists who routinely ignored the yellow painted lanes and drove madly, ignoring pedestrians.

Then there were the more bizarre cases he had seen over the past year: the two little boys aged six and five, who had found a hand grenade in Gorky Park and had died of injuries when it exploded while they were playing with it; and the bespectacled young businessman on the way home from work who spotted an odd white Styrofoam box on the ground next to a metal-mesh garbage container. The man had picked up the box to deposit it in the trash, and lifted the lid. The contents of the box were two soft, green claylike masses, the size of small melons. The suspicious and conscientious young businessman, who had a wife and a three-year-old daughter, had brought the Styrofoam box and its contents to the hospital emergency room where Leon was on duty. Leon had told the young man to place the container on a small stainless steel table with rubber-covered wheels. The container proved to be emitting a high level of radiation. The man had been exposed to the radiation when he opened the box to examine its contents and when he carried it the half mile to the hospital. The man was still being treated half a year later and not doing particularly well. And the police still did not have the slightest idea who might have placed the white Styrofoam box near the trash container.

Leon had come to a passage that always pleased him. It was flowing, beautiful, a moment of salvation in a world of madness.

In his music, in Bach, Mozart, Schumann, and sometimes Brahms, Leon could stop being the confident, wise, supportive physician whom he had made himself into, and inside of whom existed an angry and sometimes frightened man.

Even in the hospital the people of Moscow were not safe. A woman had recently bled to death while giving birth because the power company had, without warning, turned off the hospital's electricity in a dispute over nonpayment of bills.

The trio was coming to the end of the piece and the end of the concert. Leon did not want it to end. Given the slightest encouragement from the audience, Leon would be willing to give encore after encore throughout the night. He was sure his fellow musicians felt the same.

The horrors would not stop even during the most delicate of passages.

Leon remembered helping to treat the victims of a utility company blunder in which a high-pressure gas line had been attached to a residential neighborhood instead of the industrial plant for which it was intended. Fifteen homes had burst into flames. Fortunately, it happened in the early afternoon, which kept the number of burn victims down.

Leon knew well from the statistics he accessed on his computer that Russians are five times more likely to die from accidents than are Americans. Deaths in Russia exceed births by more than six hundred thousand. Of the boys who are now sixteen, only half would reach the age of sixty, which is a worse rate than a century ago.

The Mozart piece came to an end with Leon's brief solo, a slow and bittersweet conclusion.

The audience consisted mostly of university students and teachers, with a smattering of old people who attended anything—concerts, lectures, travel films—as long as the evening or afternoon entertainment or englightenment was free.

The applause was enthusiastic, appreciative, but there was something in it that the musicians frequently sensed. The people before them had decided that the diversion was over. There would be no encores this night. The audience trickled out. A few, as always, almost always the young, approached the trio, thanked them, and asked questions or simply wanted to talk about their own love of music. Part of the trio's mission, as they saw it, was to listen empathetically to those who approached.

Leon adopted his physician's manner. The others, Lev Bulmasiov and Dmitriova Berg, alternatively beamed and took on serious looks, nodding their heads, saying something that showed the person who had approached that they understood what they were trying to express.

All three—Leon, Lev, and Dmitriova—were Jews. It was the combination of their love for the same genre of music, their mutual background as Jews without religion, and their talent that brought them together. Lev was a successful carpenter in his forties who held an advanced degree in electrical engineering, a profession that would have earned him far less than he brought home to his family as a carpenter. Leon knew that Lev did not dislike being a carpenter but would have preferred the profession for which he had been trained and which he loved. Lev's oboe was his solace. Dmitriova was a medical lab technician at the hospital where Leon did his volunteer work. She was in her twenties, short, approaching a serious weight problem, and very plain with slight recurrent acne. Her compensation for the body and skin that had been given her was her cello, her music. Dmitriova was easily the most talented of the trio and should have been making her living on the concert stage.

But those who managed musicians, while recognizing her talent, were certain that they could not market someone who looked like Dmitriova.

When the last questioner, the one who always lingered until the musicians said they had to leave, had departed, the trio had said good-bye, told each other that the concert had gone well, and went their own ways.

Leon dreaded the next day. He had tried to put it from his mind, but he now had to deal with it. In the morning, he would have to call his cousin Sarah and tell her that she probably needed more surgery, that something had happened, that he wasn't sure what it was, though he was certain, as was the woman who had been the surgeon on Sarah's original operation, that an internal examination had to be made. Leon thought the problem was a growing clot of blood in the brain, a clot resulting from the original surgery, which may have weakened a crucial vessel.

Leon had a car and, unlike the other musicians in the trio, he had no instrument to carry. He did not know how they would get home. He had offered Lev and Dmitriova rides on many occasions. They had always politely refused with thanks. Leon understood. They wanted to be alone with the still-living memory of the music inside them. On this night, however, Leon would have welcomed company and conversation.

Sarah and Porfiry Petrovich would take the news well and ask that the surgery be performed as quickly as possible. Leon would arrange it and tell them the absolute truth about what the surgeon might find and have to do. He would tell them that he would be present in the operating room and that, while any surgery on the brain was serious, it was likely that this operation was not life-threatening.

Leon had no brothers or sisters. Sarah was the closest relative of his generation, more a sister than a cousin. Leon's wife had died almost ten years ago, leaving him with their son, Ivan, whose real name was Itzhak. Ivan was watched over in motherly fashion by

Masha, a Hungarian woman, who had a small but comfortable room in Leon's apartment. Leon loved his son to the point where it hurt just to see him.

Ivan showed an interest in and talent for the piano, but he did not delight and lose himself in practice as his father did. Leon doubted if his son had the emotion inside that would carry him into a musical career. No matter. The boy was smart, loving. He would do well.

Meanwhile, Leon dreaded the morning.

He had long since stopped deluding himself about his feelings for his cousin Sarah. He had loved her from the time they were children. He had longed for her. When he had married, those feelings remained tucked carefully in imaginary velvet, never to be opened for careful scrutiny.

Ivan would be asleep, but Leon would go into his room, sit at his bedside, and watch his smooth, peaceful face for as long as half an hour. Then he would go to bed, dreading what he must do in the morning.

Porfiry Petrovich did not snore, but from time to time he made a deep sigh that sounded full of promises to keep. Sarah listened to her husband sleeping. He had brought home a surprise of pizza and had done his nightly workout while the two girls sat watching.

Sarah knew the routine by heart. Rostnikov seldom deviated. First, he turned on the cassette player after having selected whatever suited his mood. Tonight it had been Creedence Clearwater Revival. Occasionally, when he was very tired, he hummed or even sang along with the music. Tonight he had hummed.

Five people in a one-bedroom apartment was both good and bad. It was good because Sarah, when she came home after working in the music shop, liked to have company, to hear what Galina Panishkoya and her grandchildren had done all day. Galina too worked while the girls were in school. Usually, Sarah and Galina collaborated to prepare dinner. The apartment was full of life. That was also the problem. Privacy was impossible, or almost so.

Rostnikov had kept his leg on for stability when he sat up or lay on the narrow, low exercise bench. Tonight he had worn his blue-and-white Prix de France sweatpants and shirt. Perspiration had come quickly and the humming had turned to grunts. This was the favorite part for the little girls, and Sarah knew her husband was doing a bit of play-acting to make it look hard. Porfiry Petrovich was working out with great zeal. Next month was the Izmailovo Park annual weight-lifting championship competition. Porfiry Petrovich was now eligible for the senior competition, but it was really no competition for the one-legged policeman. He usually won. His primary rival was a younger, likeable man with almost white hair. The younger man named Felix Borotomkin looked like the photographs of Arnold Schwarzenegger on the covers of CDs of music from his movies. Felix Borotomkin worked out for several hours every day. Since he worked in a private gym, this was not a problem for him. It was a problem for Porfiry Petrovich.

Sarah wondered if her husband might be dreaming of the competition, going over each move. For Rostnikov, the excitement was in the struggle more than in the winning, though he dearly enjoyed his victories.

Rostnikov slept on his back, no pillow, no cover except in the coldest of weather. His ritual nightwear was a clean pair of exercise shorts and the largest T-shirt he could find in his drawer. Tonight he was wearing a black one with the words THE TRUTH IS OUT THERE in white letters.

Leon had told Sarah to come when Rostnikov went to work in the morning, that he had to talk to her.

She had gone to him about her headaches, which were increasing in pain and frequency. He had given her medication. When the headaches continued, he had called his cousin in for an examination. Now, three days after the tests, he wanted to see her. It couldn't be good news.

Sarah would have gotten up and read a book, but there was really nowhere she could turn on a light. Any light and most sounds immediately awakened Rostnikov, though he had no trouble getting back to sleep instantly when he was sure no problem existed that he had to help deal with. Oddly enough, he did not awaken if Sarah reached over to touch him, which she now did.

She was certain now that the news would be bad. It was best if she got some sleep, was rested when she had to cope with the news. It would be better but it would be impossible.

Her husband's missing leg was not a problem for Sarah. She had been relieved when it had been amputated. It had been a less-than-handsome sight, and Rostnikov frequently had pain from it while he slept. Now, the sounds of pain were gone, replaced by these mournful grunts.

Sarah had lived for half a century. In that lifetime, she had never been unfaithful to her husband and she was sure he had been faithful to her. Sarah, with her red hair, smooth complexion, white skin, and ample body, had experienced many overtures from co-workers, men in cafés, customers, strangers in odd places. She had been tempted a few times, but the temptations had been slight and passing. She lay wondering if she had missed something. She knew, however, that she would never go beyond that slight temptation.

She closed her eyes and tried the relaxation techniques, the breathing, the visualization she had learned before her last surgery and had practiced till her recovery seemed complete. The techniques helped a bit and she needed them now to control her headache and to try to sleep.

She closed her eyes, imagined the full moon, and tried to let her consciousness go in full concentration on the glowing ball where men had walked and would walk again. No, she told herself, it is just a glowing ball that I must think of and watch while words and thoughts stop. She was just beginning to have some success when she fell asleep.

* * *

Anna Timofeyeva, her cat, Baku, in her lap, sat by her window. A table with folding legs was before her, the light from a lamp illuminating the pieces of the half-finished jigsaw puzzle on the table.

Jigsaw puzzles had proved to be a comforting meditation for the former procurator. A few years earlier she considered such things a waste of time that could have been productive, and she silently scorned pastimes that did not exercise one's mind, vocabulary, or dexterity. Now, however, she could be so relaxed by the process, so engaged in fitting the small pieces together that when Lydia Tkach came to complain, she could almost block out her piercing voice and stories of hardship and woe. Lydia didn't mind the puzzle as long as Anna said something sympathetic from time to time.

Each small piece attached to another was a tiny moment of satisfaction to Anna. The puzzle before her had a thousand pieces and would, when it was finished, present a picture crackled by the hundreds of edges comfortably fitting together. From the cover of the box she knew that she was working toward the completion of a Swiss chalet in the winter, snow-covered mountains in the background with blue sky and white billowy clouds. In the foreground would be two children playing on a sled. The chalet would, as it did in the picture on the box, look like it was made of fragile white-and-brown chocolate.

Elena had not been home for three days. Anna knew why and had given her niece some ideas of how she might handle the undercover assignment. Elena had listened attentively, nodding her head, absorbing. Elena was smart, a good investigator.

Her niece's relationship with Iosef Rostnikov was welcome to Anna, though she would not say so even if asked. She would not and could not exert any influence on Elena on such an issue. It would happen or it would not.

Anna petted Baku, who purred, a purr that was more a vibration than a sound. An elusive piece was found, a section of one of the chalet windows with a shutter. Without being aware of it, Anna smiled with pleasure.

Though she said and showed no reaction to her niece when Elena's current assignment had come, Anna was worried. She told Lydia nothing about the nature of what Lydia's son, Sasha, and Elena were doing. Lydia was already so obsessed with her son's safety that such a revelation would have resulted in mock hysteria, if not the real thing.

Moscow was more dangerous now than it had ever been, and the most dangerous part for a police officer was probably the gangs. Life was without value. Violence simply took place and was forgotten. Sasha and Elena were attempting to destroy the operation of one such gang, or Mafia, as they liked to call themselves now. The Ministry of the Interior, which was supposed to be responsible for gang activity, was completely overcome by the size of the problem. What Elena and Sasha were doing was worth doing, but it would probably accomplish little.

Anna examined her work of the evening with satisfaction, satisfaction that it was coming along well, satisfaction that there was still more than half the puzzle to complete, two nights' work. Anna seldom worked on the puzzle during the day. She watched the world in the concrete courtyard outside her window, took her prescribed walks, listened to music, read history books and occasional novels. Lately, she had been taking note of and notes on a young mother who was in the courtyard each day with her small child. Anna found the young woman very interesting.

It was late.

Lydia Tkach had knocked insistently and Anna had admitted her, perhaps feeling a slight touch of loneliness that she did not want to admit to herself. Lydia had entered wearing a heavy blue man's robe at least a size too large for her. Anna had returned to her chair and puzzle, and Lydia had closed the door and moved to sit across from her.

"Have you heard from Elena?" asked Lydia.

"No. I didn't expect to."

"She could be dead," said Lydia.

"Thank you for coming late in the night to cheer up a woman with a heart condition," said Anna, not looking up from her puzzle.

"Are you being sarcastic, Anna Timofeyeva?"

"Yes, Lydia Tkach."

"I did not think such sarcasm was in you."

"I have, since my retirement, nurtured and developed it with great care. Soon I will be able to reduce all but the most oblivious or determined—and that includes you—to frustration and departure."

"More sarcasm. You play games with words and pieces of cardboard and I am sick, sick with fear about my only son," said Lydia, pressing her fists into her frail chest.

"That is understandable," said Anna, finding a place for a piece of the puzzle that had eluded her.

Bakunin, who did not like Lydia, had cautiously leapt back into Anna's lap, eyes fixed on the loud intruder.

"My Sasha is a brooding, reckless young man. He has a family, children, a wife who is growing weary of his frequent absences, long hours, and . . . his rare indiscretions caused by the pressures of his work."

"And he has a mother," said Anna, examining a small puzzle piece that may have been part of a human face.

"He has a mother," Lydia said, reaching for a puzzle piece near her hand.

Anna considered taking the piece from the woman and reminding her that she was in violation of the agreement they had made when Lydia had moved into the building. Lydia was to come when invited, to keep her visits brief, and to engage in no complaints about her son, his family, or the simple dangers of being alive. Lydia had begun violating the agreement within a week of moving in. Reminders had been of no use. Anna had even taken the extreme step at one point of informing Lydia that she could not visit under any circumstances until further notice. This had been successful for almost two days.

Lydia reached over and placed the piece of the puzzle snugly into the proper space.

It was not a question of the quality of Lydia's work. The woman obviously had an almost eerie ability to do the puzzles without even thinking about them. But Anna's goal was not to race through each and hurry to the next. Anna had a great deal of time. She wanted the satisfaction of completing each puzzle by herself.

Anna put down the piece in her hand and gently took the piece Lydia was now holding.

"I cannot talk to Porfiry Petrovich about this," said Anna. "I do not wish to talk to him. It is not my business. I would not even talk to him about Elena."

"Maybe I could talk to the new director, Yockvolvy?"

"Yaklovev," Anna corrected. "I doubt, from what I know about him, that he would be sympathetic to your pleas."

"Can it hurt?"

Anna shrugged. Actually, it could hurt, but there was something satisfying to the imagination to picture Lydia loudly insisting to the Yak that he find safe work for her son, even if Sasha didn't want it. However, it could certainly do Sasha's fragile career no good.

"So," said Lydia. "You will do nothing?"

"Nothing," said Anna, stroking her cat. "There is nothing I can do, nothing I wish to do."

"Well, a mother can do a great deal," said Lydia.

"I wish you luck, Lydia Tkach. Now, I am afraid I will have to ask you to leave me. I need to go to bed."

Lydia stood up, pulled the robe tightly around her, and said, "Sometimes I think you lack normal feelings, Anna Timofeyeva."

"Sometimes I agree with you, Lydia Tkach, but that seems to be gradually changing and I am not sure I welcome the change. Please forgive me if I do not rise. I'll lock the door behind you in a few minutes."

Lydia walked to the door and opened it. "We'll talk further tomorrow," she said.

"I will try to contain my great enthusiasm for the moment of that conversation."

"More sarcasm," said Lydia. "You are a difficult person to have as a best friend."

"Best friend? I did not apply for that distinguished position."

"It evolved," said Lydia, leaving the apartment and closing the door behind her.

Could it be, thought Anna, that if I were under oath I would have to admit that Lydia is my best friend? The thought was depressing. "*Chiyigh,* tea and bed," she said. "Sound good to you, cat?"

Baku did not respond. Anna rose from her chair, careful not to jar the table. After the first time Anna had risen in the morning and found that Baku had destroyed her puzzle, Anna had chastised the cat whenever he approached the fragile table. He had learned quickly. But the mind of a cat is unpredictable in its workings. Anna took Baku into the bedroom with her every night and closed the door. Baku had no problem with this and slept comfortably by Anna's side.

Anna Timofeyeva had always been honest with herself and, when possible, with others. Now, as she prepared water for tea after locking the apartment door, she admitted that she was keeping Baku next to her at night because she wanted, needed, the company of a living creature.

In one sense, Anna, who had suffered three heart attacks, was waiting for the fatal one, waiting to die. But in another sense, Anna had come to terms with her life. She missed the satisfaction of power and mission she had when she had been a procurator, but she had grown quite comfortable with her present life. In fact, even if she were suddenly cured, she doubted if she would be interested in returning to work, though she was only fifty-five years old. She had been a loyal, hopeful Communist, well aware of the abuses of the system and the principles of the revolution, but she had doggedly pursued her duties.

The water was boiling now. Anna, who stood next to the stove, turned off the flame and poured the steaming water into her large glass, which contained an English tea bag.

Since she was an atheist, Anna did not pray as she stood drinking her tea, but she did close her eyes and will that Elena would be all right. It struck her that she suddenly knew how the many wives and mothers of police officers felt each night, the fear, the attempts not to think about what might happen.

She finished the tea, threw the bag in the garbage, rinsed the glass and said, "To bed, Baku. Tomorrow we have a satisfying and meaninglessly busy day before us, and, if we are fortunate, Elena will be home."

Chapter Eight

"No," said the woman with her head bowed, wearing a dark veil to cover her eyes and hide her face.

Fortunately, the veil was appropriate since it was a funeral and other women present also had their faces covered.

The crowd around the grave site was large and dangerous. Rostnikov had hoped but not expected that it might rain, which might cut the burial short and lessen the possibility of conflict in the cemetery. But the morning was pleasantly cool, and the sky, while cloudy, gave no sign of an immediate shower.

To the right of the temporary headstone—a ten-foot dark stone with a life-size image of Lashkovich in a leather jacket was being prepared—gathered the one-eyed Casmir Chenko and his Tatar Mafia. To the right stood Shatalov and the Chechin Mafia. Both gangs were dressed in dark suits. Four uniformed policemen from the special gang force stood a discreet distance away at the foot of the grave where the casket was now being lowered. The police were armed with automatic weapons, which two of them had put aside before the burial service began so they could search the incoming members of the two Mafias for weapons. They had found none.

This section of the cemetery was a ghostly army of tall, black gravestones etched with the likelinesses of dead young men in leather who looked down like an army of the damned.

"You are certain," said Rostnikov, who stood on one side of the veiled woman. Emil Karpo stood on the other.

"The man who was with Mr. Lashkovich is not here," Raisa Munyakinova said. "I would like to leave."

"Just a while longer," Porfiry Petrovich said gently.

The service was being conducted by a tall man somewhere in his fifties. He wore a white gown and, before the lowering of the casket began, he had spoken in an unfamiliar language, his deep voice filled with emotion.

"He said," Karpo whispered, "that a good man was being buried today, a man who treated his elders with respect, his wife and children with love, and his country, Tataria, with pride. We shall miss him."

Rostnikov knew that the man being lowered into the ground must have treated his elders, since they included Casmir Chenko, with respect because he had little choice. Lashkovich, however, had abandoned his wife and teenage son five years earlier and never sent them a penny. The widow lived in Kazan, five hundred miles from Moscow, in what had been declared the Tatar capital. The widow lived by working in a belt factory. She was not present. As for his patriotism, a quick search had revealed that the dead man had paid no taxes. It might also be considered a less than chauvinistic act to murder citizens, as the dead man had made a career of doing.

"Look again, Raisa Munyakinova, please," said Rostnikov, well under the voice of the man in the white gown who shifted in Russian to an almost tearful prayer.

"May God take the soul of this good man into his arms. May he receive in heaven all that he deserves for a life well spent in devotion and toil."

"Amen to that," said Rostnikov.

"I want to go now," Raisa said. "I'm tired. I'm afraid."

"One last look," said Rostnikov, incredibly uncomfortable and trying to bear the brunt of the weight of his body with his good right leg, using the left one to simply maintain his balance.

She lifted her veil just enough to see out from under it and scanned the crowd once again.

"No," she said, letting the veil drop. "He is not here. I am sure."

Raisa had worked a full shift and it had been a difficult one. The

Carpathian Bathhouse was nowhere near as well-maintained as the hotel health club where she had worked the night before and where the Tatar had died. She had expected another cleaning woman, Olga Sachnova, but the other woman had simply not shown up. There had been debris and wet towels. The sinks and toilets weren't filthy but they were not clean. She had put in an extra hour, though she would never be paid for it. She did not wish to lose her job, and she could not possibly bring herself to leave any sign of dirt behind her.

From the bathhouse, she had caught a bus and made it to Petrovka at the time designated for her meeting with the pale detective named Karpo. She had passed the police building hundreds of times and heard tales about the dark bowels of the building. Raisa did not want to enter, but she could not refuse. The guard at the gate had taken her name and made a call. Moments later Karpo had appeared and led her into the building for a nearly two-hour examination of the photographs of not only Chechin gangsters, but Tatars, Afghan veteran Mafia members, and dozens of Georgians, Moslems, Ukrainians, Estonians, and Russians of all ages. Nothing.

The casket was now resting on the dirt bottom of the grave and three Tatars were shoveling soil over it. The man in the white gown made a motion with his raised hand and the burial was over.

Rostnikov and Karpo had not been surprised by the appearance of the Chechins at a Tatar burial. The code of dishonor adopted loosely from an amalgam of American gangster movies required such an appearance and the presentation of a large flowery wreath to lay on the grave.

Two Chechins in their twenties were standing back with the ready wreath and a signal from Shatalov.

The service was over but no one moved.

Two of the Tatar men, hands folded in front of them, and a woman headed straight for the two policemen and the veiled woman.

"Please, please, please, let's leave now," Raisa said, gripping Rostnikov's hand.

Her grip of fear was surprisingly strong.

The Tatar contingent stopped directly in front of Raisa, and the woman, who was young and very pretty, with Asiatic features, looked at Raisa, whose head was bent forward in a fear she hoped looked like grief.

"My father, Casmir Chenko," the young woman said, "wants to thank you for coming. The journey must have been difficult. Your son was a very good man and a loyal friend. You should be very proud of him."

The young woman lifted her right hand slightly and one of the young Tatars stepped forward, a letter-sized brown envelope in his hand. He handed the envelope to the young woman and stood back.

"My father wants you to have this, a small token of his respect for your son."

Raisa wanted to look at one of the policemen to determine if she should refuse the gift. She couldn't do so. She took the envelope and nodded. The young girl stepped forward and gave Raisa a hug, whispering in her ear, "Whatever your son may have told you, do not share it with these policemen who brought you here. Valentin would not have wished it."

The young woman was adept at such whispered messages, and while the two policemen had not heard the words, they had heard the voice.

"You are one of us too," said Chenko's daughter, looking at Emil Karpo. "A relative?"

"No," he said.

"You are a Tatar," she said, looking into the ghostly face.

"I am a Russian," Karpo said.

"Then you are a traitor," she said.

Chenko's daughter stepped away and the two young men followed her back toward the grave site, where the last of the dirt was being shoveled.

"What am I to do with this?" asked Raisa.

"Keep it," said Rostnikov.

"It is evil money," Raisa said.

"It is money," said Rostnikov. "It can now be used to ease your life a bit. If you wish, give it to a worthy cause or someone more in need of it than you, if you can find such a person."

"She said it was because my son is dead," Raisa said.

"Consider it a mistake on their part which can benefit a woman who has to hold on to many jobs to live," said Rostnikov. "These people do not do good things unless they have made a mistake."

Raisa clutched the envelope as both policemen looked away from her toward the grave upon which the two Chechins with the massive floral wreath were advancing. From the other side of the grave three Tatars stepped forward and stood in a line.

The Chechins laid the wreath on the mound and stepped back.

Immediately, the three Tatars picked up the wreath and threw it in the direction of the gathered Chechins. The wreath did not sail because of its weight, but skidded on the grass and halted in front of Shatalov, who stepped forward and said loudly with a tone of mock disappointment, "Bad manners, One Eye."

"Bad manners indeed, Irving," said Chenko.

The mask of disappointment left Shatalov's face and was replaced by a cold, threatening stare. Shatalov smiled, raised his right hand, and motioned as if to an army he wished to follow him into battle. One young man with something in his hand moved forward to the flower-covered grave and in the plot next to it plunged a stake bearing a small, neatly printed sign reading, VACANCY.

Even before they could read the sign, the Tatars, led by Casmir Chenko, had begun to advance. Shatalov's men also stepped forward behind their leader.

The policemen with automatic weapons moved quickly between the two groups.

"Halt," called the officer in charge, glancing at Rostnikov and Karpo for some direction.

The policeman had not really expected any disruption or confrontation. He had been told by his captain that rival gangs attend each others' funerals all the time. The important thing was to disarm both sides before the burial and, if necessary, to fire between them.

The two sides did not halt. One of the policemen fired directly into the grave, sending up a flurry of flower petals. Rostnikov thought the fluttering colorful flowers dancing in the air looked quite beautiful. The gangs halted now and the Tatars looked angrily at the policeman who had fired into the grave of their just-buried comrade.

The situation was about to turn ugly, and the policeman in charge, who was no more than thirty, thought that he might be about to kill his first man and possibly to be killed or beaten.

"Take her away," said Rostnikov to Emil Karpo.

Karpo took Raisa's arm and led her, clutching her brown envelope, toward the entrance to the cemetery.

"Disperse," the policeman said, trying to keep his voice steady.

The two gangs hesitated. Could they back off and retain their honor? Who was the primary enemy here? The gang on the other side of the grave or the armed policemen?

Rostnikov strode forward, allowing himself a bit more of a limp than was really necessary. It was not sympathy he sought, but time.

"I was up before dawn," he said aloud, stepping alongside of the policemen. "Couldn't sleep. Too much to think about, too many problems, and the intricacies of a particularly puzzling plumbing system haunted my dreams. I couldn't make the system go away. My dream eye followed rusting pipes moving ever faster in a maze I knew had no end."

"You have a point to make, Rostnikov?" called Shatalov.

"I was up very early. I believe I said that. I put on my leg and my clothes and took the rare step of calling for a police car. It is a benefit of my position which I rarely use. But this time I wanted to get to this cemetery to watch the sun rise over the tombstones."

Chenko, with his single eye, and Shatalov, with his two alcohol red eyes, glared at each other in anticipation of what was coming next.

"I did some cleaning up of weeds that had been planted here last night," said Rostnikov. "I wish I had been here to witness this gardening, and I must say I'm surprised that the two sets of gardeners did not run into each other. Perhaps the night was long for them as well as for me. In short, gentlemen, the weapons you hid under thin layers of dirt and leaves and in the low limbs of trees nearby are no longer there. I have had then taken away to be distributed to the needy. There are petty thieves and armed robbers who can afford little more than small knives and ancient pistols."

Rostnikov paused and stepped out of the way of the policemen's guns.

"That was an attempt at mild humor," said Rostnikov. "An attempt to diffuse a situation that will bring nothing good to any of you, should it go further."

"You'll give the order if we are to fire?" asked the policeman.

"If necessary," said Rostnikov.

There was a full ten seconds of silence and then laughter. Shatalov was laughing. "You amuse me, Rostnikov," he said, chuckling. "I would like to be your friend. We could have good times."

Rostnikov looked at Chenko, who was not smiling and who had nothing to say. He nodded his head and the young man who had met Rostnikov at the Pushkin statue stepped forward and kicked the "Vacancy" sign, which sailed a few yards and came to rest. Chenko turned his back to the grave and with his daughter at his side strode away with the funeral contingent behind him.

Shatalov made a gesture with his hand and his group moved directly toward the gate beyond a line of trees. Then Shatalov, the big man with the bad skin at his side, broke away from the group and moved to Rostnikov, who was saying to the policeman in charge, "I suggest you hurry to the entrance to prevent any possible further encounter."

"There will be no encounter," said Shatalov. "I gave you my word that I would hold off killing the Tatar."

"Hold off killing anyone," said Rostnikov.

"I have other enemies. And we must defend ourselves."

"And that is why you had weapons planted here?"

Shatalov shrugged. "Caution," he said. "I live a life that requires constant caution."

"Yet you eat at public pizza bars."

Shatalov shook his head. "I am inconsistent, I know," he said. "Knowing one should do a thing and actually doing it requires a battle between logic and emotion."

"You are a philosopher," said Rostnikov.

"And an actor," Shatalov added. "It is necessary in my work. Chenko plays the wise old man of dignity. He is more cautious than I, but he has no dignity. People in our profession deserve no dignity and I don't pretend to have it."

"And," said Rostnikov, "what part do you play?"

"The explosive, good-humored man who enjoys his ill-gotten gains," said Shatalov. "Did you like that little gesture of mine? Where I raised my hand just a little and waved my finger slightly to dismiss my people? Very understated. Very dramatic. I think I saw Anthony Quinn do it once."

"Very dramatic," said Rostnikov. "Do you believe in reincarnation, Shatalov?"

"No."

"Let me tell you a story," said Rostnikov. "An old Hindu tale I read not long ago."

"I have time," said Shatalov with a smile.

"Good," said Rostnikov, ignoring the entourage that now stood back, waiting for their leader. "It seems an emperor, a very powerful emperor, decided to have built for himself the biggest monument in the history of the world. The plans were laid out for him, and he was about to order that the monument be made even larger. Suddenly at his side there appeared a very small boy who told the emperor that he was the earthly manifestation of a humble god."

"Very interesting," said Shatalov. "Perhaps you could be a bit faster. I think it will soon rain."

"It has seemed likely to rain for several days," said Rostnikov, looking up at the clouds. "The god said, 'behold.' They frequently say 'behold' in Hindu mythology. It helps establish the tale as being from another time and place. Well, the god raised his hand and into the huge marble room in which they stood marched rows and rows of beetles, all the same, several hundred in each row, in perfect order. They marched across the floor, their millions of tiny feet scratching the marble, silent alone, loud when together. 'What do you see?' asked the god.

" 'Beetles,' said the emperor.

" 'Each of these beetles was once an emperor even more powerful than you,' said the god."

Rostnikov stopped.

"Well," said Shatalov. "What next?"

"Nothing," said Porfiry Petrovich. "That is the end. When first I read this story, Shatalov, I admit to you that it frightened me just a bit. Well, more than a bit. Is life so meaningless?"

"It's just a myth," said Shatalov. "Policeman, you are mad."

"After a few weeks of being afraid to sleep," said Rostnikov softly, ignoring the gangster's comment, "I suddenly felt relieved. That I might be insignificant is not to be feared but embraced. It frees us in this life. It demands that we make our own meaning, that we are not above the morality that we must create if life is to have any meaning."

"Now I know you are crazy, Rostnikov."

"And you are a dark emperor," answered the policeman. "Will you be a beetle? Does a headstone with a picture etched on it have any meaning? It will crumble with time. Beetles have been on earth since the beginning of life."

"Good-bye, Rostnikov. If you decide you want to work for me, I can make it very worthwhile. That is what you are hinting at, isn't it?"

Rostnikov smiled sadly and looked back at the flower-covered grave of the dead Tatar gangster. "Dream," said Rostnikov, "of miles of twisting pipes in dark walls, or millions of beetles walking slowly on marble floors, their tiny legs scratching in unison. Good morning."

Rostnikov turned and limped toward the gate past trees and tombstones, moss-covered dirty mausoleums. Shatalov said to the departing policeman, "We did not kill Lashkovich. We did not kill the other one. I don't remember his name. We are not trying to start a war, but the one-eyed bastard is. He killed one of my closest . . . friends."

"Chenko, too, claims that he did not kill your man," said Rostnikov, not turning. "Perhaps I believe you both. Perhaps there is a man who wants you both at war. Think about it when not thinking of beetles, and look around at the face of each of the men who surround you."

"Yevgeny Pleshkov did not show up at the casino last night," Iosef said to Yulia Yalutshkin in her apartment on Kalinin Prospekt.

Yulia was sitting on the sofa upon which Jurgen had only hours earlier spread his arms in self-satisfied and naked possession. Yulia was wearing pink silk pajamas with a matching silk robe tied at the waist with an equally pink sash. She crossed her legs and reached for a cigarette in a small case on the table in front of her.

Akardy Zelach sat in the chair that had been offered to Oleg Kisolev the night before. Iosef sat in the matching chair, into which Yevgeny Pleshkov had crumpled after killing the German.

"He is hiding," Yulia said, lighting her cigarette and leaning back.

"From whom?"

"From you, his family," she said. "That, of course, is only a guess."

The policemen had come early and their knocking had immediately awakened her, but it had no effect on Yevgeny Pleshkov, who slept soundly next to her in the bedroom. Yevgeny was badly in need of a shave. When the knock came at the door, she had risen, put on her robe, and closed the bedroom door. Fortunately, when sleeping off a particularly bad binge, Yevgeny did not snore, at least he seldom did so. If the police searched, they would have no trouble finding the man they sought. He was only about twenty feet away behind a closed door. What troubled Yulia most was that Yevgeny might awaken and blunder into the room.

Yulia looked relaxed and in no hurry.

"The German," Iosef said.

"Jurgen," she said. "I would guess that he too is hiding."

"Why? From whom?"

"Enemies," she said. "When and if you meet him you will understand his ability to make enemies easily."

"And you don't know where he is hiding?"

She shrugged.

"I would like to talk to him."

"I would not," she said. "I threw him out last night. I could see he was working himself up to hit me. I've had more than enough of that and I had warned him. As he was about to strike me last night, I screamed. I have perfected a scream that would penetrate the walls of the Kremlin and cause the body of Lenin to rise and open his eyes. Jurgen told me to stop, that he was going, that he would not give me another ruble. Confidentially, I gambled away what little he gave me and lived on money from Yevgeny. Jurgen conveniently overlooked the fact that I gave him far more money than he ever gave me. Would you like a drink? Water with ice? Pepsi-Cola?"

Zelach looked at Iosef, who nodded his consent, and Yulia rose elegantly, crossing the floor to the small refrigerator where she pulled out a bottle of Pepsi, opened it, and poured it over a glass she had half filled with ice.

She handed the drink to Zelach, who took it with thanks.

"And you, big policeman? What can I give you?" She stood provocatively over Iosef with the touch of an inviting smile.

"Yevgeny Pleshkov," he said. "The German. Do you have either of those or know where I can get them?"

"Vodka, ginger ale, Pepsi, brandy, whiskey, and even some French wine," she said, "but I am all out of Yevgeny Pleshkovs and Germans named Jurgen."

"A man of Pleshkov's description was seen entering this building late last night," said Iosef. "He is a very famous man. People remember him."

"I was out," she said. "At Jacko's Casino."

"I was there," said Iosef. "I didn't see you."

She shrugged. "We must have missed each other. That is too bad. I would have been happy to entertain you for the evening. I understand that I have a well-developed ability to keep men, and occasionally women, happy, sometimes for an entire night."

Zelach shifted uneasily. Iosef went on. "Yevgeny Pleshkov and another man were seen leaving this building two hours after they arrived," said Iosef. "What did they do for two hours if you were not here?"

"I must make a note to give the doorman a smaller bonus," she said, looking at the end of her cigarette.

"Where were you?" Iosef repeated.

"Jacko's and then dinner with some businessmen," she said, going back to the sofa. "I don't know their names or where they live. I may have seen them about before."

"Can you explain what Yevgeny Pleshkov was doing in this building for two hours?" asked Iosef pleasantly.

"Perhaps business?" she tried. "Yevgeny knows many people."

"I am sure," said Iosef. "But in this building I think he knows only you."

"Then," she said, "who knows?"

"Perhaps we will," said Iosef. "There are twelve uniformed officers checking all the apartments in the building."

"Impressive," she said. "You must want Yevgeny very badly."

"Very badly," said Iosef.

There was a knock at the door and Yulia gracefully crossed the room to answer it. Iosef thought she looked remarkably beautiful.

"Inspector Rostnikov, Inspector Zelach," the young policeman with a thin mustache said, unable to take his eyes from the tall beauty before him. "Please come. We think we have found Yevgeny Pleshkov."

"Where?" asked Iosef, rising.

The young policeman looked at Yulia, unsure of what he should say.

"Where?" Iosef repeated.

"A shed on the roof of the hotel," the young man finally said. "He—the body—is badly burned."

"I think," said Iosef to Yulia, "you had better get dressed. Do not leave the apartment. Inspector Zelach and I will come back shortly to continue our chat. There will be a uniformed officer outside your door."

"For my protection?" she said with a smile.

"Of course," said Iosef.

Zelach quickly finished his Pepsi-Cola and placed the glass on the table as he rose.

Perhaps a second after the door to the apartment had closed and the two policemen had departed, the bedroom door opened and a very sober Yevgeny Pleshkov said, "I heard."

"So," she said, moving past him toward the bedroom and touching his bristly cheek on her way, "you are the brilliant politician, the hope for Russia. What do we do now?"

Pleshkov had no idea.

"We had better think quickly," she said, putting out her cigarette and taking off her pink pajamas.

Yevgeny Pleshkov headed for the cart containing the liquor bottles.

"Well," Yulia said with a sigh. "Let us try what has always
worked in the past."

"Which is?" asked Pleshkov.

"Yevgeny," she said, "you may be a brilliant politician, but you
lack common sense. Go in the bathroom. Shave quickly. I'll get you
out of here." Standing naked and looking quite beautiful to
Yevgeny, Yulia began to laugh.

"What is funny?" he asked.

"I am an uneducated high-priced prostitute," she said, "and I am
giving orders to the man who may soon rule all of Russia."

"You are very beautiful," Yevgeny said, pouring himself a drink.

"Let us hope the policeman outside the door agrees."

The lobby of the hotel was relatively empty as Elena Timofeyeva
headed toward the elevator. Sasha Tkach, she was sure, was still
asleep. The night before they had seen a lot and drunk more than
a human being should be expected to. They had been guided by
Illya and Boris to a lobster dinner at the Anchor in the Palace
Hotel—Sasha had never had lobster before and had to watch Elena
proceed before he began. Elena had eaten lobster more than once
when she had been a student in the United States.

Both Illya and Boris were accompanied by young women, very
young women, professionally made up and wearing dresses that
were definitely French designed. The two women had spoken fewer
than five or six words each. They smiled politely at jokes and were
serious at proper moments. After the dinner, which was liberally
accompanied by mixed drinks, the group moved on to three casinos—drinking, gambling, laughing. Elena hadn't liked it, nor had
she liked Boris checking his watch and saying, "It's time."

"For what?" Sasha had said drunkenly.

"The dogfight," said Illya. "Now, tonight. Let's go get your
dog."

"I thought that was tomorrow," Elena said.

Boris leaned toward her, his breath strong and unpleasant, and said, "The fight between your Tchaikovsky and our Bronson is tomorrow night, if they are both in shape. Tonight is just to get the bettors interested. Promotion, hype, like the Americans with boxers."

It was Sasha's call, and Elena hoped that he was sober enough to make the right one. She thought of saying something like, "We haven't prepared our dog for anything tonight," or "Dmitri wouldn't risk his prime animal before a big fight." But she couldn't speak. She was a woman. Sasha was supposedly the scheming, fearless, and ruthless man.

"Fine," said Sasha with a smile, wiping his face with a napkin and tearing the tail off of a shrimp from the huge chilled pile on the table.

"We had better go now," said Illya. "After we finish our final drinks. A toast." He raised his glass. "*Mir i Druzhbah*, peace and friendship."

When his last round of drinks was finished, everyone at the table rose, Sasha reaching for one last shrimp. Neither Boris nor Illya appeared to pay the bill. When the group was out on the street, all six of them climbed into the black limo that appeared at the curb. The failure of the threatened rain to begin falling was beginning to bother Elena. When it finally rained, it might be an omen that something bad was going to happen. It was a thought worthy of Zelach's mother. Elena shook off the idea. Touches of superstition that were also the legacy of her mother back in Odessa. Anna and her sister, Elena's mother, had the same general build, the same voice, and almost the same face, but they were nothing alike in background and thought. Elena's mother was a fish sorter on the docks. She was uneducated and surrounded by demons. Elena had escaped from her mother and her family in Odessa the day she turned eighteen.

And now Elena was surrounded by demons.

The three couples were driven to the hastily built kennel in the garage behind a pair of stores on the Arbat. The three men and Elena had gone single file down a narrow passageway between two buildings. The two young women, fearful of ruining their clothes, had remained behind in the car.

Sasha used his key, went in ahead of them, and turned on the lights.

Elena and Sasha were not sure of what they would see. The space had been prepared during the day by a quartet of carpenters who were accustomed to doing such jobs for people on both sides of the law, though one of them had commented as they had worked that it was more and more difficult to see the difference. Traffic back and forth between the good guys and the bad had almost erased the line.

The carpenter who had expressed these beliefs was a set designer and builder for television shows and movies. He took each job without questioning, without asking for reasons.

Both the criminals and the law considered him a genius, and when Elena looked around the room, which could easily have held three huge twelve-wheel trucks, she found it difficult to keep from examining the brilliant set. After all, she was supposed to have been here at least several times before.

Along the wall across from the garage doors were a series of large metal cages. In each was a dog. In all there were six dogs. The dogs were silent, which impressed Boris and Illya.

"Well trained," said Boris.

"I have a clever dog trainer from England," Sasha improvised. "And don't bother to try to find out who he is. He is my prized possession, more important than the animals. The animals, except for Tchaikovsky, are expendable."

A training ring, basically the ring of a small circus, with a red wooden wall circling it, stood in front of the wall at the end of the line of cages. Directly in the center of the garage was an oval exercise area complete with Astroturf. Two doors of the garage were blocked by shelves of items for the care of fighting dogs.

"No dog food?" said Boris, looking at the shelf.

"We feed them only fresh raw meat and water with vitamin supplements and injections," said Sasha, who had no idea what he was talking about.

Elena had to admit that he was doing a remarkably good job. Alcohol may have blurred his memory but it loosened his imagination.

"They use the exercise pen," Sasha said, nodding at the Astroturf-covered ring. "But one at a time. We wouldn't want valuable dogs killing each other without an audience and the chance to place some bets."

Illya nodded in understanding and said, "Let's go. They'll be waiting."

There were two large wooden free-standing walk-in storage rooms next to the shelves. Elena knew Sasha was trying to figure out which one might hold transport cages for the animals. Perhaps they both did. Perhaps neither. He walked slowly and a bit unsteadily on his feet to the storage room on his right. He opened the padlocked door with his key and stepped in. Elena was right behind him, as were Illya and Boris.

There were no cages. The small space held an old but still-humming refrigerator and cleaning instruments to take care of the dog refuse. The tools looked used. Sasha went to the refrigerator, opened it, and marveled that his lie about raw meat was supported by the evidence inside the cold, lighted box. There were dozens of half-gallon-sized plastic containers through the sides of which raw, red meat could be clearly seen.

"Good," said Sasha, closing the door and turning to the others. "Lokanski prepared a new supply."

"We are in a hurry," Boris said impatiently.

"I take care of my dogs," Sasha said indignantly.

"Get a cage," said Illya. "Let's go."

Sasha moved to the next padlocked storage room and once again took out the keys he had been given. Elena controlled her near panic. If a transport cage were not inside, Sasha would be very hard pressed to come up with an explanation for why he did not know where things were in his own kennel. Relying on his drunken forgetfulness would not work with these men. Elena tried to think of what she could do, but she was still certain that her intervention would not be appreciated by the two men. They had pointedly ignored her all evening, and she had accepted their rudeness with gratitude. She did not have to speak any more than the two young mannequins who were waiting in the car parked on the Arbat.

Sasha opened the door of the second storage room, stepped in, and reached up for the string that turned on the light. Stacked on the far wall were six metal-mesh cages with handles on top. Hanging almost carelessly on the wall on hooks were a wide variety of ropes, muzzles, things she could not identify and was certain Sasha could not either. One other item hung on the wall, one Elena and Sasha both recognized, an electric prod.

Sasha, with some difficulty which required him to ask Boris and Illya to help, got down a top cage and said, "Gentlemen, we are late."

Sasha, she could see, had glanced at the wall of dog-control items, possibly considering if he should take one, for he had no idea of how to get the pit bull into the cage. He rejected the idea and, carrying the cage awkwardly, had moved past a curious rottweiler, a pair of large mongrels, a German shepherd, and a sleeping St. Bernard, toward the pit bull. Elena was relieved that there was only one pit bull in the garage.

Moving to the front of the cage of the pit bull, who stood looking into the face of the man, Sasha lifted the door which covered the entire front of the transport cage. He pushed the open cage in front of Tchaikovsky's cage, which he opened, lifting the sliding door slowly.

Now, the difficult part: getting the pit bull to go into the transport cage. The dog did not move. Sasha was supposed to be the expert. He had to get the animal in the transport cage and do it quickly without destroying his cover as Dmitri Kolk.

"You need help, Dmitri?"

Elena could tell from the look on his face that for a moment he did not remember that he was Dmitri. Then he recovered and said, "No, I have my own methods for doing things. If I need anything, it is another small drink."

Sasha's improvised method was to squat behind the transport cage and talk to the dog the way Elena had seen him talk to his baby son. Elena thought quickly about finding a weapon if they were unmasked. She decided that the best, though riskiest, thing to do would be to kick the transport cage out of the way and let Tchaikovsky free to attack, hoping he would go for Illya and Boris. But miraculously the pit bull quick-stepped into the smaller cage and Sasha dropped the door, trying not to show his relief.

Illya had to help carry the animal to the car. There were metal grips on each of the top corners of the cage, which made the task easier. Tchaikovsky stood all the way to the car, maintaining his balance and dignity.

The limousine was large, but with six people and a dog there was not a great deal of room. They placed the cage next to the driver, who looked straight ahead and made no comment or response. The two beautiful young women ignored the animal and Elena, and talked softly to each other as they rode. Boris and Illya pressed Sasha for information about his operation. Since he had no information and was obviously thinking about the coming battle, Sasha did not want to make up any more tales.

The rest of the night had been a nightmare to Elena.

The small arena in a converted warehouse in Pushkino north of the Outer Ring Circle was ringed by wooden benches. The first row had blue-cushioned seats with armrests, certainly the place where the big bettors sat. All the seats were set up high so the spectators could look down at the dirt-covered ring.

When Sasha, Elena, and the others arrived, a badly mauled and dying black-and-white mongrel was being carried off by two men. The dog was on a canvas litter, his mouth muzzled to keep him from one last angry attack at the men who carried him out.

Sasha nodded and with Illya's help moved the cage to the side of the fighting ring next to a blue stick standing over the back of the circle.

"You start here, at the blue side," said Boris.

The crowd was loud, angry, crying out, "Let's go. We haven't got all night."

In fact, Elena thought, they probably did have all night and more.

The air was thick with smoke. Elena tried not to cough. There had been cushioned seats reserved for the six arrivals. The seats were comfortable. The smoke was unbearable.

"What if one of the dogs jumps over the wall and gets into the crowd?" Elena asked the young woman at her side. "The wall is low."

"Shooter," the young woman said, pointing at a man who stood in the entranceway, arms folded. He wore jeans, a white T-shirt, and a denim jacket that did nothing to hide the gun he wore under it.

Tchaikovsky's opponent was huge, a mastiff with a long, ugly white scar along its right side. The mastiff seethed with anticipation but was held back by his trainer. Tchaikovsky, on the other hand, simply stood inside his cage, looking at his opponent.

"Bets down, side bets require ten percent for the house. We don't care if you give odds. With rare exceptions, house bets are even money. We are here to watch an ancient and honorable sport," said the sweating announcer who wore an incongruous green tuxedo and used a handheld microphone. "Blue is Tchaikovsky, the pit bull whose record, if any, cannot be verified. Red is English, who many of you have seen here before. Eight victories, all kills."

It took five minutes of loud wrangling, taking bets, and having a quintet of well-built men going up and down the aisles taking the house percentage and making eye contact with the three shills in the audience whose job was to spot bettors who tried to bypass the house.

"Now," said the announcer, backing up to the entrance near the shooter to be out of the way of animals and out of the sightline of the nearly rabid audience. "Release our gladiators."

The crowd went silent. The mastiff charged and for a moment it looked as if the pit bull would not even make it out of the cage. The crowd laughed at the impassive dog still standing in the cage. The laughter stopped when Tchaikovsky suddenly dashed through the cage door and leapt at the mastiff, which raced toward him. The mastiff snapped his jaws and missed the smaller animal. Tchaikovsky did not miss. He dug his teeth into English's neck just below the ear.

The big dog tried to shake the pit bull off but couldn't. English twirled in pain. The pit bull bit even deeper. The mastiff tried rolling on the ground. Tchaikovsky held fast. Blood was coming now, spurts of blood all over the ring and the face of the smaller dog.

The crowd went wild. The mastiff made sounds of pain which drove the crowd to even further madness. The big dog, with the pit bull appended, sank down on his belly. Tchaikovsky ripped the flesh in his mouth and stood back to look at his dying opponent. The pit bull dropped the piece of flesh and fur on the dirt floor and trotted back to his cage, ignoring the shouts and applause of the crowd.

By that time, Elena was ill, ill from the smoke, ill from repulsion, and most of all, ill from the blood-and-battle-hungry crowd. The now-dead mastiff was taken away in the canvas blanket by the two emotionless men.

The announcer moved forward and tried to quiet the crowd.

"The winner, Tchaikovsky, will be here tomorrow to face the winner of our next and main battle. The champion of our circuit,

Bronson, will be in the blue. Bronson, who has twenty-two consecutive kills and almost no scars, is clearly the favorite, but his opponent, Rado, the pit bull, has seven victories, bloody and swift. He had to be restrained with nets after his last kill. He is more than a worthy opponent for the champion. However, in view of Bronson's record, the house will suspend its own rule and provide odds of five to one in favor of Bronson."

The crowd grumbled. Their chance for easy money-in-the-pocket had just been taken away. Few were surprised. None complained. This had happened before and complaining would not be wise.

The fight between Bronson, the black-and-white mongrel, and the brown pit bull took a bit longer than Tchaikovsky's battle. The pit bull had attacked quickly, but the battle-wise Bronson dashed to his left and got behind the other dog, who turned to face him and showed his teeth. Bronson leapt, leapt high. The crowd cheered. Rado the pit bull looked up in confusion at the shaggy opponent who seemed to be flying toward him. Bronson came down on the back of the pit bull and bit it in the rear.

Rado howled in pain and when Bronson let go, the pit bull ran across the ring and turned. He looked back at his bloody rump but had no time to deal with it. He attacked again. Bronson was ready. He neither moved to the side nor leapt into the air. As Rado jumped for the other dog's throat, Bronson snapped forward and brought his jaws down on the pit bull's muzzle. This time he did not let go. Rado struggled but couldn't get loose. After a minute or two, the pit bull sank back and stopped struggling.

"The fight is over," said the announcer, moving forward. "Perhaps Rado will survive his wounds and live to fight another day."

Rado was unsteady on his legs. His muzzle and rump were bloody blotches, but the pit bull still looked ready to attempt a resumption of the battle he had already lost. Rado's trainer entered the ring with a leather noose at the end of a leather-covered stick.

He slipped it around the wounded animal's neck and led Rado to his cage.

Untouched and without noose or command, Bronson returned to his cage, to the applause and cheers of the crowd.

"They should have let Bronson kill him," a man behind Elena said.

They had witnessed the last fight of the evening. Illya drove them back to the Arbat and waited for Sasha and Boris to get the pit bull back into his cage in the garage. There was no conversation in the car while they were gone, but Elena could see Illya looking at her in the rearview mirror. One of the girls was fighting sleep. The other put her arm around the tired girl. Elena thought their night might not yet be over.

Back at the hotel Elena congratulated Sasha on his performance. He waved a weary hand of acknowledgment in her direction. When they got to the room, Sasha said one word, "Sleep." He headed for the bed and, still dressed, flung himself down on his stomach. He was very gently snoring in seconds. Elena was still slightly ill and wondered if she would have to go the next night for the fight between Tchaikovsky and Bronson. Maybe she could provide some excuse to stay away.

She changed into her pajamas, took the pillows on the bed, and went to sleep on the sofa.

Then, in the morning, with Sasha still asleep, Elena had gone out for a walk to clear away her headache and nausea. The man following her today was neither of those from the day before. This one was very young and very inexperienced. She had stopped for a roll and coffee and was now crossing the nearly empty lobby. The images of the night before would not go away, and she knew she had suddenly developed a fear of dogs, all dogs.

Her bag slung over her shoulder, she pressed the button for her floor and stood back against the wall, trying not to remember what she had seen.

What happened next came so fast that Elena had no time to

think or react. A dog came through the closing doors. It was moving with great speed and it leapt at Elena, sinking its teeth into her left shoulder. The pain was searing, and Elena had a flashing vision of herself sinking to the floor of the elevator with the dog ripping at her flesh and going for her face or neck the way the animals had done to each other the night before.

She wanted to scream out for help but she couldn't.

The elevator door was almost closed. She punched the determined dog's snout with her fist and leaned over to sink her teeth into the neck of the animal. Pain drew her head back. She was vaguely aware that someone was forcing the door back open, someone was entering the elevator, the door of which slid shut as the figure entered.

Elena fought off the urge to pass out. As she sank down along the wall with the dog still tearing at her shoulder, she turned her head, opened her mouth, and leaned painfully toward the thick furry neck of her attacker.

Chapter Nine

"I will have to take the body back to my laboratory," said Paulinin, gloves on his hands, kneeling on a bath towel which had been brought to him.

Iosef, Zelach, and two uniformed policemen stood watching the wild-haired man poke, prod, and examine the badly burned body.

"I can tell you several things, however. First, I may be able to salvage a few of the photographs and maybe usable pieces of tape. Second, this is not Yevgeny Pleshkov. I have seen newspaper photographs of Pleshkov smiling. In spite of his fame and following, Pleshkov has Russian teeth, uneven, a few twisting, and certainly with a filling or more made of inferior material. This man has perfect teeth, all capped, almost certainly by a dentist in or from a Western country."

Iosef was taking notes.

"Further, this man was younger and not as heavy as Pleshkov. I will need to examine him carefully in my laboratory, but it appears this man was murdered and then burned. The skull is recently scarred and several splinters of burned wood are embedded here."

He pointed to the blackened skull.

"Also," Paulinin said, "there are splinters in the neck wound and one of the ribs has a fracture, a hairline fracture. I would guess with confidence that he was stabbed in the neck with a splinter of wood and beaten by something heavy, also wood."

"A stake. Like a vampire," said Zelach. "Maybe whoever killed him thought he was a vampire?"

It was one of the longest statements and one of the few observations Akardy Zelach had made since Iosef met him. Iosef was reluctant to simply dismiss the question.

"It is a possibility worth exploring," said Iosef. "You believe in vampires, Zelach?"

"My mother does," he said, looking at the body. "She says she has seen them. I . . . I don't know."

Paulinin shook his head, considered saying something to Zelach, and decided instead to continue his search. "Ah, some hairs."

He took one of the half-gallon Ziploc bags from his right jacket pocket. There were also smaller plastic bags, which Paulinin seldom used.

"Why," the scientist said, finally rising, "is Emil Karpo not on this case?"

"He is on another important assignment," Iosef said.

Paulinin's face showed great irritation. "I'll carry these pieces of evidence myself. You carefully get this body and anything else that may be of interest to my laboratory. Where is Emil Karpo or Porfiry Petrovich Rostnikov when I need them? They would know what I would be interested in seeing. Don't answer. I'm leaving before it rains."

The sky was indeed dark. Iosef ordered the two policemen to call for a police ambulance to take the body to Paulinin's laboratory. Paulinin left and so did the two policemen.

Zelach and Iosef stood looking down at the burnt debris and the body.

"I wonder how easy it is to get out of here without being seen," said Iosef. "Service doors, emergency exits. How did Pleshkov get out past the doorman, who claims he did not leave?"

Iosef had asked himself the question, but Zelach answered. "Maybe he didn't get out," said Zelach.

"We looked everywhere," said Iosef patiently. "We have had every corner, every apartment searched."

"No," said Zelach.

"No? Where didn't we look?"

"Yulia Yalutshkin's bedroom," Zelach said, slouching forward, his eyes fixed on the body.

Iosef looked at him with new respect. Zelach may very well be right. In which case, Iosef would look like a fool when he explained to his father that they had not checked the bedroom. If Zelach was right, Yulia had performed magnificently. Iosef dashed for the door to the roof, with Zelach right behind. If Pleshkov had been in the bedroom, he might still be there. He had to be there. There was an armed guard at the door of Yulia Yalutshkin's apartment.

What troubled Iosef even more than the likelihood that Pleshkov had eluded him was the very real possibility that the distinguished member of the congress, probably the next president of Russia, may well have been involved in or even committed a brutal murder. What led Iosef to this conclusion was the distinct possibility that the burned body was that of Jurgen, Yulia's German lover and protector, who probably had good Western teeth.

Paulinin would find out if Iosef was correct. Meanwhile, Iosef had to find Yevgeny Pleshkov.

The jaws of the dog opened and Elena felt the animal's weight lift from her. Her own teeth had been about to sink into the animal's neck and she had tasted fur when the weight was lifted. She could feel the elevator slowly going up. She opened her eyes, sat up as best she could, and saw Porfiry Petrovich holding the dog by the neck. The dog was writhing and growling, snapping at air with blood on his teeth, Elena's blood.

"Be calm, dog," said Rostnikov, placing the animal on the floor but maintaining his grip. "I have no wish to hurt you. Neither do I have a wish to take you home as a pet."

The dog suddenly grew quiet.

"Good," said Rostnikov, putting the dog at his left side. "Be reasonable and you will survive."

The dog, however, let out a growl and sank its teeth into Rostnikov's leg. His teeth and jaws suddenly quivered with pain. The dog let go and backed into a corner, cowering. He had never encountered anything like Rostnikov's prosthetic leg.

"Now," said Rostnikov, "sit and be quiet. If you try to bite me one more time, you will further destroy my clothes, which I can ill afford, and I will have to kill you. I have never killed a dog or a cat or a beetle. Remind me someday to tell you a story about beetles."

The frightened dog had appeared to be listening, and Rostnikov had spoken to him in the same way he would talk to a human.

The elevator moved up.

Porfiry Petrovich took three steps across the ascending elevator and leaned over to examine Elena's shoulder.

"We need towels," he said. "You will need a tetanus injection and some stitches."

"How, why are you here?" Elena said painfully as she stood.

"To save your life," he said. "An informant overheard two men talking in a booth of a restaurant. That is the informant's job. The two men were talking about killing you. I came here to get you out and maybe Sasha."

"Your timing was perfect," Elena said after biting her lower lip to keep away the pain.

"Not really," said Rostnikov. "I was following you when you went out for coffee. When you returned here, a man got out of a car with the dog. I moved as quickly as I could but I couldn't get to the dog quickly enough. The man said 'Kill' and pointed at you as you stepped into the elevator, and then the man stepped outside. I got to the elevator just in time to get my hands on the closing door. The rest you know."

"Let's get Sasha and leave," said Elena.

The elevator came to a stop at the floor of the suite.

"I may have an alternative idea," said Rostnikov, looking back at the dog which had crept forward on its belly. "Back," he said firmly.

The dog slunk back, not wanting the clamp of the man's fingers around his neck or the taste and texture of the strange leg. By now the dog was firmly convinced that the man was completely made of plastic and metal and could not be hurt.

The elevator door slid open.

Awkwardly but gently, Rostnikov helped Elena out of the elevator and reached back in to press the button for the first floor. The dog looked up at Rostnikov and Elena as the door slid closed and the bloody elevator started down with the dog inside.

"You said you have an alternate idea?" said Elena as Rostnikov lifted her in his arms and asked her which room was hers and Sasha's.

"Yes," said Rostnikov. "I'm afraid you are going to have to die."

"I don't understand," said the confused young man in uniform and helmet, weapon at his side, helmet strap digging deeply into his chin.

They were standing outside of Yulia Yalutshkin's apartment. Zelach had been sent down to the lobby. Iosef had checked the bedroom. Yulia was gone. It was clear that someone had slept in the bed besides the woman. The bed was still slightly warm and there were a few dark hairs between the sheets, possibly pubic hairs.

"A man came out of this apartment while you stood guard," said Iosef, trying to remain calm. "And the woman is gone."

"No man came out," the young policeman said. "And she didn't . . . I thought she was . . ."

"What happened?" asked Iosef.

"She asked me to come in," the policeman said. "She needed someone to help her button the back of her dress."

"So you went into her bedroom?"

"For an instant. I could see her the entire time."

Zelach reappeared, panting, and said, "The doorman saw Pleshkov and the woman leaving the building about ten minutes ago."

"Your name, Officer," asked Iosef.

"Nikita Sergeivich Kotiansko," the young, bewildered man said, looking at the closed door.

"How long have you been a police officer?"

"Six weeks," Kotiansko said.

Actually, Iosef knew it wasn't a matter of experience as much as common sense. Nikita had neither tool to fall back on.

"How did she get out? We can assume Pleshkov was hiding in the living room and hurried out when you went into the bedroom, but how did she get away?"

Zelach and Iosef waited for an answer.

"It must have been when she asked me to pick a different dress out of her closet. I couldn't button the dress. The holes were too small. She said she was going to get something to drink."

"So she wasn't wearing anything," said Iosef.

Nikita stood at attention, not looking at the two inspectors.

"Very little," said the policeman. "I didn't think she would run away. This is her apartment. She had no clothes on."

"She almost certainly had a dress hidden in the living room," said Iosef.

Though he said and showed nothing, Zelach thought his partner was amazingly clever.

"Did she touch you, Nikita Sergeivich?" asked Iosef calmly.

"Once, my cheek," said the policeman. "Said I should look for something in the closet I liked. She touched my cheek. I could smell her perfume. What will happen to me?"

"Go up to the roof," said Iosef. "You'll find a shed with some evidence. Touch nothing. Guard it. Hope that it rains and you get very wet so I feel sorry for you."

"Yes, Inspector," said the young man.

Nikita Sergeivich Kotiansko moved very quickly.

Viktor Petrov was as dedicated to his work as a hotel security guard as he had been dedicated to his work as a police sergeant before his wounding. Viktor was thirty-three years old and lucky to be alive. He had been involved in a shoot-out seven years earlier when he had just made sergeant. Three young boys were caught inside of a store where they were cleaning out its contents. Petrov had been shot by a fourteen-year-old. Death had seemed certain, but almost miraculously he had survived his chest wound. Petrov, recovering in the hospital, had been visited by the minister of the interior himself and given a medal. He was then told that he had a collapsed and unfixable lung and, therefore, would be honorably retired with a pension. The pension, he knew, was not enough to feed, clothe, and shelter himself, his wife, and their then infant son.

Though he told no one, Petrov had no desire to return to duty following his shooting. He was afraid because he was a young man in a job growing more dangerous. He had been given an honorable escape.

Petrov had drifted from job to job. For almost a year he was on the security staff of the Bolshoi Theater. The job paid poorly and the hours were terrible but there were perks, including food from various company parties, mainly for wealthy foreigners.

But Petrov's wife had grown ill with a disease of weariness the doctor called chronic fatigue syndrome, which he said could not be cured. Petrov's wife couldn't work.

So Viktor Petrov moved on to a job that paid much more. He became, as his father had been, a waiter. For a year he had waited tables at a private club. After being a policeman, however, he found it humiliating to be an anonymous figure to loud men and overdressed women. He found it humiliating to constantly be saying "thank you very much" for tips he had earned.

And so, Viktor had found, through a friend who was not only still a policeman but now a captain, the job of security guard at the Leningradskaya Hotel. The hotel was one of the seven huge concrete monstrosities built on Stalin's orders in the 1950s. Some found the hotel strangely beautiful. Others pronounced it a hideous tower whose rooms should be reserved for visiting mad scientists.

Petrov liked working there and asked to work nights when he would chance on few hotel employees and fewer guests. If a patron of Jacko's Bar in the hotel grew unruly, it was not Petrov's problem. Jacko's had its own security. His primary job was to check the doors to be sure they were locked, and look for thieves.

Security at the front door was good, but from time to time one of the petty criminals, gypsies, or desperate homeless who spent their hours in the Leningradsky, Yarolslavsky, or Kazansky railway stations directly across from the hotel made their way in. Petrov was armed, an American .38-millimeter pistol that he had been ordered to buy with his own money.

The rooms of the Leningradskaya were not fancy or particularly well furnished, but they were relatively clean and, by Moscow standards, which were far beyond the reach of Petrov, relatively inexpensive.

Early in the morning, before the sun was quite ready to rise, Petrov had moved slowly down the halls, hearing or imagining that he heard the loud band in Jacko's that played every night almost till dawn.

Everything was fine. The cleaning crew was already at work. Doors were locked. No suspicious people were roaming the halls or hiding in supply closets. The door to the small exercise room was open, which was not unusual. The night staff frequently forgot to lock it. Petrov had a key and was prepared to lock the door when he heard something inside. He went in slowly. The room was dark and had no windows.

Petrov considered calling out but for some reason decided against it. He remembered where the light switch was and moved along the wall to click it. The room went cold-white as the fluorescent lights sputtered and tinkled to life. The free weights were in a corner. The machines—treadmill, bicycle, and others which Petrov did not know and did not know how to use—were empty.

He had been about to click off the lights and leave when he heard a sound beyond the door that led to the small shower and toilet. No light was coming under the door. One of the three showers was running. Water was hitting the tiles.

Petrov felt sweat forming on his brow and a very bad feeling in his stomach. He imagined armed young men beyond the door, ready to kill anyone who disturbed them as they hid. He imagined even worse. He could have backed out of the weight room and into the hall where he could find the floor phone and call for help. But what if there was no one beyond the door? What if the incident was reported by whoever came to back him up? The hotel knew his background. Petrov might well lose his job. He could not afford to lose his job. In all likelihood, someone had simply left the water running in a shower. He took his weapon from his holster and pushed open the shower room door.

Darkness as the door remained open, light from the weight room barely cutting into the darkness. Petrov crouched and pointed his weapon. He really expected and hoped to see nothing. Moments like this had haunted him since he had been wounded. It was better, he frequently told himself, to be overly cautious and prepared than to be confident and dead.

"Is anyone here?" he said, expecting no answer as he reached for the switch.

The sound he then heard over the water was definitely human, definitely in pain. Petrov went down on one knee, weapon held out, trying to see into the near darkness. The sound, a low, weak groan, came again.

"Who is it?" Petrov repeated.

This time there was a weak "Oh. Oh. Oh."

Viktor stood quickly, hit the light switch, and crouched again with his gun outstretched and ready. He tried not to tremble. He tried so hard not to breathe that it made him dizzy, a frequent oc-currence resulting from the fact that he had but one functioning lung.

The doors of the two toilets stalls were open. The stalls were empty. Lying on the shower tiles, water hitting his face, was a big man, a naked man with a bad complexion and blood streaming from two wounds to his chest. The blood poured across the tattoos on his body and formed a river to the shower drain.

There was nowhere to hide in the shower room or the weight room. Whoever had done this was gone, but Viktor took no chances. He wasn't sure what he should do, but he decided to turn off the shower. He did so carefully, trying not to get his only decent pair of shoes too wet. Then he turned his attention to the big man.

"Are you alive?" Petrov said, knowing that it was a stupid question.

The man was alive, but not very. Viktor put his gun away and knelt without thinking of what damage it might do to his pants.

The man opened his eyes and saw Viktor. The eyes darted around the room. The man grabbed Viktor's hair and pulled him to within inches of his own face. Even about to die the man was extremely strong.

"I had a wound like this," Viktor said calmly. "I survived. So will you."

The big man shook his head once to show that he had no illusions about survival.

"Who shot you?" asked Viktor, prying the dying man's fingers from his hair with great difficulty.

"Little boy," the man said.

"A little boy shot you?"

The dying man shook his head again. "Little boy . . . dead."

"Who shot you?"

"Shot because of dead boy," he said. "I didn't even remember him. I didn't know."

"But who shot you?" Petrov asked.

"No," the big man said, closing his eyes. "I understand. I would do the same."

And with that he died.

Petrov stood and ran for the door, slipping and almost falling on the wet floor. He hurried through the weight room and into the hall, where he went to the floor phone and called the desk, telling them to put two security men on the front door, another one at the employee entrance, and another at the loading dock immediately. And to stop anyone who had wet shoes.

"And call the police, now," he said. "A guest has been murdered and the killer probably has not had time to leave the hotel."

"I don't . . ." the desk clerk began.

"Do it, immediately," Viktor said, reverting to the days when he had been a sergeant and had barked orders to younger officers. "You are wasting time. Look for wet shoes. Remember, wet shoes."

Viktor hung up before the clerk could say more.

He thought quickly. The doors were going to be covered. So was the loading dock. If the killer planned to leave the hotel, he stood a good chance of being caught. But, Viktor thought as he raced back to lock the weight room door, if the killer was a guest, the chances of catching him quickly or at all were not great.

Viktor prayed that he had not made any mistakes.

". . . will relieve pressure on the brain," Leon said, sitting forward in his chair and holding the hands of his cousin who sat before him.

He had always thought Sarah very beautiful, and he, like others in the family, had wondered why she had chosen the bulky, homely, gentile policeman with the bad leg when she could have done better. Gradually, however, Leon had learned to appreciate Porfiry Petrovich's wit and compassion, but above all he appreciated the policeman's sincere love of Sarah. For that, Leon could easily tolerate Rostnikov's eccentricities.

They were in Leon's large parlor furnished with French antique furniture and tastefully punctuated by a shining and beautiful black piano near the five windows that were letting in light in spite of the darkness and threat of rain. Through a door in one of the walls was Leon's office and examining room, where he had, increasingly, because of the ever-dwindling level of medical care in Moscow's hospitals, begun to perform more and more outpatient surgery. Sarah's problem, however, was well beyond his ability and definitely the job of a specialist.

"Then there is no danger?" she said.

"There is always danger," he said. "But in this case it appears the danger is only slight, very slight. Remember the last time when I told you that there was distinct danger?"

"Of course," she said.

"There was," he said. "And I was honest with you, as I am being now."

"When can we do it?" she asked.

"I've spoken to the surgeon, the same one who operated last time," he said. "Tomorrow morning. Possibly the next day."

"So soon?"

"I think it would be best," said Leon, patting his cousin's hand.

"The day after tomorrow," Sarah confirmed.

"Eat nothing after midnight tomorrow," he went on, still holding her hands. "Be at the hospital at six in the morning. No, make that seven. They always tell you to come at least an hour earlier than necessary. I'll be there through the whole operation."

"This," said Sarah, looking around the beautiful room, "will be very difficult."

"I know, but you will be all right."

"No," she said with a smile. "The difficult part will be telling Porfiry Petrovich and Iosef. The difficult part will be losing my hair again. You know it has not grown in as thick as it was before the last operation."

"It will grow back and look as beautiful as it does now," he said with a smile. "And it does look beautiful."

Sarah nodded her head, but her heart told her something quite different from what her cousin was saying.

*   *   *

Inspector Emil Karpo stood in yet another hotel shower room as a body was being removed. He recognized the dead man as Shatalov the Chechin's closest bodyguard. The big man had stood behind Shatalov at the burial of Valentin Lashkovich the day before, and he had stepped forward in front of Shatalov when it looked as if there might be a confrontation with the Tatars. Now the big man lay white and dead, and Karpo stood with the security guard Petrov, looking down at the body. Karpo had called Paulinin before coming to the hotel. Karpo had arrived as the cloudy gray dawn was breaking.

"Your name is Viktor Petrov," Karpo said to the security guard looking down at the body. "You were wounded five years ago in a gun battle with some young teens."

"Yes," said Petrov. "How did you remember that and my name?"

Karpo didn't answer. The man known, among other things, as "the Vampire," had not visited him when he was in the hospital. Rostnikov, who had also been on the siege of the boy thieves, had, however, visited him twice.

"You have done well here," Karpo finally said.

"Not well enough," Petrov said. "I heard no shots, and whoever did it managed to get by the guards at all the exits."

"It would seem," said Karpo. "Repeat again what the dead man said to you."

Viktor repeated the words precisely.

Karpo nodded. He asked Petrov more questions and examined the room and the body without touching anything. That would be Paulinin's job, and he knew the technician would be upset if something were moved or touched, including the body, before he had an opportunity to study the scene.

Something about the dead Mafia man's words touched a memory in Karpo. There had been a shoot-out between the Chechins and the Tatars nearly a year ago. In addition to one Tatar, several bystanders had been killed, including an old man and a little boy. He remembered the mother in tears after the battle, holding her dead son in her arms. It reminded him of two things. One was a scene from the movie *Battleship Potemkin* in which a mother carried her dead son toward the czar's soldiers, only to be cut down by bullets herself. The other was the death of Mathilde Verson, killed in a café in crossfire from two other Mafias. Mathilde had been a prostitute, a woman of great strength and good humor whom Karpo had visited weekly. She had always looked at the policeman, who frightened others, with amusement and understanding. Gradually they had developed a relationship and he had considered her the only living person besides Rostnikov to whom he felt close. That closeness and Mathilde's genuine concern for him had begun to bring Emil Karpo to life.

Karpo had slept little on his narrow bed during the night that was coming to an end. He had been plagued by a migraine. The migraines had been coming more regularly recently, and the pills he had been given were of no use if he did not take them before the onset of the pain. Since his warning auras of smells and white flashes had not been coming since Mathilde's death, he had to suffer the headaches in the darkness of his room, feeling the waves of nausea rise and fall inside him. The headache had gone shortly after the phone call. He had been called because Rostnikov was out and the dead man was a member of one of the two Mafias Rostnikov and Karpo were investigating in connection with what looked like the assassinations of their members.

Paulinin arrived with his familiar large metal box that looked more appropriate for going fishing than for investigating a crime scene. Emil Karpo knew better.

"Good," said Paulinin, looking over his glasses. "It's you, Emil Karpo. I had to deal with that Zelach and Rostnikov's son earlier today."

"Last night," Karpo corrected.

"Last night. Last night. You are right," said Paulinin. "Precision is essential. Three times in two days I have been called from my lab.

I don't like to leave my laboratory. You know that. Very irritating. Very irritating. What do we have?"

Which meant, Karpo thought, that Paulinin had spent the night in his laboratory.

Paulinin looked at Petrov and then at the naked corpse. "Are they going to take this one from me before I get a chance to really know him?"

"I will do my best to prevent that," said Karpo.

"I begin," said Paulinin, moving toward the body.

The police ambulance arrived at the hotel, and the two paramedics went up the elevator with their rolled-up canvas stretcher. People crowded the lobby watching, wondering what was going on. The people behind the desk were of no help, and there was no manager present to give information on the situation.

Rostnikov was gone by the time the ambulance arrived. He had left quickly, silently, carefully, and relatively unseen. There was no sign of the dog or of the man who had told him to kill Elena.

Five minutes after their arrival, the paramedics came down the stairs. The elevators were far too small to hold a stretcher with a body on it.

The body they carried under the bloody white sheet was that of Elena Timofeyeva. Many in the lobby were familiar with such sights. Others were not. Was this an accident? Suicide? Murder? Who was under the sheet? What had happened? They were given no answers. The paramedics moved to the door, which was held open for them by the doorman. The stretcher was placed inside the ambulance. The doors were closed and the ambulance quickly departed.

When he stepped out onto the sidewalk with a small group of curious hotel guests, he spotted the man who had released the dog. He did not, however, see the dog. The man watched the proceedings for a few moments, till Elena's body was in the ambulance. Then the man smiled with satisfaction.

A dozen or so people watched the ambulance pull away. One of the watchers was having his pocket picked by a gypsy. The gypsy tucked the man's wallet into his pocket and started across the street toward the railway station.

Down the street the man who had released the dog was getting into a parked car. Rostnikov could not make out the car's license.

Rostnikov considered letting the gypsy go. Rostnikov had a great deal to take care of, but if he let the gypsy escape, the crime would twist inside him. It would take weeks to go away. It had happened before.

Slowly, Rostnikov crossed the street, carefully waiting for traffic to pass.

Meanwhile, in the room he had shared with Elena, Sasha sat dressed and ready for the knock that came on his door. Cup of coffee in hand, he moved across the room and found himself facing Peter Nimitsov and Boris Osipov. Illya Skatesholkov was absent.

There was a very good reason why Illya was not there. He was dead. Illya had made a decision on his own not to send Bronson into the hotel elevator to kill the woman. He didn't want to risk the animal getting killed. It didn't take their best dog to do the job. Illya didn't intend to tell Peter what he had done.

Immediately after the attack Illya had returned the dog to the kennel and gone to Peter Nimitsov's office to report that the policewoman was dead.

"And Bronson?" Peter had asked.

"Fine," Illya had answered.

"Because," said Peter, "he was never at risk. I told you to send Bronson to do the job."

"I . . . the woman is dead. Romulus did the job."

"It is not a question of whether she is dead or not. It is a question of doing what you are told. This will be only a start. You will keep doing things like this. It is inevitable. History, Illya. Our history. Nicholas let Rasputin destroy the Russian Empire. Peter, my namesake, more than two hundred and fifty years ago was advised to move the capital from Moscow to St. Petersburg. But Moscow has remained the heart, the brain of Russia. If Russia is to survive, Moscow must live. The first Russian university was founded here, the first Russian newspaper published here. It is here the working people have first risen up against oppression for more than eight centuries. Did you know that Moscow University was the center of the Decembrist movement?"

"No," said Illya.

Peter was pacing and Illya was mute and confused. Did this young man with the white scar across his nose want to, really expect to be the leader of a new Russia? And what kind of leader? A new monarchist or the focus of a new uprising led by the working people of Moscow? It seemed to change almost daily.

"No . . . never again," said Peter. "The essence of my success is complete loyalty and obedience. Czars have fallen because of disobedience. It will not happen to me."

Illya had looked at Boris, who stood off to the side. It had been clear from the look on Boris's face that he had no intention of intervening.

"I was going to kill you, Illya," Peter had said. "But we've been together so long I didn't have the heart. So I decided Boris should do it."

"No," Illya pleaded. "It was just . . ."

"All right, all right. Don't weep. I've changed my mind," Peter had said.

Illya had just started to look relieved when Peter took out his gun. "I will kill you."

With that, Peter Nimitsov had fired four times, and Illya Skatesholkov had died.

Now, his gun replaced by a fresh one and the old one dropped into the river, Peter Nimitsov stood at the door of the hotel room registered in the name of Dmitri Kolk of Kiev.

"May we come in, Dmitri?" asked Nimitsov, standing with Boris in the doorway.

Sasha stepped back to let them enter. They did, and the young criminal entrepreneur looked around the room while Sasha closed the door.

Nimitsov was dressed in a neatly pressed dark suit and a conservative silk tie. Boris wore the same suit he had worn the night before. An attempt had been made to press or iron it, but the job had been bungled. Sasha wondered if Boris had a wife or mother.

Peter sat in a chair after examining it to be sure there was no dust or dirt on it. Boris stood. Boris tried not to show it, but he glanced from time to time at Peter Nimitsov with a look of fear that Sasha noted.

"Would you like some coffee? Tea?" Sasha asked.

Peter crossed his legs and folded his hands in his lap. "No, thank you," he said. "Did you see that your Segei Bubka had won another world title?"

"Yes," said Sasha.

Bubka was the Ukrainian pole-vaulter who had won seven world titles and Olympic gold medals. He was a national hero.

"Did you know that Lyuba Polikarpova is dead?"

"I know," said Sasha, moving to the table to pour himself more coffee. "I could never remember her last name. Then, of course, I knew her only a short time."

"She was killed by a dog in the elevator of this hotel," Peter said, watching Sasha, who took a sip of coffee.

"A dog?" said Sasha. "The man at the desk told me she was attacked, but he didn't say whether it was by a human or animal. I had assumed it was a human animal—thief, rapist, madman."

"And?" asked Nimitsov.

"And what?" asked Sasha. "It was a dog attack, a very flamboyant one, and I assume you were responsible, that you were sending a message to me. Tell me, what is the message?"

"She was a police officer," said Nimitsov.

Sasha scratched an itch on his cheek and said, "I had considered that possibility myself. There was something about her—the way she watched me, how badly she performed in bed, several things. You're sure? I could never find any definite proof."

"Yes," said Nimitsov. "I am sure."

"I'll have to find some other woman to amuse me," said Sasha, sitting. "Perhaps the woman from the other night."

"Tatyana," Peter Nimitsov said.

"Yes."

"It can be arranged," said Peter. "Right, Boris?"

"It can be arranged," said Boris.

"Now, to what do I owe the pleasure of this visit?" asked Sasha. Nimitsov stared at Sasha, who waited patiently and drank his coffee. "Tonight," he finally said, "I want your dog ready. I want a good fight before Bronson kills him."

"Tchaikovsky will not lose," said Sasha.

"He will lose," said Nimitsov. "Or you will die. Many people are betting on your dog. The odds are going down. Overfeed your animal. Give him a drug, nothing too strong. I want a decent fight, with Bronson having just the edge he needs to insure his victory. There will be people there I wish to impress, people you will wish to impress. These people have heard about Bronson. They do not know your dog."

"You don't think your dog can win without help?" asked Sasha.

"I don't wish to take a chance," said Nimitsov, a smile suddenly appearing on his baby face. "I intend to make a great deal of money tonight, and much more in the future with the help of these people I have mentioned. I can arrange for you to place a very large bet that will give you plenty of money to buy a new dog anywhere in the world. Besides, you have other dogs."

"None as good as Tchaikovsky," said Sasha, trying to contain himself.

"It cannot be helped," said Nimitsov, rising.

"A good fight and a dead pit bull. I'm more interested in our progress in getting me and my animals into the syndicate," said Sasha, reaching over to put down the coffee cup.

"We will make arrangements before the fight," said Nimitsov, moving toward the door. "We will discuss our future before the fight."

"What about now?" asked Sasha.

Nimitsov simply shook his head.

"Then tonight, before the fight," Sasha said. "I am not losing my best dog without assurance that the sacrifice will be worth it."

"You'll make a great deal of money tonight," Nimitsov said.

"I want a future with a great deal more than I can make in one night. My dog doesn't fight and die till we talk and I get some information from you."

"Dmitri," Nimitsov said, shaking his head and touching the scar across his nose. "I could kill you here and now. I would enjoy doing it. I have not yet decided whether I like you or not."

"We will have a deal tonight before the fight," Sasha repeated, folding his arms in front of him. "Or I will take my animals and go back to Kiev."

"I've decided. I don't like you," said Nimitsov, "but I would be doing just as you are if I were in your position. All right."

"What about the police?" asked Sasha. He had almost forgotten this part, which Rostnikov had said was essential. Without it, Nimitsov might wonder why he was not more curious about the fact that a police officer had been not only watching him but sleeping with him.

"We will take care of that," said Nimitsov. "Now don't say another word. I am not in my best mood and I do not like demands. Boris will be back to pick you up at eight. We will have dinner. You will get your dog and we will go to the arena."

Sasha knew he had gone as far as he could go. He sensed that the young man in the rumpled suit was on the verge of a violent explosion.

The two visitors left.

When the door closed, Sasha groped his way back to the chair. His hands were trembling. Maybe, he thought, his mother, Lydia,

was right, that he had a family, that he should get out of this before he was killed. He knew he wouldn't quit, but the thought had
come quickly and seriously to him. He could not stop his hands
from shaking.

Chapter Ten

Elena sat up in one of the two hospital beds in a small room off of Leon's office. The room was reserved for patients Leon did not believe would be best served in a hospital.

In this case, however, the request to keep Elena in the private room came from Porfiry Petrovich, who stood next to the bed, looking down.

Elena's injury was ugly but was not nearly as bad as it appeared at first glance. The teeth bites were deep but they were in the fleshy part of her shoulder. No muscles had been torn or ripped, though the dog's teeth had gone deeply in. The blood had been easy to stop and the wounds had required surprisingly little suturing.

"I can," Leon had said, "arrange for rabies injections."

On this Rostnikov deferred to Elena, who wore a clean but not becoming white hospital gown.

"No," she said. "I saw the dog that attacked me, at the arena. I don't see how he could be rabid."

"It is a risk," said Leon, looking at her bandaged and taped shoulder, her arm in a sling.

"A small one," said Elena.

"A risk," Leon repeated.

"I do not believe the dog was rabid," she repeated.

"Nor do I," said Rostnikov. "I have dealt with rabid animals before. They were wild, could not be stopped in their attacks. They looked mad except in the earliest stages. This dog did not appear to be rabid. However, I believe I may be able to get the dog tonight."

"Well," said Leon. "It is your life. I will give you an address and a name where you can take the dog for testing."

"I will ask Paulinin," said Rostnikov. "You know him."

"Yes," said Leon. "I'll leave you. I have patients. I'd say you can leave this afternoon, but sit still, take the pills, and be back to-morrow for me to look at the wound."

"Can she stay overnight?" Rostnikov asked. "I would prefer that no risk be taken that she might be seen."

"Overnight," Leon agreed. "No longer, please."

With that, Leon went back to his other patients and Rostnikov turned to Elena.

"I'll tell Anna Timofeyeva," he said.

"Yes," said Elena.

"You want a book to read?" asked Rostnikov, pulling the Ed McBain novel from his back pocket.

"Maybe later," she said, looking at the window. "I could have been killed. I would have been killed if you . . ."

"But I was," he said. "May I sit?"

"Oh, yes, please."

Rostnikov sat with a sigh of relief. He had examined his trousers, which were torn beyond repair, but he did not have time to take care of them. Perhaps he could stop at home for another pair, not that he had that many, before heading for Petrovka. He sat quietly.

"You want to check on Sasha," she said.

"In a little while."

"I think I should like to get some sleep now," Elena said. "The pills, the . . . I'll be better with a little sleep."

"You want a medal?" asked Rostnikov. "I can get you one."

"For being attacked by a dog and surviving?"

"Medals are easy to come by and there are still those who re-spect them."

"Not Anna Timofeyeva," said Elena.

Rostnikov agreed. "There was a policeman I worked with when I was a young man," he said. "He was older than I was, funny, totally corrupt. I learned from his example how not to behave and think. His name was Ivanov. Big man, bad teeth, very bad teeth, laughed a lot when we were alone, uniform was always too tight. One day, winter, he went off on his own, told me to wait at a *kvass* stand while he met with an informant who didn't want anyone else to know who he was. I stood shivering. Then I heard shouting and a gunshot. I hurried as quickly as my leg would allow into the building where Ivanov had gone. I found him lying in an open courtyard used by the building tenants as a garbage dump. He had slipped on a patch of ice. His gun had accidentally discharged.

"I called for an ambulance. Ivanov was in pain. He had shot himself through the shoe and blown off the big toe on his right foot. His shoulder was separated and he had a concussion, and there was much blood from the laceration of his scalp where he had hit the sharp insides of a broken old radio. He was bleeding from both ends.

"Ivanov was given a medal. A general who had served in the war against the Nazis came to the hospital to present the medal. Ivanov said he had seen a known criminal enter the building and that he, Ivanov, had been ambushed. Pictures were taken of the wounded policeman. The unnecessarily large white bandage that covered Ivanov's head was a banner over his brave smile. Ivanov told me when we were alone that he had entered the building to pick up a regular payoff from a black-market dealer in electrical goods. I was disciplined for not backing up my mentor in spite of the fact that he had ordered me to stay in the street drinking *kvass*.

"A few days later, a petty thief was shot down by another policeman, a friend of Ivanov, who identified the dead man as the one who had ambushed him. Ivanov's friend also got a medal.

"Now a hero, Ivanov, when released from the hospital, was promoted and insisted on working with his equally heroic, medal-winning friend who had courageously confronted and killed the enemy of the state.

"Ivanov and his friend appeared at public events, particularly when a police officer was honored. Ivanov and his friend were transferred to the Ministry of the Interior and eventually to the personal protective staff of the minister himself. Ivanov's friend eventually became minister, and Ivanov was retired with a generous pension after years of additional corruption on a much grander scale than when I had worked with him. He asked me once if I wanted a medal. He was in a position then to give them himself. I politely said no. So, Elena, you want a medal?"

"Politely," she said, closing her eyes. "No."

If she was not asleep in the next few seconds, she soon would be. She had pulled the thin blanket up to her neck and was holding the fringe loosely. She looked like a very young child.

"Stay awake a moment longer," he said. "There is someone I want you to meet. The person who told me that you were to be attacked."

Elena opened her eyes and watched Rostnikov cross the room, open the door, and motion to someone in the small waiting room. He held the door open, and Elena, fighting sleep, looked up at the blond girl who had been with Boris the night before. She was wearing a simple blue dress with a wide black patent-leather belt. The young woman approached the bed. Rostnikov remained at the door.

"They say you will be fine," the young woman said, standing next to Elena's bed. "I'm sorry I didn't tell Inspector Rostnikov sooner."

"You saved my life," said Elena, taking the woman's hand with her good one.

"I must go," the young woman said, smiling and backing away from the bed.

"Your name," said Elena, now fighting sleep.

"Svetlana," the young woman said. "Sleep."

Svetlana left the room, closing the door, and Rostnikov moved to Elena's bedside.

"Yaklovev is her uncle," said Rostnikov. "She is very valuable to him, and to us. Also, I like her."

"So . . . do . . . I," Elena managed to say as she was falling asleep. "I have reason to."

"Rest," said Rostnikov, who touched the bed and went through the door in search of a phone and Leon.

The small reception room with three comfortable chairs and a desk was empty. Leon had a part-time receptionist/nurse, but Rostnikov had not seen her today.

The phone was on the desk. He reached for it and saw Leon's appointment book open to today. As he placed his call, Rostnikov glanced at the appointment book and read the upside-down name: *Sarah*. No last name.

Rostnikov got his call through and discovered from the man he had left at the hotel that Sasha was fine, that the plan had worked, and that the meeting was set for tonight before the scheduled battle of the dogs. Sasha had managed to give the man that much information and no more.

Porfiry Petrovich's plan had been to return to Petrovka. There was much to do, much to learn. It was early, but days had a discomforting way of being over just as they seemed to be beginning. Rostnikov sat in one of the chairs. Normally, he would have read the novel he brought with him, but he had left it with Elena.

He adjusted his leg, rested on the arms of the chair, and fell asleep. He was awakened moments later by the sound of a door opening and the sight of Leon ushering out a very well dressed woman in her forties. She looked as if she had just stepped out of one of the new salons after visiting a tasteful but expensive clothing shop.

The woman, well groomed but plain in spite of her makeup, smiled at Leon and thanked him.

"It will be fine, Marianskaya," he said, taking her hand and leading her to the door next to Rostnikov.

She looked down at the block of a man seated awkwardly and then allowed herself to be ushered out.

"People like that pay the bills," said Leon, turning to Rostnikov after he had closed the door.

"You owe me no explanation," said Rostnikov.

"I know, but why is it that I feel I do?"

"A little guilt?" asked Rostnikov, rubbing his face into a semblance of wakefulness.

"Perhaps. Yes."

"You needn't feel guilt, Leon," said Rostnikov. "I know the good you do."

"Yes," said Leon, sitting in the chair next to Rostnikov and unbuttoning his jacket. "But do I do the good things because I feel guilt for being able to live like this with the huge fees I get from the Marianskayas of Moscow, or do I do it because I am a saint?"

"You are a saint," Rostnikov said solemnly.

Leon smiled.

"I suppose it is my duty to accept beatification from a distinguished member of the government. I like you, Porfiry Petrovich."

"I am humbled and honored and I like *you*."

"I did not mean to be patronizing," said Leon. "I'm tired. I have more rich patients coming, some with very little wrong with them, all who want a great deal of my time. I would rather be in my apartment through that door, playing Mozart or even Brahms. I am thinking of getting a harpsichord. Do you like the sound of a harpsichord?"

"I prefer the piano," said Rostnikov. "Harpsichords remind me of Russians in powdered wigs trying to act like Frenchmen."

They sat silently in the waiting room chairs for a few seconds and then Leon said, "You saw my appointment book."

"Yes," said Rostnikov. "Did you mean me to do so?"

"Perhaps."

"Sarah is ill."

"She will tell you," said Leon.

"You tell me."

And Leon did, concluding, "I have never lied to Sarah, but I have sometimes not told the complete truth. It is what doctors must do."

"And policemen," said Rostnikov.

"The surgeon may have no trouble relieving the pressure on the brain, but the recent tests are troubling. We're running more tests, but we have scheduled surgery for the day after tomorrow in the morning."

Rostnikov looked at the ceiling.

"Sarah will be upset that I told you," said Leon.

"No," said Rostnikov. "Relieved. Thank you, Leon."

"You are welcome, Porfiry Petrovich."

The two men rose.

"It might be a good idea if you had different pants. Those have been badly shredded. I have several pairs of trousers from my late father-in-law," said Leon. "I think they may fit you."

"Why not?" said the policeman. "Why not?"

Paulinin had cleared off three tables in his laboratory, no easy task considering the amazing clutter. On one table lay the corpse of the recently murdered Chechin gangster. His hands were at his sides, and an open incision from the center of his ribs to his lower abdomen revealed a jumble of pinkish organs, intestines, and other body parts. On the second table lay the burned corpse from the roof of the apartment building on Kalinin. Its head was missing. On the third table were at least one hundred charred and partly burnt pieces of photographs, segments of cassette tape, and various items gathered by Paulinin from the hotel roof.

Emil Karpo, Iosef Rostnikov, and Akardy Zelach stood watching attentively. Paulinin, they knew, had a passion for exhibiting his skill before small appreciative audiences. Paulinin stood between the two corpses. He wore a blue smock and white latex gloves.

"There is still much to learn here," he said. "It will take two or three days, maybe less. Had the corpses and this evidence been given to Pariatsok or Mendranov or any of the incompetents who call themselves pathologists and know nothing about careful examination and simple logic, they would have befouled the evidence, come to the wrong conclusions, and allowed the guilty to escape. That does not happen with Paulinin, who has been consigned to this room for two decades. What they do not know is that I am content here, though I could use more modern equipment."

None of the three detectives spoke or looked at each other. All three knew that those who knew of Paulinin and his laboratory also knew that he could be happy nowhere else.

"This is definitely the German, Jurgen," he began, pointing at the blackened, headless corpse. "Teeth, bone structure, size, small hair samples all coincide with his description. I will find more. I will prove it conclusively. You can continue to search for our German, but he will be found nowhere but here in front of you. He was drunk when he died. He was nude when he was burned. There are no signs of burnt clothing clinging to his bones. His skull was definitely cracked by a heavy wooden object brought down with great force, but that did not kill him. He was also stabbed in the neck, as I noted immediately upon examining the body. Now I know that the small slivers of wood in the skull and the others in the neck are from the same object, almost certainly one that broke upon striking the German's head.

"Paulinin has changed his mind about one early conclusion. It takes courage in this profession to admit a possible error, even if the error is rectified immediately. There is a definite possibility, perhaps even a likelihood, that the German, while he was killed by the stab wound, may not have been quite dead when his body was burned. Oh, he was certainly dying and would have died, even with immediate expert attention, which is not easy to come by in Moscow and impossible everywhere else in Russia."

"So," said Iosef. "He was burned alive but he was dying?"

Paulinin looked up with satisfaction. It was the question he'd been waiting for.

"It is very possible. I'll know more when I have finished my discussion with our headless friend. It would help if I could speak to him in German, but it is a language which I dislike." He gently patted the scorched rib cage. "Now," said Paulinin, "we bypass our second victim and go to the interesting pile of plastic bags."

Paulinin moved to the pile of bags and looked at the policemen lined up attentively.

"I can salvage many of the photographs," he said. "It takes time and delicacy, a skill those buffoons with all their equipment do not possess. I have already restored three of them to the point where the images can be seen with reasonable clarity. And I have begun carefully reclaiming pieces of tape, which I will put together onto a single reel and then copy."

"May we see the photographs?" asked Iosef with just the proper tone of respect.

Paulinin nodded magnanimously and lifted three plastic envelopes. "I'll hold. Don't touch," he said.

Iosef and Zelach moved forward to examine the photographs. Emil Karpo remained where he was.

Even through the blur from the dim lights, the images on the photographs were clear. Yevgeny Pleshkov was in explicit and rather uninventive sexual positions with Yulia Yalutshkin in two of the pictures. In the third, he was in bed with Yulia and another woman, a very young woman.

"We will need everything as soon as possible," said Iosef.

"As soon as possible," said Paulinin. "And I decide when that shall be."

"You've done an amazing job," said Iosef.

"Yes," said Paulinin. "It is odd, but I do not like Germans any more than I like their language. My father was killed by them. Three of my uncles were killed by them. But when they are dead and on my table, they are not only forgiven, they become my friends and we talk. Death unites us."

All three men knew that Paulinin had frequently been heard speaking to corpses with great animation.

"And now," he said, "the big gangster."

He went behind the corpse of the dead Chechin, placed his gloved hands on the table, and said, "Shot two times. Either would have been fatal. Very close range. The same gun that was used to shoot the Tatar in the river. Considering his wounds, the fact that he was capable of speaking to the guard who found him before he died indicates this man's strength and the certainty that whoever shot him did so within a minute or two of his death. He too will tell me more. Perhaps he will even yield the name of the person who shot him."

Emil Karpo had listened attentively.

Rostnikov, whom he had tried to locate before coming to the lab, could not be found. It was essential that he know about the murder of the Chechin before an all-out war began in the streets between the Chechins and the Tatars. It was not the lives of the gangsters about which Karpo was concerned. It was the innocents, always the innocents, who might well be the victims of the gangsters, notoriously poor shots.

"Now," said Paulinin, "I would like to be left to do more work." He looked down protectively at the white corpse before him.

"Thank you," said Karpo. "Lunch tomorrow?"

"I'll bring it," said Paulinin with a sincere smile.

"No," Karpo said, unwilling under any circumstance to eat anything Paulinin might make. He had frequently drunk weak tea prepared in this very lab, in specimen cups which may well have contained anything during their long lives. "It will be my treat, a sign of my great respect for your continued excellent work."

"In that case," said Paulinin, beaming, "I accept. One o'clock?"

"One o'clock," Karpo confirmed as he turned and led the way for the other two detectives through the maze of tables, piles of jars, books, and pieces and bits of mechanisms of all types and many sizes.

Iosef knew that somewhere in this museum of clutter his father's leg floated in a huge jar. He was sure, should he ask, that Paulinin would be happy to show it to him. Iosef had no desire to see it.

Before coming to Iosef's laboratory for the demonstration, Emil Karpo had finished checking the newspaper clipping files— the computer had been of no help—for the information that would confirm his memory of the shoot-out. Karpo had found what he had been looking for. The clippings had not been misfiled. They had simply never been properly filed at all. Going through them required a knowledge of what you were looking for and when it might have taken place.

One article contained the name he sought. It was mentioned but once. Karpo made a copy of the article, folded it neatly into his wallet.

Now, knowing the identity of the killer, he would have to find Rostnikov.

Yevgeny Pleshkov, the hope of Russia, the pride of Petrovar, could think of no place to hide and no one to go to. He had considered staying with Oleg, but the police had already been to Oleg and might be checking his apartment for the missing politician. Besides, Oleg had appeared greatly upset by the suggestion that his friend might stay with him. Yevgeny considered telling his friend that he knew of Oleg's preference for men, had known it for years, probably even before Oleg knew, but if the man wanted to hold onto his image, Yevgeny was not one to pull it from him.

"I have . . . visitors," Oleg had said. "Other coaches, members of the team. It wouldn't be safe."

Yulia had left Yevgeny in the park, where he sat on a bench watching some small children play and wondering if it was going to rain. He had money in his pocket but no desire for drink, women, or food.

The children in the park were kicking a soccer ball. They were no more than four or five. The ball came to the seated Pleshkov, who made an effort to kick it back to the children without rising. The kick dribbled off the side of his right foot and rolled a few pathetic feet. One of the children, a boy wearing a shiny purple jacket, picked up the ball and gave the dirty man on the bench a look of disdain. Then the boy ran away shouting, "I've got it."

Years ago, actually not that many years ago, Yevgeny and Oleg had played side by side. Yevgeny was a striker. Oleg was a left-wing. Together they had set park league records, and Oleg had gone on to the professional ranks and a coaching career.

Now, Yevgeny could barely get his foot on the ball.

He had murdered a man. Yulia had photographs and tapes that could mean the end of his career, especially the one that seemed to show Yevgeny nude in bed with an equally nude young man who was kissing him. Yevgeny remembered no such incident. It was Oleg who liked other men, not Yevgeny; Yevgeny had been outspoken in his condemnation of drug use, gangs, homosexuality, and alcohol. His positions were part of the campaign that was winning over the hearts and minds of those who had enough of the pleasures of democracy. Yevgeny was not a Communist, never had been, but he truly believed that the best path to gain-ing the rights of hardworking and voting Russians was a return to sanity and order with a new, more temperate democracy.

Yevgeny tilted his head back, rubbed his very bristly chin and face, and knew what he must do. He could not sit all day on this bench watching children play and waiting for the rain. Yulia might or might not return. She would certainly be questioned by the police. No, he could not sit here all day and possibly all night. He had to relocate some fragment of his dignity. He decided to call his wife and son and ask them to come and get him.

Rostnikov got the message from Karpo. It was sitting on his desk when he returned to Petrovka as thunder shook the walls of his office. Thunder, but still no rain. Rostnikov wore a strange suit of light blue pants and a dark blue jacket he had accepted from Leon's collection of his late father-in-law's clothes.

One who didn't know him might think that the Washtub was making some kind of fashion statement. Those who knew him or of him by sight and who saw him enter the building and go up to his office thought that there was some reason for disguise, though they wondered how anyone who looked like Rostnikov, walked like Rostnikov, and was as familiar to the criminal world as Rostnikov, could possibly think that a disguise would be effective. Maybe the Washtub was simply going mad. Even Rostnikov was not immune to lunacy.

Porfiry Petrovich wanted to call Sarah, had planned to call Sarah, but the message from Emil Karpo changed that. He called Karpo in his cubicle across the hall, and Karpo appeared with the copy of his clipping.

"The same weapon killed both the Tatar and the Chechin," said Karpo, placing the copy of the newspaper article on the desk in front of Porfiry Petrovich.

Rostnikov read the article and then placed his calls and scratched at his artificial leg where it itched. Karpo stood in front of the chief inspector's desk, waiting patiently.

It took Rostnikov almost an hour to reach the two Mafia leaders, and in neither case did he talk to them directly. He gave the message to each person to whom he spoke that Shatalov and Chenko should meet him in one hour at the tourist *stolovaya*, the self-service restaurant, directly across from the Old Moscow Circus.

"It is a small restaurant, as you may know," he told each man. "Filling it with men carrying guns will not encourage business. Only Chenko and Shatalov will be inside."

In both cases, the person on the other end of the phone said that they would pass on the message.

"It is essential," said Rostnikov. "Tell them that I know who the killer is."

Rostnikov hung up the phone after the second call and sat back.

"Emil Karpo, the world is a strange, sad, wonderful, and horrible place, and Moscow is at the very center."

"I know," said Emil Karpo, and Rostnikov believed that the gaunt specter before him did know.

"Did you also know that I am keeping voluminous notes for a book I am writing on the tastes, beliefs, interests, and hobbies of Russians? That I am planning to contact an American agent who will sell it for two million dollars? That I will buy a very small restaurant near my apartment where I will be manager, Anna Timofeyeva will come out of retirement to be the chef, and you will be headwaiter?"

"I do not wish to be a headwaiter."

"I know, Emil. I was joking."

"I know you were joking," said Karpo.

"It is part of my lifelong goal of making you smile, though I fear your laughter might cause your death," said Rostnikov, examining Karpo's pale solemn face for some sign of amusement, the slightest twitch in the corner of his mouth, a telltale pursing of the lips.

"Humor has no function for me. I was fortunate to be born without the ability to see humor in anything. I recognize irony, as I have just done with your joke, but it does not amuse me. It does not distract me."

"That is unfortunate," said Rostnikov. "Distraction is my solace."

"And justice, which is unattainable, is mine."

Chapter Eleven

There was a matinee at the Old Moscow Circus. Rostnikov and Karpo had arrived early, and Porfiry Petrovich had talked to the owner of the very small *stolovaya* with only three tables and a stand-up cafeteria-service counter that ran the length of the shop. The man who owned the shop owed Rostnikov a big favor. The restaurant owner, whose name was Cashierovsky, said he would put a "closed" sign in the window immediately. The show was beginning at the circus in fifteen minutes, and most of the remaining restaurant patrons would be attending it.

"Can I bring you something?" the man had said. "My pleasure to treat you?"

"*Pahmadoori?*" asked Rostnikov.

"Yes."

"Good, then *booterbrod pahmadoori*, tomato sandwich," said Rostnikov. "And a mineral water. Emil?"

"Nothing."

"You will hurt Cashierovsky's feelings," said Rostnikov, who had chosen the table farthest back from the door, which he faced, with Karpo opposite him.

"Tea and a roll," said Karpo.

"He is a monk," Rostnikov explained.

Cashierovsky smiled. He knew well who the Vampire was. Cashierovsky hurried to fill their order, put out the "closed" sign, and shooed out the remaining patrons, telling them that he had to shut down because he was going to the circus.

They were early. It still wasn't raining.

The day and the view of the circus reminded Rostnikov of another day several years earlier, when he had stood in the rain and watched a circus performer commit suicide by leaping from the head of the statue of Nikolai Gogol in Gogol Square. It had happened right before the eyes of Rostnikov and the traffic policeman in the nearby tower, in addition to dozens of spectators, some of whom had urged the man to jump.

Rostnikov loved circuses. He had taken Iosef many times when Iosef was a boy. He had already taken the two little girls twice. And Sarah, Sarah loved the beautiful, sad clowns and the graceful aerialists. Perhaps he could get tickets after this meeting and take Sarah, the girls, and their grandmother. Perhaps he would invite Iosef. Maybe he could even talk Karpo into coming.

Yes, perhaps, and perhaps a circus fairy would leap from the pages of a Lermontov book and give him the money to pay for such an outing.

He wanted to call Sarah, but there was no way of doing so now. He would simply go home after this meeting and discuss the surgery.

Cashierovsky, a small, pudgy man with very little hair and a wheeze of asthma abetted by the growing pollution of the city, moved as quickly as he could to serve his guests.

"Looks good," said Rostnikov. "Emil?"

"It looks very good."

"Tomatoes were a treat when I was a boy," said Rostnikov, picking up his sandwich.

Cashierovsky stood waiting.

"Delicious," said Rostnikov, chewing on the bite of sandwich he had taken.

Karpo bit into his roll. "Very satisfying," he said.

"Peto," Rostnikov said, "some men will be here in about ten minutes. Two men, I hope. Would you leave the door unlocked and stand near it in case others wish to ignore the 'closed' sign?"

"Of course," said Cashierovsky, already moving back behind the counter.

"You remember my friend Cashierovsky?" asked Rostnikov, savoring his sandwich and mineral water.

"Yes," said Karpo, slowly eating his roll and sipping his tea. "Three students from Moscow University beat him, his wife, and his sons, because they are Jewish. They broke his windows and told him to move."

"What a memory," said Rostnikov, genuinely impressed, since the incident had happened almost a decade earlier when Rostnikov was still chief inspector in the Office of the Procurator General. Karpo had not helped with that case. Rostnikov had quickly found the three students and given them the choice of court and certain prison, or dropping out of school and going their separate ways outside of Moscow, after turning over a sum sufficient for Cashierovsky to repair his restaurant. He had also warned them that they would be watched for the rest of their lives, that they were now in the central computer.

The trio had left within a day.

Had they remained, Rostnikov was certain the insane justice system would have been sympathetic to them and probably let them go with a mild warning and a token fine that would not even repair one window they had broken. As for keeping their names in a central computer, it was little better than a joke. Rostnikov wondered what university students were being taught if they did not know the system was nearly useless. The only ones at the time who had decent monitoring systems were the KGB, and they would have no interest in cluttering the memories of their computers with such matters.

But that was long ago. Times had changed. The bureaucracy was different. Things were worse.

Chenko, the one-eyed Tatar, was the first to arrive. The young man who had met Rostnikov before his first encounter with Chenko came out of a car illegally parked at the curb. The windows of the car were tinted. The young man looked both ways and around the street. Then he looked through the window, saw Rostnikov, and returned to open the back door of the parked car. A moment later Chenko came out of the car and quickly entered the door of the restaurant, which the young man helped open for him.

The man stood outside the door, his back to the restaurant, and Chenko moved forward to the table.

"What is this?" said the Tatar.

"A tomato sandwich," said Rostnikov.

"I don't like jokes," said Chenko, cocking his head from side to side to look at the two men.

"Neither does my associate," Rostnikov said, nodding at Karpo. "Please sit."

"If this is a trap," Chenko said, "my men have been ordered to kill both of you very painfully and then to do the same to all the members of your families till your line is erased."

"That," said Rostnikov, "is very colorful. *The Godfather*, something like that. I believe you, Casmir Chenko. Your problem is that if we were to be killed, our friends would destroy your families. We could start a regular old-style feud with our descendants killing each other, forgetting eventually why they were doing so. This is not a trap. Please sit."

The gnarled, one-eyed man sat at the table with his back to the side wall. He was between the two policemen.

"Mineral water? Something to eat?"

"Nothing," said Chenko. "I will remain here for five minutes, no longer."

At this point, Cashierovsky appeared with a large, round metal tray covered with small plates of food—*ukha*, fish soup; meat boiled in *kvass* and served with *kasha*. He placed the plates and forks out for the men, and, after putting the empty tray on the counter, the shopkeeper moved to stand next to the front door of his establishment, as Rostnikov had asked him.

Rostnikov's eyes moved to the door as did Chenko's single eye.

Karpo did not turn. He finished the last piece of his roll and served himself a plate of *kasha*. Rostnikov ate with one hand, the other in his lap within easy reach of the weapon under his jacket.

Chenko started to rise. "I will not talk to him," he said.

"You don't have to," said Rostnikov. "I would like you to simply listen to me. Sit, please."

Rostnikov knew that Chenko's gesture had been for show. In his call asking the Tatar to meet here, he had been clear that Shatalov would also be present.

Outside the door Shatalov posted his own man, who stood facing Chenko's young man. There was certainly a carful of Chechins close by.

Shatalov moved to the table. His smile was gone. He did not look at Chenko. "There is no point to this," said Shatalov. "It is too late for talk. I agreed to a truce and he . . . that smirking Tatar murdered one of my best men."

"You are here, sit," said Rostnikov. "Casmir Chenko did not murder your man as you had not murdered his man."

"I . . ."

"You will please sit," said Rostnikov loudly, bringing a fist down on the table that made the two men outside the restaurant and Peto Cashierovsky start nervously.

Shatalov sat and motioned to his man outside that everything was calm. Chenko did the same.

"I now know you have a temper, policeman," said Shatalov, "and terrible taste in clothes."

"My anger comes unbidden. As for the clothes, I had an accident," said Rostnikov.

"Others can be arranged," said Shatalov, looking at Chenko for the first time.

"Easily," said Chenko.

"One-eyed, wattle-necked rooster," said Shatalov, whose white hair looked even whiter than it had the day before.

"Irving," said Chenko.

"Do you want to know who killed your men and why, or do you want to simply leave here ignorant and continue the war that is costing you lives and rubles?" asked Rostnikov.

"Why do you care?" asked Chenko.

"Innocent people will die," said Rostnikov. "I don't care about you or your men. Innocent people have already died because of you."

Rostnikov picked up the newspaper article which he had placed facedown on the table. He handed it first to Chenko, who cocked his head to one side to read it with his good eye. When Chenko was finished, he handed it back to Rostnikov, who handed it to Shatalov, who read it quickly and returned it to the policeman.

"The name of the boy who died when your men had a street fight, a fight over an insult, not even over territory, a fight . . . the name means nothing to you, either of you? The underlined name?"

"Nothing," said Chenko.

"Nothing," said Shatalov.

"Emil, tell them the name of the killer of their men."

Karpo did as he was told.

"I don't know this person," said Shatalov.

"I don't either," said Chenko.

"Yes, you do," said Rostnikov. "I will tell you and convince you, and you will stop your war before it begins. I have no illusions. At some time, you will start killing each other again, and though it may make no difference to either of you, if one more innocent person dies, I will see to it that you are both brought to justice. This I promise you and myself."

"Talk," said Shatalov, looking at his watch. "I told my men I would be in here no more than ten minutes."

"I told my men five minutes," said Chenko. "And those minutes are almost up."

And so Porfiry Petrovich Rostnikov pushed his plate away and explained. They listened. There was not much to tell. When he was done, Chenko rose immediately.

"You are both convinced?" asked Rostnikov.

Neither man spoke. Both nodded that they were convinced.

"There is a condition to my telling you this truth," Rostnikov went on, pulling the plate of food back so he could reach it. "You are not to seek out or harm the one who did this."

"That cannot be," said Chenko.

"It cannot," said Shatalov.

"An eye for an eye. Five gangsters for one child," said Rostnikov, his hand still in his lap. "I want your word."

"You will accept our word?" asked Shatalov.

"Yes," said Rostnikov.

"No more killings?" said Shatalov, looking at Chenko.

"Not from the person I have just named," said Rostnikov.

"You have my word," said Chenko.

"You have mine," said Shatalov.

"I arrived first," said Chenko. "I leave first."

Shatalov opened his mouth to speak, but Rostnikov stopped him. "Go," Porfiry Petrovich said, and the one-eyed man left.

When he had entered the car with tinted windows, followed by the young man he had posted at the door, Rostnikov nodded at Shatalov that he could leave. The white-haired gangster rose and departed. Rostnikov eased his weapon into the pocket of the ugly slacks of Leon's dead father-in-law.

When Shatalov was no longer visible outside the door, Rostnikov said thank you to Peto, who took down the "closed" sign, hurried to the table, and asked no questions about what had just happened in his restaurant, though he was pulsing with curiosity.

"Another tomato sandwich?" asked Cashierovsky.

"Why not? Another roll and tea for you, Emil Karpo?"

Karpo shook his head.

"I'll wrap the food you didn't eat to take home," said the restaurant owner.

"That would be very nice," said Rostnikov.

The pudgy restaurant owner hurried off to make another sandwich for Rostnikov.

"Were you genuinely angry when you struck the table, Porfiry Petrovich?" asked Karpo. "It was very unlike you, but most effective."

"I was genuinely angry, Emil," said Rostnikov. "I have a family crisis. Elena Timofeyeva has been injured and I am wearing a jacket and pants that would befit a clown across the street. I have a bad feeling. I was angry, but perhaps not as angry as I appeared."

A bag containing the uneaten food and a second tomato sandwich appeared in front of Rostnikov. On the plate next to it was a firm peach.

"You remembered," said Rostnikov.

"I remembered your love of peaches," Cashierovsky said. "Enjoy."

"He's back," Ivan Pleshkov said to Iosef over the phone.

"Does your father know you are calling me?" asked Iosef, sitting at the desk in his cubicle. He had been about to go out the door and head for the home and office of Leon the doctor. Porfiry Petrovich had left a message for his son telling him where Elena was, that she had been injured but that she was fine.

Iosef had wanted to see for himself, to be with her, but the phone had rung and Yevgeny Pleshkov's son was on the line.

"Is he planning to leave?"

"I don't think so," said the son. "He looks tired. He looks like cat vomit."

"Has he said anything to you or your mother about where he has been, what he has done?"

"He doesn't have to," said Ivan. "He's been whoring, drinking, gambling, behaving like a fool. The great potential leader of the people is a buffoon, but what is new about that?"

"Can you keep him there?" asked Iosef.

"I can't keep him anywhere," said Ivan. "He goes where he

wishes, does what he pleases, helps the masses and abuses individuals. But from the look of him he is at least content to be home for the immediate future. My mother has asked no questions. She will, though, and he will give her stupid lies. She will pretend to believe them. It is over. He is back till next time. Good-bye."

Ivan hung up the phone and so did Iosef.

The proper thing to do at this point was to tell everything to the chief inspector, his father, but Porfiry Petrovich was out somewhere with Karpo and it was possible that Yevgeny Pleshkov might run off again. He either had to act on his own or talk to Director Yaklovev, which he preferred not to do. But he had little choice.

Instead of calling, he walked to the director's office and asked if the Yak was in. The dwarfish Pankov began to sweat almost immediately. He had been given a specific list by Director Yaklovev. Except in an emergency, no one else was to be admitted to his office. Porfiry Petrovich was on the list. No other member of the Office of Special Investigation was.

"Is this an emergency?" asked Pankov, looking at the director's office door.

"It is," said Iosef. "And we are wasting time."

"What is the emergency?"

"Something for the ears of the director only."

"I can ask him," Pankov almost pleaded. "But I must have some idea . . ."

"Tell him it is about Yevgeny Pleshkov," said Iosef. "Tell him it is urgent. Tell him . . ."

The director's door opened and Yaklovev, spire-straight, said, "Come in, Rostnikov."

Oh, by my mother's saints, thought Pankov, he can hear everything that is said out here. He has wired my space.

This was terrifying news to the little man, who now searched his memory, frantically wondering, fearing, that he had said something in the last months, something that would eventually mean his ruin.

I should have known, Pankov thought. I should have suspected.

Oh, god. He doesn't care if I know. He is planning to replace me, to drive me into a breakdown and replace me.

The door closed behind the two men.

Porfiry Petrovich Rostnikov had many things on his mind when he returned to his office. He wanted the day to be over so he could talk to and be with Sarah. He wanted to bring in the killer of the Chechins and Tatars. He wanted quite a few things, but he did not want to find Lydia Tkach sitting in front of his desk with her arms folded when he returned from his meeting with Shatalov and Chenko.

He sat behind his desk, put his hands flat in front of him, and looked at the thin woman attentively. That she was furious was obvious. Sasha's mother did not hide her opinions or feelings. And her primary feelings were reserved for her only son.

"Elena Timofeyeva was attacked by a wild tiger," she said.

"A tiger?" asked Rostnikov. "Contrary to rumors you may have heard, I can assure you, Lydia, that there are no packs of wild tigers roaming the streets of Moscow. There are animals far more dangerous, but not tigers. It was a dog."

"Anna Timofeyeva said it was a tiger."

Rostnikov seriously doubted this, since Lydia was shouting and not wearing her hearing aid. Actually, she almost never wore the hearing aid, which made conversation with her very public.

"A dog," said Rostnikov.

"Then a dog," Lydia conceded with exasperation. "Anna Timofeyeva says she will probably die."

"Elena Timofeyeva is probably home by now," said Rostnikov, trying hard to keep from looking at his watch. "She has some injuries but she is fine."

"We shall see," said Lydia with suspicion. "She was working with my Sasha, wasn't she?"

"Yes."

"Then he may be attacked by some animal, may be killed," she said, challenging the chief inspector.

Sasha was certainly in danger from animals with guns, but a second dog attack was unlikely.

"I think he is in relatively little danger," Rostnikov said, reaching under the desk to try to adjust his leg through the trousers of Leon's dead father-in-law.

"Relatively?" Lydia shouted. "Relatively? There shouldn't be any *relatively* for Sasha. There should be no danger."

"He is a police officer," said Rostnikov patiently. "There is always some danger when one is a police officer."

"Not if one sits behind a desk," Lydia said, leaning forward with a cunning smile.

"He does not want to sit behind a desk. I don't know if I could get him moved behind a desk even if he wanted to. We have had this conversation many times, Lydia Tkach."

"And we will have it many more times till you do something to protect my Sasha."

There was a knock at the door of his office. Rostnikov called, "Come in."

Pankov entered with a very false smile and a steaming mug.

"I'm sorry," he said. "I thought you might like some tea."

"That would be nice," said Rostnikov.

"Can I bring some for the lady?" Pankov asked, placing the tea before Rostnikov.

"What?" said Lydia, looking at the little man as if he was an intrusive insect.

"Tea," Rostnikov said loudly.

"No."

"This is Sasha Tkach's mother. This is Pankov, the director's secretary," said Rostnikov.

The tea was hot and sweet, a strong tea. It was clear that Pankov wanted something. This was the first time the little man had been in his office, and Porfiry Petrovich was confident that Pankov had never been in the room across the hall with its cubicles for the other inspectors.

"I would like to speak to you, Chief Inspector," Pankov said, trying to smile apologetically.

"I'll come down to your office when we are finished."

"No," Pankov shouted loud enough for Lydia to hear him clearly and look up at him. "No. I will come back. Don't come to my office."

Pankov left quickly.

"Strange man," said Lydia, looking at the door. "He could have offered me some tea."

"He did," said Rostnikov, but her back was turned and she clearly did not hear him.

Then she turned.

"I cannot tell Sasha Tkach what to do," said Rostnikov, wrapping his thick fingers around the hot mug. Thunder grumbled somewhere far away. "He is a grown man."

"He has a wife, two children, a mother," said Lydia.

"I do not have time for this conversation which, as we have agreed, we have had many times before," said Rostnikov.

"And you always sit there like a . . . a . . . Buddha, a sphinx, a clerk at the postal office."

"I have an only son, too," said Rostnikov. "He is a policeman. It was his choice."

"And you were happy with his choice?" Lydia said with most unsubtle sarcasm.

"Yes," said Rostnikov. "And no."

"If Sasha is hurt, I will hold you responsible," she said, pointing a thin finger across the desk.

"I will probably do the same, Lydia Tkach," he said. "But that does not alter the fact that I cannot force Sasha to take a job in the office."

"You mean you *will* not," she said.

"Perhaps."

Lydia rose suddenly, lifting her Saks Fifth Avenue shopping bag filled with vegetables, a few pieces of fruit, some cans of Hungarian soup, and two new pairs of socks.

"Sasha has not been himself," she said, changing her tone from aggression to a deep, solemn concern.

"I have noticed, Lydia."

"He has been sullen, depressed. I think, and I don't want this to go beyond this room, that he has . . . that he has been with women other than Maya. He is his father's son."

"So are we all, Lydia."

"I think Maya is planning to take the children and leave my Sasha," she said. "Take them back to the Ukraine. I know she is. I won't see them. If Sasha . . ."

"You want me to talk to Maya?" he asked.

"Could it hurt?"

"I don't think so," he said.

"Then talk to her, Porfiry Petrovich. Talk to her soon."

"I will," he said.

Lydia pulled herself together, stood tall, and said, "I have money, Porfiry Petrovich. I could buy my son a shop or help him get started in a business."

"I know," said Rostnikov. "You want me to talk to Sasha too?"

"Yes," she said.

He nodded to indicate that he would do so. Lydia left.

Rostnikov raised the mug of still-very-hot tea to his lips. A knock at the door and Pankov entered before Rostnikov could tell him to come in.

Pankov closed the door, smiled at Rostnikov, and quickly sat in the chair that Lydia had just vacated.

"Director Yaklovev had to go to a meeting at the ministry," Pankov said.

"That's nice," said Rostnikov. "That is what you wanted to discuss?"

"No," Pankov said nervously. "We have known each other for many years."

"About eight," said Rostnikov. "The tea is good."

"Thank you," said Pankov with a smile that suggested a man in desperate need of root-canal surgery.

The little man shifted in the chair uncomfortably and looked at the closed door as if he feared the sudden entrance of uniformed, helmeted, and armed men.

"Pankov, can I help you with something?"

The little man turned back to face Porfiry Petrovich. The office was warm but not warm enough to account for Pankov's perspiration. Then again, Pankov perspired very easily.

"Can you recall ever having said anything in my office or, more important, my saying anything to you in my office that would, might be considered . . . indiscreet?"

"Knowing you from our many pleasant exchanges," said Rostnikov, drinking more tea, "I would doubt if you ever spoke indiscreetly. I, on the other hand, am on occasion given to utterances that might well be considered indiscreet, though I can recall no specific instances. Would you care to tell me what we are talking about?"

"I have reason to believe," said Pankov softly as he now leaned toward Rostnikov, "that there is a microphone in my office and that the director can hear everything that goes on, everything that is said."

"Yes," said Rostnikov.

"Yes? All you have to say is *yes?* You knew this?" asked Pankov, removing his glasses.

"Yes," Rostnikov repeated, putting the mug aside, pulling his pad of paper toward him, and writing something in pencil.

Pankov assumed Porfiry Petrovich was simply making one of his cryptic drawings. After meetings in the director's office, Pankov had many times examined the pads left behind on the table. There were seldom any words on Rostnikov's pad, and the words that were rarely there made little sense and seemed to have no relevance to anything that had gone on at the meeting. Pankov had saved all the notes and drawings left behind by all the inspectors. He remembered one of Rostnikov's notes in particular. It contained two drawings of birds in three-dimensional squares. One bird was black. The other white. And the words "monks, monks, monks" were neatly printed below the birds.

"Porfiry Petrovich . . ." Pankov had begun when Rostnikov tore off the sheet on which he had written and held it up for the little man to read. The letters were large but Pankov's eyesight left much to be desired. He leaned closer, adjusted his glasses, and silently read: "ALL OF OUR OFFICES ARE WIRED."

Pankov sat back in his chair. Actually, he fell back and began to look around the room.

"Pankov, you may well be wrong."

"Yes, yes, yes. I may be wrong. Probably am. I've been working hard." Pankov rose in confusion and turned toward the door.

"Wait," said Rostnikov.

"What?"

He held up the now-empty mug and handed it to the little man. "It was very good. Thank you."

Pankov nodded and headed in dazed confusion out of the office. He had trouble closing the door behind him and came very close to dropping the mug. But he managed to juggle and catch it before it fell to the floor.

Yaklovev was many things. Corrupt, self-serving, ambitious. He was also loyal to those under him upon whom he depended for his success. Yaklovev was smart, very smart. He was not a man to underestimate, and Rostnikov did not intend to do so. Porfiry Petrovich had known his office was monitored two days after the Yak had become director, given Rostnikov a promotion, and assigned him this private office. The microphone was well hidden behind a panel in the ceiling almost directly over the desk. It had taken Rostnikov almost half an hour to locate it. He could have done so faster, but climbing atop the desk with one good leg was an invitation to disaster.

Since Rostnikov respected the director's intelligence, he doubted if the conversation he just had with Pankov would fool him for an instant. The director would know, when he listened to the tapes, which must now be rolling to record silence, that Rostnikov knew about the microphone.

"Like the old days," Rostnikov said aloud for the ears of the Yak.

Fifteen minutes later, after he had spoken with Sarah on the phone, Rostnikov and Emil Karpo were on their way to pick up a murderer.

"It's early," said Sasha with a yawn, his mind moving quickly to adjust to the unexpected appearance of Boris Osipov. "I thought you were coming at seven tonight."

"Meeting is earlier," said Boris. "We'll pick up the dog now."

"He may not be ready," said Sasha. "He needs his rest."

"Dmitri, let us get your dog. Hurry."

Sasha had been looking out the hotel room window when Boris had arrived. There was nothing he wanted to do, nothing he wanted to read, nothing he wanted to see, though the television set was on. When the knock had come, Sasha had picked up a magazine and opened the door. Now he slowly prepared to go with the older man, wondering how he could leave word that he had been forced to leave early.

What is the worst that can happen? he asked himself. Rostnikov and a dozen armed men would simply show up at the dog arena. Nimitsov and the others would be arrested, and Sasha would hand over the small tape recorder in his pocket which should then have the entire conversation of the meeting he was about to attend. If he was searched, which he doubted he would be, he would simply and readily admit that he was planning to tape the meeting for his own protection. It would be reasonable, coming from the criminal he was supposed to be. For further protection, a gun had been hidden in a sliding tray under the portable dog cage in which he would transport Tchaikovsky. Sasha hoped he would not need the weapon. And then again, he hoped he would. This man waiting for him and Nimitsov had tried to kill Elena. And for some reason, Sasha was sure they had killed Illya Skatesholkov. They would certainly kill Sasha with very little provocation.

Sasha Tkach had left the room earlier, had an expensive lunch in the hotel, and called Maya at work from a phone booth. In case someone was watching him, Sasha smiled a lot when he spoke and tried his best to suggest that he was speaking to a woman, which he was, but not the kind of woman a watcher might assume. The clerk at Maya's office said she was not in. He called her at home.

"It's me," he said. "Why didn't you go to work?"

"Because your mother couldn't stay with the children," she said. "She said she had to go see Porfiry Petrovich. Do you know why she had to see him, Sasha?"

The baby started to cry in the background.

"No," he said, but he knew.

"Are you enjoying your assignment, Sasha?"

"No," he lied.

"Are you doing dangerous things, suicidal things?"

"No," he repeated.

"I love you, Sasha."

"I love you, Maya."

"I'm leaving you, Sasha," she said. "I'm taking the children and going back to my family in Kiev."

"No," he said finding it difficult to hold his smile and keep his voice down. "Please wait till this assignment is over. We should at least talk before you do something like this."

"If you change, can prove that you have changed, we will come back. My brother is doing very well in the automobile business. He wants us. He has a job for me. Don't follow us. I'll call you. When, and if, I think you have changed, we can talk about our returning."

It was growing ever more difficult to keep smiling, but Sasha managed. "Wait till I get home," he said. "I should be finished late tonight."

"We will be gone by late tonight," she said. "You feel trapped by us. You will no longer be trapped. Maybe you will find it unsatisfying. Maybe you will feel liberated. We'll see."

"Maya," he said, "have you been with another man?"

"No," she said.

He believed her. She pointedly did not ask him if he had been with another woman.

"Wait till I get home," he said, "please. We'll talk. I can change."

"Maybe you can, but I don't think so. I do not want to talk. Good-bye, Sasha. I do love you."

"Maya . . ."

She hung up.

That was less than an hour ago, and now Boris stood waiting for him in the hotel room. Sasha adjusted his jacket and tie and nodded that he was ready.

Boris drove. Sasha sat in the seat next to him and tried not to look for backup that might be behind him but probably wasn't. It had been too early. It would be hours before backup came. Nimitsov had said they would be picking Sasha up much later.

At the converted garage at the end of the narrow passageway off the Arbat, Sasha made as much noise as he could, talking loudly to Boris, telling him an off-color story he had actually heard from the mistress of a car-hijacking gang when Sasha had been undercover several years earlier. The woman, with Sasha's cooperation, had seduced the policeman. Boris was in no mood to laugh at the joke. He had seen Peter Nimitsov kill Illya Skatesholkov. Boris had no particular fondness for Illya, though they had worked reasonably well together. But Boris did have a fondness for Boris, and if Nimitsov could go wild and kill a man who had simply protected Peter's prize dog, what might Boris accidentally do that would earn him a bullet in the brain? The baby-faced Nimitsov was definitely getting crazier and crazier. Boris had spent much of the day trying to figure out how he might be able to get some money and go somewhere far away—Canada, Australia, Japan. Hidden in his small apartment was a very legal passport Boris had bought with bribes, for one thousand dollars. One could get a passport by simply applying for one, but that meant long lines and weeks of waiting. Boris had received his passport in less than a day.

And so Boris was in no mood to laugh at the loud off-color joke he would normally have found funny. And he was too preoccupied to notice that Dmitri Kolk's voice had grown uncharacteristically loud when he told his joke.

Sasha made as much noise as he could reasonably make as he opened the unlocked door, held it half open, and said something to Boris that he hoped would alert the trainer inside the garage. It did, but the trainer was not doing anything that would have alerted Boris in any case. He was exercising one of the dogs, a German shepherd, in the mesh-surrounded area in the middle of the garage.

"I need Tchaikovsky now," said Sasha.

The trainer, wearing black denims, a white T-shirt, and thick leather gloves, nodded and climbed into the exercise pen. The shepherd looked up, sensing that his time uncaged was shorter than usual. It was a sensation he did not like. The dog began to growl.

Boris and Sasha stood watching as the trainer slapped the side of his leg. This time the dog trotted to his side.

Less than five minutes later, Boris and Sasha were carrying the cage containing the pit bull to the car. The gun in the tray under the cage was inside a holster firmly taped to keep it from sliding. Sasha had a fantasy of getting the weapon, shooting Boris, Nimitsov, and anyone else at the meeting, and running to stop Maya from taking the children to Kiev. Kiev wasn't even safe. People were still dying there from the Chernobyl fallout.

But Sasha knew he would do no such thing, and he had little hope that his wife and children would still be there when he got home.

*   *   *

"Deputy Pleshkov," Iosef said, "we would like you to accompany us back to Moscow."

Akardy Zelach stood back but forced himself to keep from looking down. Yaklovev himself had, according to Iosef, ordered them to take a car, with a driver, out to Pleshkov's dacha.

Both policemen anticipated that the confrontation at the end of the journey would not be easy. And it wasn't.

Pleshkov looked sober, somber, cleaned, and well groomed. This was the Pleshkov of television interviews, the confident man with the smile of understanding.

Pleshkov's wife stood behind him in the small reception area of the dacha. The son, Ivan, was nowhere in sight.

"No," said Pleshkov. "I am sorry. I'm too busy. I have a speech to give at the assembly tomorrow. I must get it finished today. A trip to Moscow and then back would interrupt my thoughts and eat too deeply into my time. The day after tomorrow might be possible."

"Deputy Pleshkov," said Iosef politely, "this is very important."

"I'm sorry," said Pleshkov, looking genuinely sorry.

"May we speak to you in private?" asked Iosef.

"My wife can hear anything you might have to say," he said.

"Murder," said Iosef.

"Murder?" repeated Olga Pleshkov.

"Murder?" said Yevgeny Pleshkov.

"A German," said Iosef. "Wouldn't you like to come with us?"

"Perhaps I should," Pleshkov said with a sigh. "If this is about a murder and you think I may be able to help."

"What is this, Yevgeny?" Pleshkov's wife asked.

"You heard the young man," Pleshkov said. "Apparently a German has been murdered."

"So?" she asked. "What has that to do with you? Germans are murdered in Moscow all the time. Frenchmen are murdered. Finns are murdered. Americans are even murdered. You are not called to

Moscow for every murder. What is so diplomatically significant about this German that your presence is immediately required?"

"That is what I intend to find out, my dear," said Pleshkov, looking not at her but at Iosef.

When they were in the car watching Pleshkov's wife through the window, the deputy, seated between Zelach and Iosef, said, "Would you have arrested me had I refused to come?"

"Yes," said Iosef.

"I see," said Pleshkov as the car pulled away onto the dirt road. "I'm sure we can settle this quickly and I can be back at my desk in a few hours, finishing my speech."

"I don't know," said Iosef, looking forward, as was Zelach. "That will be up to Director Yaklovev."

Pleshkov turned to look back at his wife standing tall, hands clasped in front of her. Ivan Pleshkov suddenly appeared in the doorway of the dacha. They both watched the unmarked police car head toward Moscow.

Pleshkov looked up at the sky. Still no rain. He had never seen anything quite like this in Moscow. The sky had been dark for days. Thunder crashed. The wind swirled, but it did not rain. Yevgeny Pleshkov did not believe in omens, but he silently cursed the sky and to himself said, Rain, damn you. Rain.

The room was not large and contained relatively little. A bed with a pillow and a green blanket, a small table with two chairs, an electric hot plate, a cabinet that certainly held a few plates and cups, a sink, a battered chest of drawers, and a curtained-off area in a corner.

Raisa Munyakinova should have been in bed after her night of work, but she was dressed and tired when Rostnikov knocked at her door. She did not appear surprised when she opened the door and saw him and Karpo standing before her.

"You know why we are here?" Rostnikov asked gently.

"You have found the killer," she said. "Come in. Would you like some tea, coffee? I don't have too much to eat or drink at the moment. I've had little time to shop."

"I've already had tea," said Rostnikov.

"Thank you, no," said Karpo.

Raisa moved to sit heavily on her small bed.

"It is not the man I described, is it," she said. "Not the man in the coat."

"No," said Rostnikov.

He and Karpo stood before her. She looked up at them, nodding in understanding.

"May I sit?" asked Rostnikov.

She pointed to one of the wooden chairs. Rostnikov sat with some difficulty, holding onto the table to keep from toppling backward. Karpo continued to stand.

"You were on the cleanup crew at the Leningradskaya Hotel last night," said Rostnikov, looking at Raisa, who showed only a distant blankness. "You work there regularly in addition to doing shifts at several hotels."

"Yes," she said.

"In fact, you were working the hotels on the nights when five Tatar and Chechin Mafia men were murdered," said Rostnikov.

Raisa shrugged.

"We have the records and a newspaper photograph of you carrying your dead son who was killed in a gun battle between the two gangs."

"I should have protected him with my body," she said, shaking her head. "I keep seeing it, feeling myself trying to think."

"There was no man in a coat," said Rostnikov, "was there?"

Raisa shrugged again and looked up at Karpo. There was no sympathy, no condemnation in the pale face of the policeman.

"No," she said.

"Would you like to tell us what happened, or shall we keep fishing?" asked Rostnikov. "I fish fairly well, but it helps if the fish cooperates. It is less painful for the fish and the final results are the same."

Raisa Munyakinova began rocking forward and back, looking at the floor as she spoke.

"I made up the man in the coat and told the night manager of the health club that he was there, and later that he had left. The night manager seems to believe that he saw this man. You want to know why he believes?"

"Yes," said Rostnikov.

"Because I am nobody," she said. "My son was a nobody. I am a drudge, a woman with no face who cleans men's hair from toilet seats and mops up vomit and sprays showers that smell of alcohol. They don't look at me. They don't see me. I'm sure the monsters who murdered my little boy forgot about him in minutes, if they ever thought about him at all."

"Why did you take the body of Valentin Lashkovich to the river and how did you do it?" asked Karpo.

"I knew someday it was possible that a smart policeman would figure out as you have that I was working in each hotel on the night of the executions," she said. "I wanted to make it look as if he had been killed and dumped in the river, killed somewhere other than the hotel. I'm very strong. The death of my baby made me even stronger. I shot him and he staggered through the door and into the pool. There he died. I pulled his body out of the water and put it in a garbage can, covered it with garbage and a few torn towels, and put the can on a two-wheel lift I knew was in the cleaning supply room. There is an old man named Nikolai at the back door near the loading dock. I am as invisible to him as I am to everyone else. He asked me nothing, even opened the door for me. I told him I was taking the garbage out. I sometimes do that. So did the other women. I hurried, but I did not run. I saw few people on the streets. I dumped the body and the garbage in the river and hurried back. Nikolai didn't even notice that I had been gone far longer than was needed to dump garbage."

"The gun?" asked Rostnikov.

Raisa kept rocking.

"The gun," Rostnikov repeated gently.

"I bought it from a neighbor's husband," she said. "I know I paid far too much for it. I didn't care. He showed me how to use it. He's a cab driver. He has more guns."

"Do you know where it is now?"

"I threw it in the gutter on the way home last night."

"Then you decided you were through killing?" asked Rostnikov.

"I decided I needed a new gun," she said. "If I go to jail for a hundred years, I will live, and when I get out, I'll kill every man who was on the street the day my only child was killed. He played the violin. Did you know that?"

"No," said Rostnikov.

"A little boy who played the violin beautifully," she said, looking at the impassive Karpo. "Little boys who play the violin should grow up to play in orchestras, concert halls. They should not be shot in the head by monsters who do not even care what they have done. Do they hear music, these monsters?"

"No," said Karpo.

"No," repeated the woman. "And now?"

"Now," said Rostnikov with a sigh as he stood awkwardly. "You come with us to Petrovka. There is a place where you can sleep tonight. Tomorrow, we shall see. Take some things with you."

Raisa stood up, nodding dumbly. She was standing in front of Emil Karpo, looking into his eyes.

"I did what had to be done," she said. "You understand?"

"Yes," said Emil Karpo. "I understand."

Chapter Twelve

Iosef stood in Director Yaklovev's outer office. Seated to Iosef's right were the soccer coach Oleg Kisolev, Yevgeny Pleshkov, and Yulia Yalutshkin, who sat erect and quite beautifully calm, smoking an American cigarette. Pleshkov, now quite sober, once again the politician, looked at his watch. There were only three chairs in the outer office where Iosef waited with his prisoners. Even had there been another, Iosef would not have sat. He was on the brink of his first real success as an investigator. The suspects were before him. The evidence was inescapable, and though he had no great fondness for the Yak, he did respect his ability, intellect, and ruthlessness. Yaklovev would follow through.

"I have a committee meeting at the Kremlin in one hour," Pleshkov said to Pankov, who sat behind his desk trying not to look at Yulia Yalutshkin, or, at least, not let anyone know he was looking at her. "And I have an important speech to prepare. One that will have great consequences for our country."

"The director will see you shortly," Pankov said with what was intended as an ingratiating, apologetic smile.

Oleg Kisolev was neither a politician nor a prostitute. He was very bad at hiding his emotions. Now he sat slightly slumped, his tongue running over his lower lip, glancing frequently at the forbidding door of the director of the Office of Special Investigation.

After ten minutes, the Yak opened his door and stood looking at the three people seated against the wall across from him.

"*Vighdyeetyee*, come in," the Yak said.

The three rose from their chairs, with Pleshkov leading the way and Yulia and Oleg behind him. Iosef started in after them, but Yaklovev held up a hand.

"Wait here, Inspector Rostnikov. I will call you in later. Pankov, no visitors, no calls unless there is a real emergency."

"Yes, Com . . . Director Yaklovev."

Pankov still had no idea what he would do to determine if something was an emergency. If he believed in a god, Pankov would pray. All he could do was hope.

Yaklovev entered his office and closed the door.

Iosef looked at his watch. He had been running madly through the night, gathering information, evidence, listening to Paulinin ramble at two in the morning. Iosef wanted to be with Elena. He had not seen her since the dog had attacked her. By the time he had arrived at the doctor's office and rooms, Elena had already left for home. He had no time to go see her, but the fact that she could go home was a good sign. She might be wondering where he was and what was so important, if he really loved her, as he claimed, that he could not get away for a few minutes to see her. No, that was not Elena's way. Many others Iosef had known would have been hurt by his absence, pouted, complained. Not Elena. At least he did not think so.

There was nothing to be done at the moment. Iosef did what his father did. He took out a paperback, a German translation of three plays by Tom Stoppard. Iosef shared his father's passion for reading but not American mysteries. Iosef's favorites were plays, particularly those by Gogol, all of which he had read many times. Reading now would not be easy. How was Elena? What was going on in the Yak's office?

There was no point in talking to Pankov, who had returned to the paperwork on his desk. Pankov was sweating, though it was not particularly warm in the outer office.

Iosef sat in the chair where Yulia Yalutshkin had sat. He could smell a faint scent of perfume. Iosef opened his book and tried to read *Jumpers*.

*   *   *

Inside the office Yaklovev directed his guests to sit in the chairs he had placed in front of his desk. When they sat, Yaklovev went behind his desk and stood with one hand on the neat, five-inch pile of yellow folders held down by a lead paperweight with the likeness of Ivan the Terrible looking up at him. Beside the files was a small battery-operated tape recorder, which the Yak made no effort to hide. He handed the pile of files to Yevgeny Pleshkov and sat behind his desk, hands folded on top of it.

Yulia reached for a cigarette and said, *"Nyeht lyee oo vahss speechyehk,* have you a light please?"

The Yak said, "Smoking is not permitted in my office."

Yulia shrugged and lit the cigarette herself. Pleshkov looked up to watch how Yaklovev would deal with this typical Yulia Yalutshkin behavior. The outcome might well affect Yevgeny's own method of dealing with the duplicate Lenin behind the desk.

"Miss Yalutshkin," the Yak said calmly, hands still folded before him. "If you do not stop, I will have Inspector Rostnikov take you to an uncomfortable and possibly very dirty cell. All that you have with you will be confiscated and two policewomen will check you and all of your body cavities for weapons. I understand that they are not gentle. Is your defiance worth the outcome?"

Yulia looked at her cigarette, shrugged, and looked around for an ashtray.

"Not in my office," said the Yak. "Take it out to Pankov and get back here immediately, please."

Yulia stood, glaring at Yaklovev.

"Now," said the Yak. "I have much to do and I am growing impatient. I do not wish to waste our time on childish behavior."

"Damn you," said Yulia, striding to the door and exiting.

Yevgeny began examining the files—the photos, letters, reports on the body of the German, the evidence of what Yevgeny and the others had done. It was not just his career that was in jeopardy. It was his very freedom.

Yulia came back in, making a show of closing the door slowly.

Oleg wanted no quarrel with the man behind the desk, but he dearly wished he had something to occupy him or pretend was occupying him while he waited what would surely be his turn.

Yulia sat, and as Yevgeny finished each file he handed it to her.

The room was silent except for Oleg shifting in his chair and paper being slowly shuffled. After five minutes, Yevgeny and Yulia returned the files to the Yak, who again piled them neatly with the Ivan the Terrible paperweight on top of them.

"We have the physical evidence downstairs," said the Yak. "The wooden stake, the body with its crushed skull and the wound to the neck, and, as the report you just read clearly indicates, much, much more."

"You have your supposed evidence," said Yevgeny Pleshkov. "What do you want of us?"

"Perhaps to save you," said the Yak. "If you cooperate. First, I want a statement from each of you about what actually happened. Now, if you refuse, I will be forced to proceed with legal action, which the press will certainly hear of. Yevgeny Pleshkov first. The truth."

"You said you may be able to save us," said Pleshkov.

"The truth, now. We will see what can be done," said the Yak, hands still folded before him. "You have examined the evidence report. You have little choice."

Yaklovev turned on the tape recorder and nodded at Pleshkov, who looked at Yulia and Oleg and began to speak. Pleshkov's statement was the longest. The others reluctantly confirmed and added some of the details that Yevgeny, in his alcoholic daze, had forgotten. The box with the photos and tapes, the fight with Jurgen, the attempt to destroy the evidence were all laid out with excuses from all three presenting the statement. The German attacked first and would have killed Pleshkov, who was only defending himself. They had burned the body in panic, to preserve Yevgeny's reputation.

"I was drunk, in the apartment of a . . ." Pleshkov began.

"Prostitute," Yulia supplied.

"Yes," said Pleshkov. "I had just killed a man who had attacked me. I would be destroyed."

When they were finished speaking, the trio waited for Yaklovev to probe, ask questions. Instead, he turned off the tape recorder. Yaklovev took out the tape and replaced it with a fresh one. The taped confession went into the desk drawer. The Yak spoke slowly, not turning on the tape recorder.

"Your story does not explain the evidence. I believe that evidence clearly shows that the following took place: Oleg Kisolev and Yevgeny Pleshkov went to the Yulia Yalutshkin apartment where the German and Yulia Yalutshkin were waiting. There was an argument. I don't know what it was about. The German, Jurgen, said he wanted to talk to Oleg. Yevgeny Pleshkov was drunk. Oleg asked Yulia to help Yevgeny to the elevator. She did. When they were gone, the German threatened to expose the fact that Oleg Kisolev is a homosexual."

Neither Yulia nor Pleshkov showed any sign of surprise at the Yak's revelation, and Oleg was now sure that they had known before. Yevgeny had hinted at his knowledge of his friend's sexuality in the past, but Yulia clearly knew. For how long? Had Yevgeny told her?

"Exposure of your homosexuality," said the Yak, looking at Oleg, "would end your career. You refused to give in to the German's threat of such exposure. He attacked you. You fought. There was a box. You struck him in the head with it. It broke. You found yourself holding a small, sharp piece of the shattered box. The German attacked again. You struggled. Somehow the pointed end of the piece of wood went deeply into the German's neck.

"You ran to the elevator. Yulia stood there impatiently. Yevgeny Pleshkov was in a stupor. You told Yulia to take him to a hotel. Neither Yulia nor Yevgeny learned about the death of the German till the next day. When Yulia and Yevgeny were going down in the elevator, you returned to the apartment where, to protect Yulia, you took the German's body to the roof and you burned it. You did not murder the German. His death was an unfortunate accident. Your motives in burning the body were honorable. Now, I will turn on the tape recorder and you will—of course providing it is true—tell this version of what happened. If you would like to discuss this with each other before I turn on the tape recorder . . ."

"That won't be necessary," said Yevgeny Pleshkov. "Will it, Oleg?"

"No, Yevgeny," said Kisolev softly, his head down. "It will not be necessary."

"Good," said Yaklovev. "Then we will begin."

The Yak turned on the tape recorder and nodded at Oleg, who began speaking very softly in a monotone. The tape recorder was a very good one. It picked up every word of Oleg's confession and Yulia and Yevgeny's confirmation, which established their innocence in the death of the German. The entire relation of this version of what had happened took about the same time as the version that was on tape in the Yak's drawer.

When the three had finished, the Yak again asked no questions. He turned off the tape.

"What I require now," said the Yak, "is a complete list of Yulia Yalutshkin's clients. One of them might be able to confirm the German's violent tendencies."

"No," said Yulia.

"Yes," said Yevgeny emphatically. "You will provide the list. Don't you see what the possible consequences of refusal might be?"

"Yes," Yulia said, glaring at the Yak, who sat calmly looking at Pleshkov.

"Then," said Yaklovev, "I can see no reason to hold any of you. Yulia Yalutshkin, you can go into the outer office where Pankov, my assistant, will provide you with a pen and paper to write the list of your clients. If the list is not complete, I shall have to review your version of events very carefully."

"It will be complete," said Yevgeny Pleshkov.

"In that case, Yulia Yalutshkin, you may go in the outer office and begin making the list. You may smoke there if you wish. Oleg Kisolev, you may leave. On your way out, tell Inspector Rostnikov that I would like to see him."

Oleg Kisolev rose, clearly dazed by what had happened. He looked at Yulia, who led him to the office door and opened it. A few seconds later, Iosef entered the Yak's office, closing the door behind him. Iosef approached the Yak's desk, looking at Yevgeny Pleshkov, hiding his curiosity.

"Take this, Inspector Rostnikov," the Yak said, handing him the second version of what had taken place. "Give it to Pankov. Tell him to transcribe it and give a copy to you, to me, and to Chief Inspector Porfiry Petrovich Rostnikov."

Iosef looked at Yevgeny Pleshkov, who appeared to be his well-known, often-seen old self, confident, alert, with what might be a knowing smile.

Iosef took the tape, waited for more information or some questions. There was no more. He left the office, again closing the door behind him.

There was silence in the Yak's office for several minutes.

"It seems that I owe you a great deal," said Pleshkov.

"Yes," said the Yak. "I would say that you do."

Maya was packing when Porfiry Petrovich arrived. Pulcharia was sitting at the kitchen table, trying to get through a book about bears. The child had looked up when Rostnikov entered the small apartment. She squinted, smiled, and went back to her book. She would, he knew, soon need glasses, which was odd since neither of her parents nor her grandmother wore them.

The baby appeared to be sleeping.

Maya closed the door behind Rostnikov. She was wearing a very plain amber dress and her hair needed brushing.

"I know why you are here," she said. "I will listen to you while

I finish packing, not that I have much to pack, not that there is anything you can say."

She turned and went into the bedroom. Rostnikov followed.

There were three suitcases on the bed. One was closed. Maya went to dresser drawers and continued to pack the children's clothing and her own.

Maya was darkly beautiful and she looked no older, though quite a bit wiser, than she had before she had the children.

"He will be finished with this assignment tonight," said Rostnikov. "Can you wait?"

"What is there to wait for?" she asked. "He would try to stop me. He would fail. The children would be upset. The baby would cry. No, it is best if I am gone when he comes home."

"And Pulcharia?" he asked.

"I've told her we are going to visit her cousins in Kiev," said Maya, folding a red sweater. "She is looking forward to it."

Rostnikov looked around for someplace to sit. There were no chairs in the small bedroom, and the bed itself was cluttered. He would have to stand.

"There is something you are not telling me or yourself, Maya Tkach," he said.

"You are wrong," she said, putting the sweater neatly into the suitcase. "I can no longer take Sasha's absences, absences in which I know he is sometimes with other women. Each time he confesses. Each time I forgive. Each time he does it again. And if Lydia comes through my door one more time and I am here, I will go mad and order her out. Sasha has been depressed and brooding for more than a year. I am not a saint, Porfiry Petrovich."

"Which means you have had your revenge," said Rostnikov. "And now you don't want to face telling Sasha what you have done."

"No," she said, moving past him to the dresser and picking up a pile of underwear.

"You do not meet my eyes. You want to be out of here before

Sasha sees you. You suddenly decide that this is the day you must leave. What is your secret, Maya? Why are you running away? What has your revenge been?"

"I told you why I am going," she said, folding a child's dress.

"And I am sure that what you told me is true," he said. "But what have you not told me?"

Maya laughed and kept packing. "This is your method?" she said. "I have heard about it from Sasha, but now I am the victim of your sympathetic, insistent probing. I . . ."

"Mama," said Pulcharia, appearing in the doorway, book in hand. "What is a *vahdahpahd?* See, there is a picture here."

"It is a waterfall," Maya said, pausing to look at her daughter. "A place where the water comes down from a hill or a mountain and joins a river."

"Are there really places like that?"

"Yes," said Maya.

"Are there any near Kiev?"

"No."

"Why are you crying?" asked Pulcharia.

"I am not," Maya said.

"Is he making you cry?" Pulcharia asked, pointing at Rostnikov.

"No," said Maya. "You go back in and read. I have to finish packing and talking to Porfiry Petrovich."

The child ran out of the room.

Maya stopped packing and turned to look at Rostnikov. She was crying. Rostnikov had never seen her cry. She had always seemed so strong.

"Sasha has cheated, lied, driven me nearly to the level of depression in which he moves all the time. He is dissatisfied with me, the children, everything but his work, and I would guess that his attitude is affecting even that, isn't it?"

"It is," said Rostnikov, "but he does his job well."

"And," said Maya, "by my count, he has had sex with six women other than me since we have been married. The most recent was within the last two days. I could hear the guilt in his voice. It is enough. What do I get out of this marriage? What do my children get?"

"A father," said Porfiry Petrovich. "What did you do, Maya?"

"I spent a few hours in bed with one of our clients," she said, folding her arms in an attempt at defiance which she couldn't quite maintain. "He is Japanese. He was very gentle. He has a wife and family in Japan. If I stay here, I will sleep with him again."

"Does Sasha know?"

"No," she said. "I lied to him, but I'm afraid I lied badly, whether because I am a bad liar or I wanted Sasha to know."

"May I suggest that you never tell him," said Rostnikov. "He does not know."

"It makes no difference now," she said, continuing her packing.

"Maya Tkach," Rostnikov said with a sigh. "I too am having a very bad day. Sarah may need more surgery. Elena has been mauled by a dog. I have just arrested a woman who lost her only child, and the skies refuse to rain. I think the fact that it will not rain is up-setting me more than anything else at the moment."

"I'm sorry," Maya said with real concern.

"Give me a bright moment," he said. "Stay till you talk to Sasha face to face. Give him one more chance. Give yourself and the chil-dren one more chance. I am asking you shamelessly. I am laying bare my wounds."

"I'll think about it," she said, sitting on the bed. "But . . . will Sarah be all right?"

"There is all right and there is all right," he said. "Think seri-ously about staying, at least for a while."

Maya nodded. A lock of hair fell over her forehead. She shook it back in a gesture that surely came from Sasha Tkach.

"You don't want to lose a good inspector," she said.

"I don't want to lose close friends," he corrected. "I have lost too many of them. I must go."

"I will consider," she said, "but . . ."

"I will accept that much for now," he said, moving toward the bedroom door.

"I plan to finish packing," she said.

"Yes," he said, walking out to the other room where the baby in the crib near the door was stirring. Pulcharia's head was buried in the book and she was frowning, trying to read. She looked up.

"Mama is crying," she said.

"Mama is crying," said Rostnikov.

"I want her to stop," the child said.

"She has probably stopped," he said.

"Did you make her cry?"

"No."

"Did my papa?"

"I think you should ask her," he said.

"I am very little," she said. "I am going to be four." Pulcharia held up four fingers.

"I know," said Rostnikov.

"I don't really want to go to Kiev," she said.

"Perhaps you won't have to."

"Can I touch your leg?" Pulcharia asked.

"You may knock upon it if it pleases you."

The child got off the chair, leaving her book open on the table, and hurried to the policeman. He looked down at her as she was about to rap at his leg.

"The other one," he said.

She nodded and tapped at the leg with her tiny fist. "Is it strong?" she said.

"Very. A dog bit it yesterday. He was very disappointed."

Pulcharia laughed.

Sasha sat in the rear of the white Lincoln Continental between Boris and Peter. Sasha had never before seen the driver, a squat young man with almost no neck. Sasha was desperate. He had to call Maya, convince her to stay, or at least wait till he could talk to her. He wasn't sure what he would tell his wife but, at this point, he knew he was not above begging.

At the same time, Sasha had to hold himself together, not let the men on either side of him know that there was something wrong with the man they knew as Dmitri Kolk. Sasha had worn a charcoal-gray silk suit and an Italian silk tie with alternating diagonal stripes of red, green, and blue. He attempted to maintain an air of calm and confidence. Could he look at himself through the eyes of the men who flanked him, he would know that he was doing a reasonably good job under the circumstances.

The drive was long, taking them well beyond the Outer Ring Circle to the town of Zagorsk, seventy kilometers north of Moscow just off of the Yaroslavl Highway. Sasha knew a bit about Zagorsk, but he was supposed to be a Ukrainian relatively unfamiliar with towns beyond Moscow.

"There are two places you should see here sometime," said Nimitsov, patting Sasha's leg. "I'll be happy to be your guide."

The young man smiled at Sasha, a smile so false that it chilled the policeman.

"First," said Nimitsov, "the Museum of Art and History, magnificent relics of Russian culture from the fifteenth to the seventeenth century. Magnificent, right Boris?"

"Magnificent," said Boris without enthusiasm as he looked out the window.

"But," Peter Nimitsov went on, "the real treasure is the Troitsa-Sergyeva Monastery built in the 1340s and fortified in the sixteenth century with the stone wall that still exists. It became the principle protection of Russia from foreign invaders. Early in the seventeenth century three thousand Russian soldiers in the monastery held off a sixteen-month siege by a fifteen-thousand-man Polish army."

"You know a great deal about Russian history," Sasha said.

"I will be a part of it," said Nimitsov. "There are a number of cathedrals in the monastery. My favorite is Uspensky Sobor, built by order of Ivan the Terrible. You must see it. There is a saying among Muscovites: 'You must see the cathedral before you die.' "

Sasha knew of no such saying. There was no doubt in his mind that this was simply a game the strange young man liked to play—and that he suspected something.

"Down there, see," Nimitsov said, pointing down a narrow street. "You can see the wall. What I would give to be the commander of a fortress under siege . . . but it is no longer so simple, is it? Armies do not attack fortresses. Heroes do not stand on parapets. There are no more Ivan the Terribles, no Alexander the Greats. We need a new, modern hero, one who, like them, is willing to be ruthless to . . . here we are."

They had driven beyond the town to an ancient road on which the large old stone houses were set well back from the road and hidden, for the most part, by birch trees and bushes growing close together.

Peter Nimitsov got out first, leaving the door open for Sasha to follow him, with Boris and the driver behind him. The driver and Boris stood on either side of Sasha. Peter moved ahead of them.

The door to the huge house, which was at least several hundred years old and massive, was made of a dark wood Sasha did not recognize. There was no need to knock. The door was opened by a man who looked like a larger version of the almost neckless driver. There was something decidedly not Russian about the man who opened the door. The clothes, walk, face.

The large entry hall which stood two stories tall was sparsely furnished.

The big foreign-looking man closed the door and led them to another door across the hallway, in which their footsteps echoed as if they were in a mausoleum.

The man knocked and a voice said, *"Entrez."*

Nimitsov motioned for the driver and Boris to stay behind with the guardian of the door. Peter motioned for Sasha to follow him.

The big doorman closed the door behind Sasha Tkach and Peter Nimitsov.

There were three men seated in a circle in the surprisingly small room. The five chairs were all the same, large—high backs, thick arms. A large, round, and very old table stood in the middle of the circle. The heavy table was empty. The wood of the chairs and the table was dark. Two chairs in the circle were empty. Nimitsov sat in one and Sasha in the other.

"Dmitri Kolk," said one of the men, a rugged-looking man in his forties with an accent Sasha recognized. "There is no reason for you to know our names or anything about us. There is, however, much reason for us to know you. And we know very little about you."

"Perhaps," said Sasha, "you should have a discussion with the police in Kiev."

"We have done so," said the rugged-looking man with the accent. "Our discussions have left much to be desired."

Sasha looked at the other two men. One was a duplicate of the rugged man, but at least twenty years older. Father, uncle, older brother? The other man was a little younger than the older man. In spite of his age and white hair, his skin was smooth and clear. One of his parents had obviously been black.

"My partners," said the rugged man, "do not speak your language, and, as you see, I do so only haltingly."

"Your Russian is very good," said Sasha. "I wish that I could speak a language other than ours."

The rugged man closed his eyes and bowed his head slightly, smiling. "You flatter me," he said. "I will be very frank with you, Kolk."

Sasha very much doubted the statement.

"The dogs are but a small part of our international investments," the man went on. "But we expect the dog combat to get quite large, with our enterprise moving across Europe, the former Soviet States, even Asia and the United States. We need to bring individuals like you into our business. We are very pleased that you are interested in joining us."

"I am interested in getting rich," said Sasha.

"If we agree to let you join us," the man said, "you will be rich, and not in rubles. Now, if you'll forgive me, I must translate for my partners."

The man began a conversation in French with the two older men. He spoke very quickly and in a dialect with which Sasha was unfamiliar but which did not stop him from understanding almost all that the three men said.

Sasha looked bored, being careful not to let the three men know that he understood the essence of their conversation. Had they been English, Italian, German, or anything else, Sasha would have understood not one word.

"I told him what we agreed," the man said in French. "What do you think?"

"I don't trust him," the half-black man said.

"I don't trust him," said the oldest man. "Young, sleek, confident. He could be the police. He could be an infiltrator from one of our competitors. He could be simply a dangerously ambitious young man like the young crazy Russian over there. I don't trust him either. He would eliminate us and take what he could when the opportunity came. We must see that the opportunity does not come."

"Yes," said the rugged younger man, still in French. "Nothing new in that. We have remained cautious for a long time. We will continue to do so. What do we do now?"

"Tell him he is in," said the half-black man. "After tonight we eliminate the young Nimitsov and replace him with this Kolk till we can select someone whose loyalty we can be sure of. Nimitsov is insane."

Nimitsov had recognized his name being spoken and looked up cautiously, still smiling.

"I say we eliminate both of them tonight," said the oldest man.

"We can replace them with our own people. Why let this young Kolk have the chance to grow in power?"

"All right with me," said the half-black man.

"*Et moi,*" said the young, rugged-looking man. "Tonight we eliminate them both. Then we let the word out around the world. Join us and make even more money than you are making, or be eliminated. I suggest we make it particularly unpleasant deaths."

Both older men nodded in agreement.

"Pardon my rudeness," said the rugged man in Russian with a smile of regret. "We have decided to accept you into our enterprise. Peter, will you please ask Honoré to bring in the brandy to celebrate our growth?"

The man seemed quite aware of Peter Nimitsov's displeasure at being ordered about. Sasha was certain that the man had done this intentionally.

After drinks, with silence from the two older men and a non-stop charming discussion dominated by the rugged man, Sasha said, "I would like to stop back at the hotel to change clothes."

"Ah, I'm afraid that will not be possible," said the rugged man, looking at his watch. "We have already removed your dog from the car, and if you wish to spend some time here preparing him . . ."

"Yes," said Sasha. "I'd like, however, for my dog trainer to be here."

"Too late," said the rugged man, shaking his head. "We expect a good fight from your animal. We want to see the quality of what your enterprise can produce."

Sasha avoided looking at Nimitsov, who had told him that Tchaikovsky must, in fact, lose. Sasha had no idea how to accomplish such a thing, even if he were willing to do so. Peter Nimitsov seemed to be about to betray either the three men or Sasha.

"All right," said Sasha, rising. "Then I should like to prepare my dog."

"Certainly," the rugged man said, rising. "Do not take too long. They will be waiting for us at the arena."

Peter Nimitsov rose slowly.

The two older men remained seated.

The situation did not seem particularly dangerous for the present. He would try, however, to find a phone, to call Maya, but he would have to do so carefully. Rostnikov and others would be at the arena tonight. It would be over now that Sasha could identify the three Frenchmen, who would not have the opportunity to kill Sasha and Nimitsov.

What Sasha Tkach did not know was that Tchaikovsky would be fighting in a different arena tonight.

Viktor Shatalov would no longer have to worry about being called Irving by the Tatars. Viktor Shatalov would no longer be eating pizza and telling jokes. Viktor Shatalov lay dead in Fish Lane almost in front of the Old Shopping Arcade and across from the New Shopping Arcade, which was one hundred fifty years old and had replaced the original fish market.

Two of Shatalov's men lay dead nearby. All three bodies were violated by many gunshot wounds.

A police ambulance was just arriving, its annoying horn signaling an urgency that did not exist.

"He liked to come here for *blinis*," said Emil Karpo, looking down at the bodies.

"If you knew that, others knew that," said Rostnikov, looking at the remarkably small crowd of the frightened and curious, mostly shopkeepers who had come out of their stalls to witness death. The curious wore everything from suits to white aprons and loose-fitting dresses. There were even a few children in the crowd.

"Others certainly knew it," said Karpo.

"No one else hurt?" asked Rostnikov.

Two men came out of the ambulance. They were dressed in white and wore the businesslike look of those who touch death daily. They moved around Rostnikov and Karpo, knelt at each body to be sure that all signs of life had departed.

Shatalov's face showed silent, final pain, and blood dripped from the hole directly over his right eye. Both eyes were open. One could mistakenly think the look of pain was a smile. One of the other corpses was curled in a fetal ball, trying to protect himself. The third dead man had been very young. He lay on his back with his arms spread as if taking in the sun on the beach at Yalta. This third dead man bore a striking resemblance to Shatalov.

"His son," said Karpo, watching Porfiry Petrovich as he looked down at the young dead man being checked by one of the medics.

"Witnesses?" asked Porfiry Petrovich, smelling an aroma of bakery coming from inside the New Market. It smelled remarkably good and he considered going in to find out, after he was finished in the street.

"Raisa Munyakinova has succeeded," said Rostnikov. "The war has begun. You are, however, not displeased, Emil Karpo."

"Murder is a crime against the state," said Karpo.

"And the victims," added Porfiry Petrovich. "But you are not displeased at the prospect of the Mafias dwindling their numbers."

"You know that to be the case, Chief Inspector," said Karpo, taking notes. "However, it will not diminish my commitment to finding whoever did this."

"And we have a good idea of who that might be," said Rostnikov. "Witnesses?"

"Two," said Karpo. "A boy and an old man. Do you wish to talk to them?"

"Yes," said Rostnikov. "Inside. Bring them. Follow that smell. Don't bother to call Paulinin on this one. He will consider it beneath his talents. A simple gangster assassination. There is little challenge. Call the pathology office."

Karpo closed his notebook and nodded. As Porfiry Petrovich entered the market, Karpo motioned to a slightly overweight police officer whose cap was so tight it had turned his forehead pink.

"You remain here," Karpo said. "No one touches the bodies or approaches but the ambulance men and forensics."

The man with the pink forehead nodded and stood at near attention over Shatalov's corpse.

"Can we take them now?" asked the older of the two medics.

"Wait for forensics," said Karpo.

"They take forever," said the driver with a look of disgust. "People are dying every ten minutes in Moscow. We run, eat bread and cheese while we drive, and it gets worse. Can we go and come back?"

"No," said Karpo.

The medic was about to protest, but he looked at Emil Karpo and tried not to shudder at the intensity of his stare.

"We'll wait," said the driver. "Maybe a little break won't hurt us. But if we get in trouble, we will say that you ordered us to remain here."

Karpo turned his back on the medics.

The two witnesses were standing apart from the small crowd. The boy was very thin and no more than twelve. The man was almost as thin and certainly no younger than eighty. It was a puzzle to Karpo that in a country where the life expectancy was sixty years, the streets were filled with men and women in their seventies and eighties.

The market was reasonably busy in spite of the crowd outside. Karpo, the boy, and the man walked slowly past sights and smells of food. The strongest smell came from the busy fish stalls, where the fish were generally big and probably beginning to turn.

Karpo followed the sweet smell of baking that could not be suppressed by the other odors. He found Rostnikov sitting on a low wooden fence behind a pastry stall, a brown paper wrapping open on his lap before him and four triangular baked objects the size of an adult hand laid out on the paper. The low wooden fence appeared to be in serious danger of collapse under the chief inspector's weight.

"Take one," said Rostnikov, looking at the witnesses.

The old man took the gift eagerly. The boy took another, but cautiously. He knew there was always a price to pay. The old man knew too but was beyond caring.

"I can't offer you a seat," said Rostnikov, selecting one of the last two triangles, "but I will try to be brief. Inspector Karpo, I bought one for you."

"No, thank you, Chief Inspector," Karpo said.

Rostnikov wrapped the final triangle and put it in his pocket. "Now, gentlemen, are you related?"

The boy and old man shook their heads.

"These are good, aren't they?" Rostnikov said after his first bite.

"Yes," said the boy.

The old man nodded in agreement. Both the witnesses now had dots of white sugar and flakes of light-brown crust on their faces.

"I think they are Armenian," said Rostnikov seriously, examining the pastry that was no longer a triangle.

"Armenian?" said the old man. "No, I am Russian."

"I mean the pastry," said Rostnikov.

"Oh, Armenian, yes," said the old man, taking a bite and tearing the pastry with his few remaining teeth.

The boy's clothes were clean but shabby. The old man's baggy pants and oversize sweater were clearly flea-market items. Both man and boy had eager looks on their faces, anticipation tinged with caution. This was a high point in each of their lives.

Rostnikov knew he should interview them individually, but there was little chance, almost no chance that either of them would ever appear in court as witnesses in a Mafia shooting regardless of what they might have seen. The courage of the old man would fade quickly if it became known that he could identify anyone. And Rostnikov knew better than to even consider putting the boy before a judge. It would be an assurance of the boy's death. But Rostnikov could, possibly, use information they might give him.

"What did you see?" asked Rostnikov, taking another bite. He could taste honey, yoghurt, sugar beneath the flaky brown crust.

The old man spoke first. It was hard to understand him because his mouth was full of pastry. "I was going to get food for my dog," the old man said. "Do not go near him if you should meet. He has grown old and sometimes bites strangers."

"I will avoid him," Rostnikov assured the old man. "I doubt if he could provide any information that might help in this case."

"I was going to get food for my dog," the old man continued. "Three men got out of a car. They started to walk to the market. Another car came. The windows were open. Shooting, shooting, shooting. Glass breaking. Stones from the market wall exploding like in a movie. Then the car that the three men had come out of chased after the car the shooting had come from."

"You see any of the men in the car with the shooters?" asked Rostnikov.

"No, too fast."

"Can you tell us anything about the car?"

"Big, black, maybe American, maybe German, not Russian."

"Anything else you can tell us?"

"I have to get home to my dog with some food. His name is Gagarin. I was almost a cosmonaut. I was a pilot in the real war, killed many Germans, many Germans."

Rostnikov did not doubt it. Neither did he believe. Anyone the age of this man had no choice but to fight against the Germans. Rostnikov, as a very young boy, had been a soldier. It was in the process of destroying a German tank that Rostnikov had suffered the wound that eventually led to the loss of his left leg.

"Give your name and address to Inspector Karpo. We will come to you if we need to talk to you again."

"You think my dog would eat some of this sweet?"

"It is worth the attempt," said Rostnikov.

"My dog bites. If you come to see me, be careful."

"I was bitten by a dog yesterday," said Rostnikov.

"You were?" said the old man. "Are you all right?"

"He bit my plastic leg," said Rostnikov.

"That was fortunate," said the old man, moving to Karpo, who took several steps back.

"And what did you see?" Rostnikov asked the boy.

"You really have a plastic leg?"

Rostnikov reached down and pulled up his pant leg to reveal his prosthetic leg. The boy examined it, taking another bite of pastry. He nodded to indicate that he had seen enough of the leg.

"And a dog really bit you?"

Rostnikov smiled and lifted his pant leg again and pointed to the teeth marks in the plastic.

The boy nodded again.

"What did you see?" Rostnikov repeated.

"The men in the black car fired many times, like the old one said. It looked like the men who were shot were dancing to the music of the guns."

"You are a poet," said Rostnikov, smiling at the boy, who nodded.

"No money, poets don't make money," said the boy. "I want to be a policeman like you. Policemen make lots of money."

"We do?"

"Bribes, payoffs, everyone knows," said the boy.

There was enough truth in the statement that Rostnikov ignored the boy's observation and said, "How close were you when the shooting began?"

"I was right next to the three men who died."

"You are lucky to be alive," said Rostnikov.

The boy shrugged and finished off the pastry, licking the residue of sweetness from his fingers.

"I wasn't afraid," said the boy.

"Sometimes it is good to be afraid. It makes you careful."

The boy shrugged again.

"What else did you see?"

"The man in the front seat, the passenger seat. When the car slowed down to kill the three men, both the back and front windows came down. The man in the backseat fired. The old man in the front seat watched."

"What did these men look like?"

"The shooter wasn't young. The old man had one of those black things over one eye."

"A patch?"

"If that's what you call it."

Casmir Chenko.

"Why aren't you in school?" asked Rostnikov.

"I don't like school. I go sometimes. But I don't like school."

"If you want to be a policeman, you have to go to school," said Rostnikov. "If you go to school, come and see me when you are twenty years old. I'll probably be retired, but I'll do what I can for you."

"Who are you?" the boy asked suspiciously.

"Chief Inspector Porfiry Petrovich Rostnikov of the Office of Special Investigation. Are you impressed?"

"Are you going to want me to sign a statement, point to the old man with the patch in a courtroom, something?" the boy said, not answering the question.

"I don't think so," said Rostnikov. "I would like to see you reach the age of twenty so you can become a policeman. Here."

Rostnikov shifted his weight, pulled out a crumpled card from his wallet, and handed it to the boy. The printing job was crude but it told the story, Rostnikov's name and title, the name of the Office of Special Investigation, and the phone number and address of Petrovka. "Now go give your name and address to Inspector Karpo."

"Is he dying?" asked the boy. "The other policeman?"

"No," said Rostnikov. "His aspect is a combination of heredity, a lack of humor, tragedy, and careful, if unconscious, cultivation."

The boy understood nothing of the explanation.

Rostnikov had little hope that the boy would become a diligent scholar and appear on his doorstep sometime in the future with the

crumpled card in his hand. But if one never tried, one never succeeded. He checked his watch. He was late. He was too late to take
the metro and he had no car.

Getting up was a monumental chore, but he managed without
slipping. Rostnikov thought he was getting more friendly with his
new leg with each day. This was a leg that reminded him of Karpo:
solid, emotionless, efficient, and reliable. The withered real leg that
was now gone had been more of a Sasha Tkach leg, feeling put
upon, emotional, needing help more than helping.

That was an unfair thought. Sasha was a good policeman, a
troubled young man but a good policeman.

When the two witnesses were gone. Emil Karpo approached
Rostnikov, who was walking out of the market past the stalls.

"I will meet you back at Petrovka," said Rostnikov. "I want Casmir Chenko in my office in two hours. You know how to find him.
If he is in hiding, locate him. Get whatever help you need from
Opatchoy in MVD Uniform Division. He owes me a favor. Be
careful. Take whatever men you need."

"He will be in your office," Karpo said.

Back on the street, with the sun making a futile effort to come
out from behind very black clouds, Rostnikov took one last look
at the corpses and moved down the street in search of a cab. In less
than a block, he had found one, even though they were not very
close to the tourist hotels. Cabs were plentiful in Moscow.

This one sported a dour driver with the weatherworn, pinkish
face of an alcoholic, a face very familiar in Moscow.

Rostnikov climbed in awkwardly, closed the door, and told the
driver where he wanted to go. "I am a police inspector," Rostnikov
said as the man shifted into second. "You will charge a fair amount
or I will declare this vehicle commandeered for police business, in
which case you will be paid nothing. You understand?"

The driver nodded.

"Are you married?" asked Rostnikov.

The driver nodded.

"Children?"

"Two," said the driver in the most gravelly voice Rostnikov had ever heard. It was even more rough than that of his sergeant when Rostnikov was a boy soldier.

The driver waited for more questions. None came.

Fifteen minutes later the cab pulled up in front of the hospital.

"What do I owe?" asked Rostnikov.

"Whatever you want to pay," said the driver.

"I want to pay nothing," said Rostnikov. "But you deserve payment for your work." Rostnikov gave the man more than the trip would normally cost.

"Thanks," said the driver.

"May your family be healthy," said Rostnikov.

"May my family stop complaining," said the driver.

Rostnikov got out of the cab and began the short walk to the door of the small hospital. Sarah's surgery was one hour away.

Chapter Thirteen

Iosef stood before the desk of Director Yaklovev, doing his best to hide his anger. It took all of the skills he had learned in the theater. He should have discussed this with his father before he came to see the director, but he was fairly certain what Porfiry Petrovich would have advised.

Iosef didn't want common sense and he didn't want caution. He wanted to express his ire even if it cost him his job. Since he preferred not to lose his job and he hoped for some satisfaction, Iosef decided to play the role of an unflappable diplomat, unsurprised by events, only slightly disappointed by the actions of his superior. It was what he decided, but Iosef was certain that his indignation would overcome him. There really was nothing to gain here and much to lose.

Yaklovev sat behind his desk, looking at the transcript of the confession of Oleg Kisolev and the statements of Yulia Yalutshkin and Yevgeny Pleshkov. It was Iosef's copy, the copy Pankov had handed to the young inspector less than fifteen minutes earlier.

"Yes, I have heard the tape," said the Yak. "I have read the transcript."

"And?" asked Iosef.

"Too many typing errors, but I will edit them and Pankov will produce another version," said the Yak.

"This," said Iosef, pointing at the transcription, "is not what happened. Oleg Kisolev has no money. The German wouldn't get anything by trying to blackmail him. And how would he know that Kisolev was homosexual? If Oleg told Yulia to take Pleshkov away from the hotel after he killed the German, there is no chance she would do it. She would never be ordered about by Oleg Kisolev or anyone else. You saw that. And Kisolev is incapable of participating in such a sequence of events—killing the German, trying to destroy the body, ordering Pleshkov to leave the scene. In this version, Pleshkov and the woman did nothing, and Kisolev acted in self-defense and to protect his friend. And none of this is what they told me and Zelach. It is a different story."

"Are you finished?" asked the Yak calmly.

"I don't know," Iosef said.

"You are finished," said the Yak. "And if you pursue this case any further, your career will be finished before it begins. You are a very good investigator. You could be, with time, as good as your father, possibly a chief inspector. I have great respect for Porfiry Petrovich's discretion and ability. He could not be pleased if I were forced to dismiss you from Special Investigation. Pause now and think. Think and discuss this with your father."

Suddenly, Iosef understood. It should have been clear and would have come to him had he not been enraged and stormed into the Yak's office. Yaklovev had not been taken in by a flimsy story. The director of Special Investigation had made a deal, had gambled on the possibility of Pleshkov being in an even greater position of power in Russia. The Yak had given the politician freedom from jail in exchange for future considerations relating to the Yak's ambition.

"I believe the statements," said the Yak. "I suggest you do the same. The German could well have spied on Kisolev and discovered that he was a homosexual. The German could have assumed that Kisolev could borrow money from his friend Pleshkov. And our soccer coach, in a state of panic, showed an aggressive side of his nature that is normally hidden. His very future and present were at stake. The case is closed. You understand?"

"Yes," said Iosef, holding out his hand.

The Yak gave him the transcript. "I have a new assignment for you," he said. "Someone broke into the office of the United States Peace Corps. He or they took thirty thousand dollars and stayed to cook a ham, which they ate. There appear to be no clues and the MVD and State Security want no part of it. They see no gain in catching a fool, and they are sure of ridicule if they fail. I, on the other hand, have an instinct for such crimes. Chief Inspector Rostnikov will discuss it with you after I meet with him."

"I'm to catch a ham thief?" said Iosef.

"Who also took thirty thousand dollars," said the Yak.

"I am being punished," said Iosef.

"No, you are being given an assignment."

"I would like to offer . . ." Iosef began.

"No," said the Yak, still not looking up. "I want you to leave now, talk to the chief inspector, and then consider the offer you were about to make. Iosef Rostnikov, I have learned that our work follows a simple principle. We take one step forward and one step back. We are always in the same place we started. Our hope for success is to plan carefully, taking what we might be able to use, as we step forward and back in a simple two-step."

Iosef nodded and left the office.

The Yak opened his desk drawer and removed the tape containing the voices of Pleshkov and the others telling what really had happened. He sat for the next hour making two copies, using the two tape recorders he kept in his desk. The copies would not be perfect but they would be clear enough. He would keep one copy in his desk and place the others in separate, safe places. While his office was reasonably secure, the Yak knew that someone in Petrovka could be bribed to break in when he was away and remove the tape from the desk drawer. The Yak almost welcomed the possibility. He began to imagine the conversation that would take place with Pleshkov. The Yak would produce another copy of the tape, and Pleshkov would be in a very awkward position from which the Yak would help him to escape . . . at a price. But Pleshkov was probably too intelligent. He would realize that there would be other copies. He would not make that mistake. Still, he had been witness to other, even worse mistakes from people supposed to be intelligent and capable.

While the copies were being made, the Yak contemplated the future of Iosef Rostnikov. The young man would either be made aware of reality by his father or the Yak would have to find a way to transfer Iosef to another department.

Director Yaklovev had great confidence in Porfiry Petrovich's powers of persuasion and his understanding of the need for compromise.

They had not yet cut Sarah's hair. She lay in a bed in a preparation room, waiting. There were no other patients in the room. Rostnikov sat at his wife's bedside, holding her hand.

"What have they done so far?" asked Rostnikov.

"Tests. They put me on the machine. The same one as before, the one with the lights that hums. Leon and the surgeon are looking at the results."

"I brought you something," he said, taking out the triangular pastry with his free hand. "You can have it when you wake up after the surgery."

"It looks good," she said. "Hold on to it for me, Porfiry Petrovich."

"I will," he said.

"The last time we were in a hospital room," she said, "a big naked man came in."

"Yes," said Rostnikov.

"You handled him perfectly," she said. "I hadn't seen you acting in your job before, except for the time when you were a uniformed officer and we ran into the two drunks on the street harassing a young woman. You were wonderful."

"Thank you," said Rostnikov.

"You know what I hate the most about this surgery?" asked Sarah.

"Yes," he said. "The loss of your hair."

"Yes," she said. "And what do you hate most?"

"That I might lose you," he said.

"You would survive, Porfiry Petrovich," she said, patting his hand.

"Yes," he said. "But it would be a lonely and less than meaningful survival. I am being selfish."

"No," Sarah said. "You are being honest. I . . ."

The door opened and Leon came in holding an X ray.

"The growth is smaller," he said. "Much smaller. The pressure on your brain is gone."

Leon showed them the X ray.

"We have canceled the surgery," he said. "We'll keep checking you, but you can go home. This kind of spontaneous remission is uncommon but not unheard of."

Sarah and Porfiry Petrovich looked at each other, stunned and only in the first stage of understanding what was happening.

"Could it come back?" Sarah asked.

"It could," said Leon, "but the decrease in size in just a few days is remarkable. It could have been the blood thinner I gave you."

"It could be a miracle," Sarah said.

"I don't believe in miracles," said Leon. "You both deserve good news. I'm happy to be the one who brings it to you. How about a celebration? Would you like to come to a chamber music concert tonight? I think you might enjoy it. All Mozart."

"I would very much like that," said Rostnikov, smiling at Sarah and holding her delicate hand in both of his thick, heavy ones. "A celebration. But I have to attend a dogfight. There is, however, a chance that the dogfight will be over early. What time is your concert?"

"Ten," said Leon.

"Perhaps I can do something to make the dogs decide to retire early so that we can make the concert."

"I'd like that," said Sarah, reaching for Leon's hand.

He took it and Rostnikov could see that Leon was very much in love with his cousin. It was a condition that Porfiry Petrovich fully understood. He too loved Sarah very much. He would do his best to end the dogfight early.

Iosef knocked at the door of the apartment of Anna Timofeyeva. He had called Leon's home in panic because he had not been at the hospital before his mother's surgery. He had been talking to Yaklovev. When he had reached Leon, he had been told the good news.

"Shall I come there now?" Iosef had asked.

"Your mother is on her way home," said Leon.

Iosef had expected the worst and had been feeling great guilt. What if his mother had gone into surgery and not come back? But she was fine. Something, the most important thing, had gone well this day. Perhaps another thing would now go well.

The door was opened by Elena, who had her right arm in a sling.

"I got here as quickly as I could," he said.

Elena stepped back to let him in. Anna Timofeyeva sat at the window, her cat, Baku, in her lap, her puzzle before her.

Elena closed the door.

"How are you?"

"Alive," said Elena. "Thanks to Porfiry Petrovich."

"How are you, Anna Timofeyeva?" he asked the woman at the window.

"There was a time when even if I were in the throes of a heart attack, I would answer 'fine.' Ever the stoic Communist bureaucrat. There were other times when I welcomed the question so I could complain about my condition. It was a very short period. I quickly learned that few cared for details and few would accept a simple answer. You ask me now and I answer as I am answering you, fine."

"That's good," Iosef said.

"It's not true," said Elena, cradling her injured arm with her healthy one. It looked to Iosef as if she were cradling an infant. "My Aunt Anna had words with Lydia Tkach last night. Sasha's mother demanded that she find him immediately, that . . . well, it was a domestic issue. Anna Timofeyeva said she could do nothing. And . . ."

"I banished her from these two rooms," said Anna, looking out the window, stroking the cat, whose eyes were closed in ecstasy. "Now I'm feeling like an irritable old woman who sees from her window the wife of a fugitive hiding from a charge of armed robbery. I should make calls, ask if she is using her real name, let the police take over. But what do I do? I decide to watch her, wait for her fugitive husband to appear, then call Porfiry Petrovich. The hero in the window."

"Like *Rear Window*," said Elena.

"What is *Rear Window*?" asked Anna Timofeyeva.

"A movie about what you are doing," said Elena. "The man watching is almost murdered by the killer."

"Was he a policeman?" asked Anna.

"The killer?" said Elena, hiding a smile.

"The man watching," said Anna.

"No, a photographer."

"That explains it. Come, look."

Iosef and Elena went to the window. The curtains were drawn back as they were always during the day. In the large concrete courtyard, children played, chasing each other, riding tricycles, hiding behind the concrete blocks that were supposed to be decorative. Five young women sat on the concrete seat with a concrete table between them. The sky promised rain, but it had for almost a week and had not delivered.

"The one with the baby," said Anna. "Her child is the little blond boy chasing the girl."

"He's cute," said Elena.

Elena stood up, wincing. Bending to look out the window had brought blood rushing painfully to her wound, which began to throb. She would have to take one of the pills Sarah Rostnikov's cousin had given her.

"He is presentable," Anna went on, changing quickly into the deputy procurator she had once been. The transformation was dramatic. The block of a woman who had begun her career as a factory worker and loyal Communist who believed in the revolution was now sitting up. Her voice had grown stronger, deeper, official.

"The woman is using the name Rosa Dotiom. Her real name is Rosa Dodropov. Her husband is Sergei Dodropov. Two years ago he robbed a bank. He was positively identified. He got away with lots of money. No one knows how much. The bank lied. The money was illegal business money from gangsters. He is wanted by the police. He is wanted by the bankers, who are afraid he will be caught and talk. He will come back here. She is waiting for him. See, she waits."

"How can you tell?" asked Iosef, who was still looking out the window.

"By how often she glances around in anticipation," said Anna. "It is not a look of fear. It is a look of hope. She has been looking like that for more than a week. He will show up soon. Do you want to be the one to call or should I?"

"Call my father, Anna Timofeyeva."

"You believe me?"

"I have been taught by my father that you were a great procurator, one who did not act rashly."

"Good," she said. "But I'll give you a demonstration of my training. You are angry, Iosef, very angry. And you are nervous and determined."

"Yes," said Iosef.

"You realize, Elena, I have just done more talking and shown more emotion that I believe I have done in the rest of my adult life."

"Yes," said Elena.

Anna looked down at the cat, which may have been asleep in her lap. Anna sighed.

"You want privacy?" she said.

"Well . . ." Iosef began.

Baku awakened as Anna rose.

"I am required to take a nap," Anna said. "I do not like wasting the time, but I cannot avoid it. Give my regards to your father."

Anna stood straight and walked without any hint of her problem to the bedroom, where she closed the door behind her.

Elena moved back to the window and looked out.

"She has me doing it," said Elena with a smile. "I feel I have to take her place on the vigil."

"You are really all right?" he asked.

"I will be fine," she said. "I will be in pain for an undetermined period of time, but I will then be fine."

"Elena," he said, "I don't have much time and I don't know why I am doing this again now. It is probably not a good time. Maybe it is my fear of losing you."

"I am not yours to lose," she said, standing straight and facing him.

"But I would like you to be," he said.

"You are proposing again."

"I am proposing again."

"It is not a good idea," Elena said. "You will worry about me on the job, and I will worry about you, and I will worry about you worrying about me, and . . . you see?"

"I worry about you now," he said.

"Then I will accept your proposal," she said.

"You will?"

"You expected rejection again," she said, stepping in front of him.

"Yes," he said. "I don't know how to react to acceptance."

"Start by very gently kissing me and avoiding contact with my arm," she said. "And continue by taking a seat, so we can discuss what this means."

Iosef was dazed. Elena came into his arms and he was very careful as he kissed her. It was a long, open kiss that Iosef did not want to end.

Elena sat in her aunt's chair. Iosef sat across from her in the chair that visitors were often directed to.

"You're not on some pain medication that is causing this reaction? You are not going to change your mind in a day or two?"

"No, Iosef, I will not. But there are things I must tell you about my past, about . . ."

"And I have things too," he said. "Unless you must, I would prefer that you tell me nothing about you that would cause either of us pain."

"And you do the same," she said, reaching forward to touch his hand.

"And I will do the same," he said.

"Do you believe in signs?" Elena went on.

"Mysticism?" he said, adding perplexity to his emotions of the moment. "God? ESP?"

"Perhaps," she said, looking out the window again.

"Not really," he said.

"Look out the window, Iosef," Elena said. "Less than a minute after you propose and I accept, Aunt Anna's bank robber appears. It is a sign for policemen."

Iosef leaned over to look out the window. A small blond boy was running toward a young man who stood next to one of the concrete blocks that surrounded the courtyard. The woman Anna had been watching said something to the other women and got up.

"I'll call for backup," he said, picking up the phone. "Elena, I love you."

"I'll lose some weight," she said.

"No," he said, "don't. You are beautiful as you are and . . . this is Inspector Rostnikov . . . no, the other one. I need backup, quickly."

Elena and Iosef smiled at each other. Iosef's anger was gone, the Pleshkov situation of minor interest compared to the beauty of this moment.

He hung up the phone.

"They'll be here soon," he said.

"Meanwhile," she said, "we can watch and talk. We have plans to make."

It was dangerous. It was stupid, but Sasha was frantic. When the meeting with the Frenchmen was over, hands were shaken, drinks downed, and talk was almost nonexistent.

"At some point, if we are to work together," said the rugged youngest man, "you will both have to learn a little French, come visit us in Marseilles."

"I am very bad with languages," said Sasha.

"And I am not interested in any language but the one of my people," said Nimitsov.

More amiable silence. A few toasts to the future. The old men showed nothing.

When the rugged Frenchman looked at his watch and said, "Time to go," Sasha followed Boris and Nimitsov into the entry hall. The door closed behind them.

"I have to make a call," said Sasha.

"No time," said Peter Nimitsov.

"There's plenty of time," said Sasha.

"Who are you calling?" asked Nimitsov.

"A woman," said Sasha, flashing a huge false and leering smile.

"No time," Nimitsov repeated. "We must get back, prepare."

"I could have had the call finished by now," said Sasha. "I must make the call."

Nimitsov played his teeth against his lower lip and nodded at Boris. "There's a phone in the kitchen. Boris will show you. Be quick."

There was no doubt that Nimitsov was suspicious. There was no doubt that making this call was madness. There was no doubt that Sasha didn't care.

Boris led Sasha through an arch, down a stone-floored hallway lined with cabinets containing dinnerware, large serving bowls, service for dozens.

They entered the large kitchen. There was an oven, a refrigerator, a freezer locker, a stone table in the center of the room and knives, pots, and pans hanging on hooks along the wall.

"There," said Boris.

Sasha went to the phone on the wall, picked it up, and dialed his home. After three rings, Maya answered.

"Maya," he said, trying not to betray himself to Boris. "It is me, Dmitri."

"Dmitri? Sasha, are you drunk in the middle of the day?"

"No," he said with a laugh.

"Someone is listening to you?"

"Of course," Sasha said, grinning hugely.

"They could . . . maybe someone is listening on an extension?" she said.

"It's possible," he said, winking at Boris.

"Why are you doing this?" she asked.

"Don't you know?"

"Dmitri," she said, using his cover name, "you are mad."

"It's worth the risk. Don't leave."

"Your uncle Porfiry came to talk to me about our problem," she said.

"And?" he said, knowing that his mother had certainly interfered again.

"Are you going to be home soon?"

"Late tonight," he said. "Will you be there?"

"You are in danger."

"Of course," he said.

"Be careful. We will be here."

"I have to go now," he said, looking at Boris. "Wear your silk nightgown, the clinging one."

"If I had such a thing, this would not be the night I would wear it. Be careful."

Sasha hung up and sighed deeply. "It's good to keep them happy," he said.

"Till you tire of them," said Boris.

"True," said Sasha. "Let's go."

One hour later Sasha was in a dogfight arena, definitely upscale compared to the one where he thought he would be, the one he had been in the night before. This room was air conditioned and immaculately clean. There were fewer seats, but the men in them were better dressed and the betting in the first fight had been handled by men in matching dark suits. Drinks were served. If there were a shooter present to control any dog that might go wild, that shooter was not immediately visible. It was all very respectable, and the noise level, except when the fights were taking place, was relatively low and conversational, with much laughter.

The first was not civilized. A pair of malamutes from the same litter were matched against each other. One dog was completely white except for a healed pink scar on his rump where hair would not grow. His brother was black and white. The trainers had held the straining dogs back till a man in dark slacks and a white jacket over a black shirt with a white tie announced that all bets were in and the trainers could release their dogs.

There was no familial recognition in the animals, which attacked each other with fury. They were noisy even above the frenzy of the crowd. Sasha turned his eyes from the animals and looked at the front row where the three Frenchmen sat, not joining in the insanity, not interested in the battle before them. In seats flanking the three were four men, one almost as old as the two older Frenchmen. The other three were young, wearing masks of indifference. Twice, Sasha had caught one of the young men looking at him. When Sasha decided to meet his eyes, the man did not turn away.

Definitely a bad sign. It was also a bad sign that all of the French-men were armed. Sasha had looked for and immediately seen the signs of weapons under their jackets.

When Sasha turned back to the fight, it was over. The all-white dog was bloody. His brother lay dying with a terrible gash across his nose and right eye. The white dog was restrained but tried to get at his brother, to finish him. The dying dog snapped at the trainer who tried to help him up. The dying dog whimpered from the effort. The trainer backed away.

Sasha still had to deal with whether to let Tchaikovsky try to win or to do something to insure the dog's loss. Sasha had not the slightest idea of what he could do to hamper the dog, and besides, he had decided that he had no intention of contributing to the murder of the animal.

Sasha looked at the seven men in the front row. The one who had been looking at him looked again. Nimitsov was suddenly at Sasha's side.

"We are next," said Nimitsov. "You know, this used to be a chil-dren's circus arena? I've considered staging fights between children. There are plenty of them on the street. You could give them knives and promise them more money than they dreamed of if they won."

Sasha looked at the smiling young man at his side. Nimitsov was not just evil, he was quite serious and quite mad.

While the blood was being cleaned from the dirt ring, Sasha de-cided that he had to act, even though the action was loathsome.

"I understand French," Sasha said, pretending interest in the cleanup.

"Interesting," said Nimitsov. "I may learn the language. Now that we have French partners."

"They plan to kill both of us," said Sasha.

Nimitsov turned to look at Sasha. They were only a few feet apart.

"You are telling the truth."

"I am telling the truth."

"When?" asked Nimitsov.

"After the fight sometime," said Sasha. "Tonight."

Nimitsov looked at the rugged Frenchman, who nodded. Nimitsov nodded back and said to Sasha, "Dmitri, we could all have been very rich men. These Frenchmen are fools. You and I will have to kill them first, after Bronson destroys your dog."

"I do not intend to do anything to contribute to my dog's destruction," said Sasha.

"Then I will have to kill you too."

"You were planning to anyway. However, I think we stand a better chance of survival if we form a temporary partnership."

Nimitsov's smile was sincere as he put his hand on Sasha's shoulder. "I almost like you, Dmitri Kolk, but you are too clever, too dangerous. Bronson can win without your help. You and I are partners, but just for the night."

"You should tell Boris," said Sasha.

"He would be useless in a battle," said Nimitsov. "He can't shoot straight. Actually, he is a good front man but a terrible coward. No, I'm afraid it will be just you and me. A partnership made in hell, to face the demon hordes."

Sasha went to get Tchaikovsky. The pit bull was lying in the cage ears up.

"Tchaikovsky," said Sasha, "you are on your own, and, it appears, so am I."

The cage was heavy. A strong young man who watched over the dogs in a back room helped Sasha bring the cage out and place it on one end of the ring. Bronson was uncaged, standing alert, teeth showing in clenched anger. The trainer, a crook-backed man with no hair, spoke soothingly to the dog. The betting was furious. The room, now full of smoke, was alive with debate about the animals, particularly the almost legendary Bronson.

Nimitsov stood, Boris at his side, hands folded in front of him. He was directly across from Sasha, who was suddenly afraid, very much afraid.

The announcer stepped forward and said loudly, "All bets are in. The battle begins."

Sasha opened the cage door and Tchaikovsky stepped out, facing the dog across the ring. Sasha was holding the cord around the pit bull's neck, but the dog was not straining at it. The man who had helped Sasha pulled the open cage back and out of the ring. The moment had come.

Sasha let the rope loose at a signal from the announcer.

"Survive, Tchaikovsky," he whispered. "It is what I plan to do."

Bronson leapt across the ring and landed on the pit bull's back. The crowd went mad with killing frenzy, all except the seven men in the front row.

Bronson had bitten into the smaller dog's back but he suddenly released his hold. Tchaikovsky had calmly ignored the pain and sunk his teeth deeply into the left foreleg of the dog on his back. Bronson turned, unable to free himself from the teeth that dug into his leg. He snapped at Tchaikovsky's left ear and took a small piece of it. The pit bull showed no pain but bit even more deeply into the leg.

"Fight," shouted someone. "Let go of his leg and fight."

Tchaikovsky paid no attention.

Bronson was now trying to get away. On his three good legs he pulled the smaller dog around the arena, turning every few seconds to try to sink his teeth into the pit bull.

"Stop it," shouted someone. "It's boring."

Others told the shouter to shut up. The crowd was in a fighting mood. This was not the fight they expected, not the fight they had been led to expect.

Bronson's foreleg was bleeding badly. He kept thrashing, trying to escape. It was clear to all that the only way he would get away from the pit bull's grip was to lose his leg.

Bronson lunged awkwardly, teeth apart, at the pit bull's head. Tchaikovsky, without loosening his grip, calmly turned his head

down toward the dirt floor and out of reach of the madly snapping larger dog.

The fight was clearly over. Tchaikovsky seemed almost sedate
and clearly determined to never loosen his jaws.

"Tchaikovsky, stop," shouted Sasha.

Instantly the pit bull loosened his grip and walked away from his
bloody opponent, who tried to move after him on his remaining
three legs. The almost severed foreleg made it impossible for him
to pursue. He took two steps and rolled over on his side, now trying to lick his bloody wound.

Meanwhile, Tchaikovsky walked indifferently toward his cage,
ignoring his own significant but clearly not crippling or life-
threatening wounds. There were shouts, demands for the return of
bets, while others shouted that there had been nothing wrong with
the fight. Drinks spilled. Cigar and cigarette butts were thrown.

Bronson would never fight again. He might survive to walk
three-legged through life, but that was the best the animal would
ever achieve.

Tchaikovsky entered his cage, turned to face the action in the
arena and to watch Bronson hobbling toward his trainer, who stood
next to Nimitsov.

"You did well, Tchaikovsky," said Sasha.

The dog blinked.

Nimitsov looked at Sasha, smiled and shrugged.

What happened next came so fast that Sasha was not really
aware that Nimitsov had saved his life. The pudgy young madman
had stepped into the ring where the dogs had fought and bled. He
faced the seven men in the first row.

Over the crowd roar, Peter shouted, "Betrayers. French scum."

The Frenchmen in the front row and the crowd heard the elated
shriek of madness from the man in the ring. The Frenchmen began
to go for their guns. Sasha was frozen for an instant and then dived
for Tchaikovsky's cage and the compartment where the gun was
hidden. There was a momentary standoff in the arena because

Nimitsov now stood feet apart, a gun in each hand, a very happy look on his face.

The crowd began to scramble for the exits, pushing, trampling each other, growing louder in their panic.

Sasha had just opened the drawer when the first shot was fired. For an instant he did not know who had started the insane battle, and then he felt the body fall on his back. He heard an explosion of gunfire from the ring and the first row. Sasha pushed the body off of him. It was the young Frenchman who had stared at him. He was still staring, but now with a third, round eye in his forehead, a simple, bleeding dark hole from which blood and something yellow was seeping. The dead man held a gun loosely in his right hand.

Peter Nimitsov had saved Sasha's life.

Sasha took the dead man's gun in one hand, his own in the other, and rolled over shooting toward the first row, over the wooden rim of the ring.

The madness of the battle equaled the madness of the dogfights. Seven men were in that front row, each with a gun in hand. Two of them were now dead. The remaining five were shooting at Nimitsov, who stood unprotected.

A fat man dashed out of the stands and waddled past Nimitsov, who was firing rapidly. A bullet took the fat man in the back.

Sasha aimed more carefully and put a bullet into the rugged Frenchman who had ordered the death of Peter and himself. The rugged man bit his lower lip and closed his eyes, falling forward. Now some of the Frenchmen began firing wildly at Sasha.

Except for the combatants, the arena was almost empty. Sasha glanced at the now-wounded Nimitsov, who was on his knees, still firing. One of Nimitsov's bullets took the oldest Frenchman in the chest and then Nimitsov fell forward on his face. His fingers kept pulling the triggers of his weapon and the random shots shattered through the roof and into empty seats.

The four remaining Frenchmen turned their full attention on

Sasha. They had all scrambled for some cover when Nimitsov fell. Sasha fired almost blindly, hitting nothing.

And then silence. Nimitsov was no longer firing, and since no gunfire was coming from the Frenchmen, Sasha forced his shaking hands to stop pulling the trigger. He had no idea of how many shots he had fired or how many were left or if he was wounded.

His hope that the four men had fled was destroyed when he heard a voice in French say, "You two that way, around. Martin, hold him down. Maurice, go the other way."

The gunfire resumed. A single person resumed firing at Sasha to keep him in place till the others came around him from the sides or rear. Sasha didn't shoot. There was no time to think through the slightly controlled panic. Sasha went into a crouch and raced toward the man shooting from the cover of the aisle chairs. While the others flanked him, there was only one man between Sasha and a chance at the exit. Sasha ran right, turned and ran left, took two steps back to the right and then dived forward, now no more than a dozen feet from the man who had him pinned down. Bullets echoed. Sasha's last bullet tore into the man's left arm. The man's gun was in his left hand. Sasha fired again. Nothing.

A wild thought. He turned to go for the guns in Nimitsov's hands, but it was too late. The Frenchmen had moved into the open and now stood in a circle along the rim of the low wall around the ring.

It was Sasha's turn to entertain.

"I am a police officer," Sasha said in French, panting, sitting back, still hoping for a chance at Nimitsov's guns.

"We suspected," said the very old man in French. His gun, like the others, was pointed at Sasha. "You have killed my nephew. You have left our business in the hands of old men. Your being a policeman makes no difference."

"It makes a difference," came a voice from the darkness of one aisle of the arena.

The Frenchmen turned their guns toward the voice.

Porfiry Petrovich Rostnikov stepped into the light. So did five uniformed and helmeted men in flak jackets, all carrying modified Kalishnikov automatic rifles.

There was a moment, only a moment, in which the eyes of the old Frenchmen turned toward each other. They had the least to lose in death. The pause was long and then the oldest man dropped his weapon. So did the others.

"I'm sorry to be a bit late, Sasha," Rostnikov said awkwardly, going over the rim of the ring and reaching down to help Sasha to his feet. "We had an informant, but she had some difficulty telling us where the fight would be."

The policemen herded the Frenchmen out of the arena. Sasha saw the old man look toward the body of the rugged man. There were tears in the old man's eyes as he left the arena.

Sasha, breathing heavily, turned over the body of Peter Nimitsov, who looked up at him. The two guns were still in his hands. Nimitsov let the guns go. The number of bullet holes in the young man was remarkable, including one in his neck and one through his cheek. What was even more remarkable was that Peter Nimitsov was still alive.

"What did you tell them, in French?" Nimitsov asked in a gurgle that Sasha could barely hear.

"That I am a policeman."

Nimitsov nodded as if everything were clear now. "I'll never get the chance to save Russia," the dying man said.

"You saved me," said Sasha. "Why?"

"Destiny," said Nimitsov, choking.

"Destiny?"

"You ask a madman a question and you'll get a mad answer," said Nimitsov. "It was a good fight, wasn't it?"

"A very good fight," said Sasha.

"Now, if you will excuse me, I must die."

And he did.

"Are you wounded, Sasha Tkach? An ambulance is coming."

"No. I should be but, no, I am not. The dog is hurt."

Rostnikov left Sasha looking down at the corpse of the lunatic killer who had saved his life, and moved toward the cage of the pit bull. Tchaikovsky was still inside, lying down now, watching the end of the show.

"Dog," said Rostnikov, "someone will be here soon to take care of your wounds."

The dog looked up at Rostnikov.

"The Hindus believe in reincarnation till one achieves Nirvana," Rostnikov said conversationally, watching Sasha kneeling at the side of Nimitsov's body. "I would value your opinion, dog. What were you before? Who were you before? I doubt if one remembers when one is reincarnated. What will Nimitsov be? I think a bird, a small, vulnerable bird would be appropriate."

Rostnikov looked down at the dog who was looking back up at him, his head cocked to the left. No one had ever spoken to him this way before.

"But," said Rostnikov, now looking at the bodies in the front row. "The truth is that I don't believe in reincarnation. Atheism when taught from an early age is a difficult religion from which to escape. Perhaps we'll talk again, dog. As I said, help is coming soon for you."

Rostnikov checked his watch. If he did the paperwork tomorrow and hurried, there was still a chance he and Sarah could make most of Leon's concert. He would have preferred the blues, or 1950s American modern jazz on his cassette machine, but this was a celebration. He had hoped for the best and expected the worst when he discovered that his wife needed more surgery. The best, as it seldom does, had come.

"Are you all right, Sasha?" he asked, moving back to his detective, who rose.

"I don't know what to think, to feel. I think I . . . I feel alive."

"And things that seemed important no longer seem so."

"Yes."

"The feeling comes more frequently as you grow older," said Rostnikov. "Go home. Come in early tomorrow. Write a long report. Kiss your children for me. Kiss your wife for yourself."

"If she'll let me," said Sasha. "You spoke to her."

"Yes. Go home. Try," said Rostnikov. "You want a ride? I have a car and a driver."

"Yes," said Sasha, following Rostnikov out of the ring and into the darkness behind the stands.

When all the humans were gone, the pit bull walked slowly out of his open cage, ignoring the wounds to his ear and back. He moved to the side of Peter Nimitsov and smelled death. He looked at the bodies in the first row and smelled their death too.

Tchaikovsky sat back and waited as the sound of a siren approached from too far away for a human to hear.

Rostnikov recognized the melody, could hear the playful interchange of themes and instruments. It was not unlike the best work of Gerry Mulligan and Chet Baker. Sarah took his hand. They were in the large auditorium of the Moscow Technical Institute. The room was about half full. Rostnikov estimated about one hundred people were listening, mostly older people, but a few of college age or a bit older. There were even two little girls in the audience. Sarah and Porfiry Petrovich had brought them. It had been Sarah's idea. The girls' grandmother claimed she was too tired for a concert and that she had never learned to appreciate "smart" music. The girls sat next to Leon's son, Ivan. The three children had been promised ice cream after the concert, if they weren't too tired for the treat. They had all insisted that they would not be too tired, but a glance showed that only Laura, the older girl, was still alert and even attentive.

The piece ended with a solo closing by Leon at the piano. When the last note stopped echoing, the applause began.

"Are you enjoying?" asked Sarah.

"Yes," said the older girl.

The younger one had fallen asleep and was now in danger of toppling from the wooden seat. Ivan was still awake, but he had begun fighting his heavy eyelids. Rostnikov reached past his wife, picked the sleeping girl up, and put her on his lap. She stirred slightly and put her head on his shoulder.

"It is beautiful," said the older girl.

"It is beautiful," Sarah agreed, reaching over to touch her husband's arm.

The next piece began.

Destruction, creation. Death, beauty, thought Rostnikov. He decided that if he could make the time tomorrow, he would find the young Israeli rabbi, Avrum Belinsky, and have a serious talk which would probably clarify nothing but, Rostnikov was sure, would make a one-legged policeman a bit more at peace with the chaos that is Russia.

The trio on the low stage began another piece.

"Brahms," Sarah whispered.

Brahms would be most appropriate, Rostnikov thought as he smelled the clean sweet hair of the child on his lap.

The children were both asleep in the living room and, thank whatever gods there may be, Lydia Tkach was not in the apartment.

Sasha sat next to Maya on the bed. Neither spoke. Neither reached out to touch the other. There was a night chill of impending Moscow rain in the air. People were going nearly mad waiting for the rain that refused to come. Maya wore flannel pajamas Sasha had given her for her birthday two years earlier. Sasha was in his white boxer shorts and the extra-large Totenham Hotspurs soccer shirt he had confiscated from a shipment of illegally imported goods from England a few months earlier. The three suitcases were on the floor in the corner. They were closed, waiting, threatening.

"Something has happened to me, Maya," he said.

She said nothing. He went on.

"I would normally be depressed now, afraid of losing you and the children, dreading the need to face my mother, cursing my work. But I'm not. I feel calm, as if the things that usually get to me are not important. I don't want you to go. I will surely weep. But if you must, I'll try to understand. You surely have reason to leave."

"You are reacting to being alive when you should be dead, Sasha," she said softly, her head down. "Lydia is right. You should try to do something less dangerous, but I know you will not."

She was right.

"Maya, I did it again. The weakness came. I became a different person, Dmitri Kolk, criminal."

"You were with a woman," said Maya. "I knew. I could tell from the guilt in your voice on the phone. Did she have a name?"

"Tatyana," he said.

"Was she pretty?"

"Thin, but pretty, yes."

"Did you have to do it? Would the people you were with be suspicious if you didn't?"

"Maybe. No," Sasha said, "I was drunk. I was playing a role. Forgive me if you can, but I was enjoying playing that role."

Maya turned her head toward him. "Sasha, you just told me the truth."

"I know."

"You have always lied in the past."

"Yes. I told you. Something has changed. Don't go, Maya."

"Twenty-two days' trial," she said. "I'm not threatening you, Sasha. It just seems reasonable, enough time to see if you've really changed."

"Twenty-two days," he said. "An odd number."

"I took a leave from work," she said. "I have twenty-two days. We can spend time together. I'm not sure I have much hope. I'll call my office in the morning and say I might like to come back. They'll be happy to have me. No one else knows the billing system program."

Maya worked for the Council for International Business Advancement. She liked the job. She did not want to lose it. She would decide what to do about the Japanese businessman when the need to decide arose. What she would do would depend primarily on Sasha.

"Would you like to get under the covers and make love?" she asked.

"What?"

"I still love and want you," she said, "I'm just not sure I can live with you."

"I would like very much to make love. The moment you asked the question, I was immediately . . . I love you, Maya."

"I know, Sasha Tkach," she said. "But that is not enough."

Iosef sat in his small, comfortable one-room apartment trying to read a play by a new writer named Simsonevski. Simsonevski had three plays produced in the last year, all in the little theaters in storefronts or the back rooms of shoe stores or churches. Iosef had seen all of the plays, liked none of them. The one in his lap—he was wearing only his underwear and a plain white T-shirt—was even more grim than the others. There had been one suicide, one murder of a husband by a wife, one young woman going insane (with a stage note indicating that she should bite off her tongue), and a soldier who has an epileptic seizure onstage.

Iosef laughed. It was that or cry, but on balance the laugh was called for. He put aside the play knowing he would not pick it up again. It was very late but he thought he would try to find something on television, anything but the news.

He could not match the tragedies of Simsonevski's play but he could beat it for simple irony. First, the Yak had purposely allowed Yevgeny Pleshkov to go free of a crime he surely committed. The Yak was not one to take bribes. From what Iosef could see, Yaklovev was not interested in material things. Porfiry Petrovich had told him that the Yak lived alone and simply. His wardrobe each day confirmed this in part. No, money was not the culprit in this injustice. Did Pleshkov or the woman have something on the Yak? Iosef didn't think the Yak would stand for blackmail even if they did have something. He would find a way out. It was something Iosef would discuss tomorrow with his father.

But the problem of the Pleshkov case was less vexing than Iosef's embarrassment over arresting the man in the courtyard outside of Anna Timofeyeva's window. The man proved to be the woman's brother, a construction worker, not the woman's husband. Anna had been right about who the woman was, but Iosef had now revealed that her place of hiding and change of name were known. They had alerted her, and she would alert her fugitive husband.

Anna Timofeyeva slept through the capture, and when she was told about it when she awakened, she shook her head and said, "You should have awakened me. I know what the husband looks like."

That was all she said. She asked them if they wanted tea, which she disliked but drank because she thought it might be good for her. As Anna had moved toward the stove, Iosef and Elena declined the offer of tea and told her that they planned to marry.

Anna went to the small sink in the corner, filled her teapot with water, and turned on the gas on the stove.

"I know," Anna said.

"How would you?" asked Elena, standing next to Iosef. "I didn't know he would ask. I didn't know I would say yes."

"I knew," said Anna, rummaging for a tea she might find drinkable.

"You approve?" asked Elena.

"I approve," said Anna, making a choice of teas, the least of the four evils on the shelf.

"When?"

"We haven't discussed that," said Iosef.

"No," said Anna, pushing the tea she had selected back in the narrow cupboard over the sink.

"No?" asked Elena.

"Tonight I take you both out for dinner," she said. "An old woman with a bad heart, a young woman with a bad arm, and a man who has made a fool of himself. The perfect trio for celebrating. I still have friends, even a friend or two with a restaurant."

And they had celebrated at an Uzbekistani restaurant where Anna knew the owner, a former cabinet minister who had once needed the help of the stern procurator.

They had eaten well—*tkhum-duma*, boiled egg inside a fried meat patty; *mastava*, a rice soup with chopped meat; *maniar*, a strong broth with ground meat, egg, and bits of rolled-out dough; a *shashlik* marinated and broiled over hot coals. They had laughed, though Elena was in pain from time to time, and they had made some preliminary plans. She had said that she would like to wait a few months before a wedding, to be sure they had not been carried away by a romantic moment. This seemed reasonable to Iosef.

By the time he got to his room, it was too late to call his parents.

Iosef's stomach was contentedly full. That, and Elena's acceptance of him, made it just a bit easier to face the embarrassment at Petrovka in the morning.

Iosef's room had theater posters on each of the four walls, bright theater posters except for the one for the self-indulgent play Iosef had written and starred in. That poster held a place of prominence to remind him that he was not a playwright. He had a two-cushion, sturdy yellow sofa with black trim, two chairs, a worn but still colorful handmade Armenian rug that covered most of the floor, and a desk in one corner. The couch opened into a bed in which Iosef slept. There were three bright floor lamps, one black-painted steel, one a mock Tiffany, and the third a brass monstrosity from the 1950s. The room was bright. Next to the desk was a small table on which the television sat. The rest of the wall space on all four walls was filled by floor-to-ceiling bookcases he had made himself.

He supposed that after he and Elena were married, this is where they would live.

It could have been worse. He had his own toilet and shower behind the door off the kitchen area. The sink, toilet, and shower functioned perfectly since Porfiry Petrovich had worked on them.

Tomorrow, when he was the object of jokes at Petrovka, he would concentrate on thoughts of his and Elena's future. There was no doubt that word of his calling out a squad to arrest an innocent construction worker would be all over the building, and that there were some who would make lame jokes about the event.

Think of Elena, he told himself, removing the pillows from the couch and opening it into a bed. Think about telling your father and mother. He finished making the bed, propped up his pillows, and turned on the television. There was nothing worth watching. He turned it off and then turned off the lights.

Tomorrow he would ask Elena if she had changed her mind, tell her that he would understand. He was certain she would not change her mind and that she had already taken plenty of time to decide.

Overall, thought Iosef, it had been a good day.

He lay back in his bed and fell asleep almost instantly.

Emil Karpo sat at the desk in his cell-like room, entering new data in his black book on the new Mafias. Even though he had a computer, Karpo did not fully trust it. He had heard tales of computers losing data, breaking down, crashing in bad weather. He would enter the data on the computer tomorrow night.

Karpo was fully dressed, scrubbed clean with rough soap, teeth brushed, face shaved.

He wrote his last word for the night, closed the book, and turned to look at the painting of Mathilde Verson on the wall. Emil Karpo had only one bright image in his dark room, the painting of Mathilde, the reminder of a great failure.

Emil Karpo needed the smiling image of Mathilde on the wall

to remind him that she had been real. Her red hair was flowing, her cheeks were white. Karpo's memory held the black-and-white images of hundreds of criminals, but they were flat, dead images.

He turned away from the painting, rose, removed all his clothes, and hung them neatly in his closet. Everything in the closet with the exception of the few things Mathilde had bought for him were black. He closed the closet door and moved naked to the cot. Before he turned off his single light next to the cot, he tried to imagine Raisa Munyakinova in her holding cell. He could not. He simply knew she was there.

She had done no more than he had considered. Mathilde had been gunned down on the street between two Mafias. Raisa's son had been torn by bullets. But Karpo was certain he would not be able to kill as she had. His belief in Communism was gone. Mathilde was gone. All he had was the daily solace of doing his job, a job that would never end.

He turned off the light.

Chapter Fourteen

It was raining, finally it was raining, a light but insistent morning rain.

The Yak stood at the window of his office, hands clasped behind him, looking into the Petrovka courtyard below.

"You will turn over all of your notes on the dogfights, the killings, and the foreigners you have arrested to me," said the Yak. "This is now an international issue and I shall present it to the proper agencies of investigation. You have done a good job, as usual, Chief Inspector Rostnikov."

Rostnikov was seated behind the dark conference table in his usual seat. He was slowly drawing pictures of birds in flight. He imagined that one of them was Peter Nimitsov.

"As for the Pleshkov investigation," Yaklovev said, his back still turned, "there are some irregularities, but the case is closed. Your son has done an excellent job. Please prevail on him to go on quietly to his next assignment. Tell him that his mistake yesterday in calling out the special squad is of no consequence."

"I will," said Rostnikov. "He will find the ham thief."

"Finally," the Yak said, turning to face the man whose eyes and pencil were fixed on the notebook before him. "The Mafia killings. They continue. They grow worse. But you have taken into custody someone who committed some of the murders. We can inform the media, give her name."

"A mistake," said Rostnikov without raising his eyes.

"Mistake? I've read the report from you and Emil Karpo. What is the mistake?"

"She didn't do it," said Rostnikov. "Mistakes can be made, as they clearly were in the case of the prominent Yevgeny Pleshkov."

Silence except for the rain hitting the window.

"I see," said the Yak. "All right. The woman is of no consequence to me. What do you intend to do to insure that she . . . ?"

"She has relatives in Odessa," said Rostnikov, "but I don't think she will leave the grave of her child."

"Would she go to Odessa if the body of her son were moved with her and a reasonably impressive headstone placed over his grave?" asked the Yak.

"Perhaps, yes, I think so. I will have to ask her."

"Do so," said the director, moving behind his desk. "If she decides to cooperate, and I'd like you to be your most persuasive, tell Pankov that I want him to make the necessary financial arrangements."

Rostnikov closed his notebook, put his pencil in his pocket, and stood up. It was the director's turn to look down at the work on his desk, pen in hand.

"Your wife," he said. "I understand that she did not need the surgery."

The fact that the Yak knew did not surprise Rostnikov.

"Fortunately not."

"Good," said Yaklovev. "I am not without compassion, Porfiry Petrovich. I may have little of it, but that which I do have I husband and give out only to those I respect."

"Thank you, Director Yaklovev. Will that be all?"

"New assignments tomorrow," said the Yak. "New successes. New enemies. That will be all today."

The cemetery was empty except for two badly matched figures, a man in a black raincoat and a hood and a woman in a raincoat of crackling gray plastic.

They walked together to the sound of pounding rain, knowing where they were going. They had been there before, the grave of

Valentin Lashkovich. In the day since they had last been here, a headstone, life size, with an image of Lashkovich etched in the dark stone, had replaced the old one. Lashkovich on the stone was thinner than he had been in life, his dark suit nicely pressed.

The flowers on the grave were fresh, bright and varied, though the rain was beating down the petals. There were many wreaths and bouquets. The grave was completely covered with brightness. As in the deaths of other Mafia members, Emil Karpo knew the number of flowers would dwindle till, in less than a week, there would be none.

Raisa and Karpo looked down at the grave, their feet growing wet as the rain soaked the ground.

Karpo leaned over, gathered an armful of flowers, and handed them to Raisa. He took an even bigger armful. Then the woman led the way as the rain came down even harder.

The grave she led him to was in a far corner where the graves were close together and there were only stones set flat in the ground with the names of the dead chipped neatly but simply into them.

The one for Raisa's son was no different than the dozens of others.

Karpo knelt and placed his armload of flowers on the small grave. Raisa did the same. Mathilde was buried in another place and time, and flowers from the grave of a killer would never do. But Raisa did not seem to mind.

"The sky is crying for my child. It waited for me to be able to come here and cry with it."

She expected no answer and received none.

The two stood over the grave as the rain seeped through their protective covering. They said nothing. There was nothing that either of them wished to say. They stood for almost forty minutes, when the rain suddenly stopped.